BEGIN AGAIN WITH YOU

ALEXA RIVERS

To my husband.
My best friend.
My everything.

"WELCOME TO HAVEN BAY," CHARITY ST. JOHN muttered to herself as she drove past the brightly colored sign announcing she'd arrived in the quaint beachside holiday destination that was her hometown. "Where everyone hates you, and flaming pitchforks are at the ready."

When Charity moved away three years ago, she'd vowed never to return. Unfortunately, that vow hadn't lasted as long as she'd have liked. First, she'd been summoned back for her cousin Erica's wedding—which she'd happily have ignored if not for the less-than-subtle threats from her parents to drag her there kicking and screaming—then she'd been talked into spending Christmas with her sister's new family, and now the simple fact of the matter was that she had nowhere else to go.

Okay, amend that. She could move in with her parents, who'd left the bay a while ago in favor of the bustle of Wellington, but much as she loved them, they'd drive her crazy within a week. Plus, Samuel would expect that, whereas after everything that had happened here, he certainly wouldn't think to look for her in the bay. So here she was, with a crappy car that was lucky to have survived the trip, and all of her worldly belongings crammed in the back seat and trunk.

Jobless, homeless, and penniless.

"Oh, Samuel," she murmured. "If you could see me now."

How her ex-husband would laugh, knowing what had become of her. His buddies had been messing with her head for weeks, ever since her former roommate, Simone, sold out her location to them. They'd been messaging her constantly—creating new social media accounts each time she blocked them—and had turned up at the café where she worked and made a scene more than once. Not to mention the days they'd staked out her apartment building and jeered, or tailed her in their car when she was forced to leave for work. They'd driven her to the point where she could hardly sleep, was too distracted to do her job—hence getting fired—and felt like she was going crazy. Then, without Simone around to help pay the rent anymore, she hadn't been able to keep her apartment. And frankly, no landlord wanted to take a chance on a broke, unemployed woman with a patchy work history. Her one consolation was that Samuel was rotting in a prison cell. As far as she was concerned, he could stay there.

Charity indicated and pulled onto one of the roads leading to the town square, which was the thriving hub of Haven Bay, especially during tourist season. She glanced over at the neatly printed papers on the passenger seat. Her resumé. Nerves clustered in her stomach and her fingers tightened on the steering wheel. The sooner she found a job, the sooner she could earn enough money to get the hell out of here again. But she wasn't fooling herself. Convincing anyone to hire her would be a mission.

She parked on a side road, grabbed her resumé, and got out of the car, locking it behind her. Most people would consider it safe enough around here that everything could be left unlocked, but when you were on the residents' shit-list, it didn't pay to take chances. She ducked her head and walked toward the square, not making eye contact with anyone and hoping they wouldn't recognize her. She'd changed a lot since she stopped being Mrs. Charity Hagley. Not enough to conceal her identity from people who knew her, but enough that the general public often didn't realize who she was.

The square had a cobbled center and Old English-style lampposts, which she'd once found charming. She went directly to Cafe Oasis—the only cafe in town —and let herself in. A bell chimed as she entered, and she joined the line waiting to order. She kept her face lowered until she reached the cashier, then she sucked in a breath as she raised it and looked into the familiar eyes of Lana McQueen. *Damn it.* Lana had owned the cafe during Charity's youth, but she'd hoped the older lady might have sold it and moved on. Apparently not.

"Well, look what the cat dragged in," Lana drawled, a chill in her green eyes. "Charity Hagley, fancy seeing you here."

Charity managed not to squirm. "Actually, it's Charity St. John. I'm divorced."

Lana huffed. "That doesn't surprise me. I guess you couldn't get anything more out of him after he was convicted. But shouldn't you have found another con artist to attach yourself to by now?"

Charity tried not to show how much Lana's words

affected her, and she didn't protest. She deserved every ounce of censure she got. After all, she'd married a man who'd defrauded dozens of people by persuading them to invest in a non-existent real-estate scheme. "I'm moving back to the bay," she said, getting to the point. "I've worked for the past three years as a barista in Auckland. Is there any chance you're hiring?"

Lana snorted and put a hand on her hip. "Let me get this straight. *You're* asking *me* for a job? After your husband tricked me into investing my retirement savings and then stole them out from under me? You've got some nerve, girl."

Closing her eyes, Charity reminded herself not to snap back. There was no point in arguing that she'd been oblivious to Samuel's shady dealings. Even though she hadn't faced charges—and had actually testified for the prosecution—she'd been tried and convicted in the court of public opinion.

"Yes," she said, opening her eyes and swallowing her bitterness. "I am."

At this point, a good number of people were watching them, and the cafe was strangely silent.

"It isn't happening," Lana told her. "Get out of here. I wouldn't so much as sell you a scone."

Tail between her legs, Charity nodded and left before she could spit a retort that would only make the situation worse. She'd always been a little fiery, but she'd tried to rein it because nothing good ever came of it.

Once she got back to her car, she started the engine and drove to Sailor's Retreat, the local restaurant. Unfortunately, they had no more interest in her than Lana did. Deflated, but not surprised, she wandered across the beachside pavilion that separated Sailor's Retreat from The Shack, the ice cream and cupcake parlor owned by her sister Faith. A gust of wind stirred the black skirt she'd picked up from the Salvation Army shop because she'd hoped it would make her look more professional. She smoothed it back into place before pushing open the door to The Shack.

"Charity!" Faith exclaimed from behind the counter, her vivid red lips spreading in a grin. "You're here! I wondered if you'd come by." She rushed onto the shop floor and swept Charity into one of the best hugs ever. With her curves, bubbliness, and the scent of cream and sugar that clung to her like a second skin, Faith's embraces could make the worst days seem better. Charity sank into her, squeezing her eyes shut and wishing everyone was as forgiving as Faith.

"God, I missed you," she said. "You're the one good thing about being back here."

"Come on, there must be more than just me," Faith said, releasing her. "What about the lack of traffic? The warmth? The beach?"

"The lack of traffic is nice," Charity allowed, and glanced around the store. She'd only been here once before and thought her memory must have exaggerated how cute and funky the parlor was, but it hadn't. The color scheme was pink and green, very retro, and Faith wore a fifties-style polka dot dress to match. Behind her, Charity noticed another woman. Slender, with dark blonde hair and eyes that were brownish-gold. She assumed this was Faith's business partner, Megan, who she'd heard a lot about but not met yet.

"Hi," she said, approaching her. "I'm Charity, Faith's sister."

"Nice to meet you." The woman came around to join them and offered her a smile. "I'm Megan. Faith has told me so much about you. She's really excited to have you here."

"She's the only one. If looks could kill, I'd never have made it this far."

Faith grimaced. "That good, huh? Sorry, Char. Where have you been?"

"First to Cafe Oasis, then Sailor's Retreat. I was hoping to find work, but they're not interested." She shrugged, trying to pretend it didn't bother her, but based on Faith's sympathetic expression, she wasn't fooling anyone.

"You might need to target people who weren't around three years ago," Faith suggested.

"Actually," Megan said, and they both turned to her. "There's a job posting board near The Refuge. You should have a look and see if there's any you might be able to apply for."

Charity nodded. At this point, she was willing to try anything that would allow her to build a nest egg and escape. "I'll head over there now and have a look. Thanks, Megan."

"No problem."

"Once you're done there, feel free to go straight to my place and get settled in," Faith said, reaching into her pocket and extracting a key, which she handed over. "We've cleared space for you in the spare bedroom. It'll probably be easier to unpack before the boys get home from school."

"Great, thank you." Charity slid the key into her purse and zipped it shut. "I really appreciate everything you're doing for me. Did you tell Shane I'm happy to chip in once I start earning some money?"

Faith rolled her eyes. "Yes, and he said the same thing I did. You're family, and we're happy to have you until you get back on your feet. No payment necessary."

Charity made a mental note to find out their bank

account number so she could transfer something into it on the sly. Faith and her new family were being more than generous, but with two young boys around, they couldn't afford to put her up indefinitely without some kind of repayment.

"If you say so, sis. I'll let you know how things go. Fingers crossed."

"We'll cross ours for you too," Faith said. "See you later, gorgeous."

"Good luck," Megan said, as Charity exited the shop.

She returned to her car and drove to The Refuge, which was the local retirement village. Halfway down the block, she noticed what looked like a newsstand on the side of the road and pulled up beside it. She headed over and scanned the scraps of paper pinned to the board. Many were old, but one looked to have been added recently. It was a job advertisement for an assistant librarian role. Charity quirked her brow and considered that. She liked books. She had no experience, but if it was only an assistant role, perhaps that wouldn't matter. It was worth a shot, anyway.

She took a photo of the advertisement on her phone, then tucked it away in her pocket. It was a short drive to the library, and she managed to find a parking spot right outside. Resumé in hand, she headed through the main entrance, aware that she could be walking into another potential confrontation. She'd barely made it five steps before she smacked into a solid wall of man. Her papers scattered on the floor, and she dropped to her knees to gather them up, fingers trembling because she had no doubt everyone was staring at her. As she straightened, her forehead knocked against the man's as he bent to help her. He grunted in shock.

"Oh, my God, I'm so sorry," she exclaimed, backing away so quickly she tripped over her own feet. The only reason her ass didn't hit the ground was because the stranger grabbed her by the arm before she fell.

"Are you okay?" he asked in a deep, velvety voice.

"I'm fine," she assured him, afraid to look up in case she'd given him a black eye in addition to making a fool of herself. But what she could see of him was very nice. A broad chest and tapered waist. He smelled good, too. Like lemongrass. "I'm not normally so clumsy. I hope I didn't hurt you."

He chuckled. "No, you just took me by surprise."

Finally, Charity dared to lift her eyes to his. Her heart stuttered.

Just freaking typical.

She'd bowled into the hottest guy she'd ever seen. With dimples, golden hair, and eyes the vibrant blue of the water in the bay, framed by sexy glasses, he knocked the breath right out of her lungs. He grinned, revealing straight white teeth set in a brilliant smile. Charity melted. Her brain lost its capacity for rational thought. All she wanted to know was whether his body was as gloriously muscled beneath his button-down shirt as it appeared to be.

Because of course, *of fucking course*, she'd steam-rollered into the most attractive specimen of a man in Haven Bay.

KYLE PRIDE'S HEART HAMMERED WILDLY AS HE WAS struck by recognition, and he discreetly wiped his sweaty palms on his pants. He couldn't believe he was standing in front of Charity St. John. He hadn't seen her for years, and she'd changed drastically in that time. Her hair was strawberry blonde where it had been platinum back in school, her face was devoid of makeup, and her outfit... well, teenage Charity wouldn't have been caught dead in it. Nondescript black skirt, shapeless blouse, and no jewelry in sight. But that wasn't the only change. She also carried herself differently. When they were young, she'd always held her head high and her shoulders back, confident of her place in the world. But before she walked into him, her gaze had been down, shoulders hunched, and she gave the definite impression of being skittish. Her hazel eyes—which he was convinced were one-of-a-kind, ringed by green and growing darker near the pupils—were shadowed. Despite that, she was as beautiful as ever, and now that he'd recognized her, his voice was trapped in his throat.

Damn it, why couldn't he have gotten over her by now? Once upon a time, she'd crushed his heart beneath her heel with less care than he'd take squashing a mosquito, but his body still responded to her as though she was its warp engine, and all systems were go.

"Charity," he choked out, when the silence between them extended for long enough to become awkward. "It's been ages."

Her brows furrowed, and she cocked her head. "I'm sorry, have we met?"

Even her voice had changed. It was deeper, and more cautious.

"You don't recognize me?" Sometimes he forgot how much he'd transformed since high school because he felt like the same guy on the inside. He had the same hang-ups. The same insecurities.

"Should I?" Her tone had adopted a degree of wariness, and rightfully so. There were plenty of people in these parts who'd like to see her taken down a notch.

"It's Kyle Pride," he told her. "From school."

Fortunately, this was enough to prompt a flare of recognition in her eyes. He didn't want to have to spell out the fact that he was the boy she'd brutally rejected in front of thirty of their peers. Her gaze flicked up and down his body, and her cheeks flushed. Was that shame in her eyes? If so, he wanted to know whether it was because of how she'd treated him, or because of how she'd fallen from grace. He preferred to think the former, but who would know? Some people were selfish and rotten. She nibbled on her lip, looking like she'd rather be anywhere else, and vindication flashed hot and ugly in the pit of his stomach. He tamped it down, reminding himself it was petty to be pleased that everything went to shit for the girl who'd made him a laughingstock. Even if she kind of deserved it.

"It has been a long time," she mumbled, so low he could scarcely make out the words. "Sorry for running into you. It was nice to see you, but I have to, uh, go."

With that, she brushed past him. He turned, watching her head for the counter. Apparently she didn't know he was the librarian. Now that she had her back to him, he noticed the papers clutched in her hand, with "Resumé" printed across the top in bold letters. A grin crept over his face. She was here for a job. As his subordinate. Oh how the tides had turned. He rounded the solid oak counter. Haven Bay wasn't one of those towns with a modern, new-build library. Theirs had character, and he liked it that way.

Resting his forearms on the counter, he grinned at her. "How can I help you?"

All the color drained from her face. "You're the librarian?"

"Guilty." He loved his job. Some days more than others. Like now, for instance. She appeared to be wavering, and glanced at the exit. He figured she was deciding whether to make a run for it or not. This probably wasn't a situation she'd ever wanted to find herself in. Taking pity on her, he nodded toward the papers in her hand. "Are you here about the assistant librarian position?"

"Uh…" Her knuckles turned white, and the paper crinkled slightly where her grip tightened. "Yeah."

He held out a palm. "Is that your resumé?"

Teeth sinking into her lower lip, she passed it over, although he had to tug so she'd release it. He scanned the first few lines, noticing immediately that she was going by her maiden name. She must have changed it back after the divorce. She'd been married to a scam artist nearly twenty years her senior. Everyone had figured she'd married him for his money—of which he'd had plenty, until his tower of lies came crashing down. Had Charity managed to blow through the fortune she'd no doubt won during their separation?

"I'll pass this on to my manager," he told her. His boss, Hamish, worked in a nearby city and oversaw all of the smaller libraries. Much as Kyle would love to reject Charity, he wasn't that kind of person, so he'd hand it along and hope she had absolutely no relevant experience and that Hamish would see how unsuitable she was. "We'll be in touch."

When he said "we" he meant preferably someone other than him.

She traced a particularly deep scar in the surface of the wooden counter with her finger. "This was a mistake."

Then she spun away and hightailed it out of the library. He stared after her, wondering if he was still supposed to give Hamish the resumé, or if she'd rather he didn't. And also, what the hell was with him? Getting tangled up on the inside just from talking to a pretty girl with a black soul? Disgusted with himself, he carried her papers back to his desk and started to read, curious as to what Charity St. John had been doing with herself since her world fell apart.

2

____

The universe was officially playing jokes on her. Charity could think of no other explanation for this karmic cherry on top of a crappy day. Kyle Pride—he of the bad haircuts and geeky t-shirts—had blossomed into the hunkiest librarian she'd ever met. And in the past few years, she'd met plenty of librarians. As someone who liked to be around people but had been ostracized on account of her poor taste in men, libraries had become a haven where she could be near others without interacting with them. But never in all of her library adventures had she met someone like Kyle. The guy was seriously swoon-worthy. He'd lit her body up like nobody had in a long, long time. But of course, she'd been epically bitchy to him in another life—which couldn't be justified, no matter how miserable she'd been feeling at the time—so all of that manly goodness was well and truly out of her reach.

Trying not to think of Kyle's lady-killer smile, she hustled to her car and got inside, then ducked her head when she spotted Betty and Mavis, a pair of local retirees, across the road and approaching fast. Betty's late husband had been one of the people Samuel swindled, and Charity had no intention of being berated by someone else today. She quickly pulled away from the curb and headed for the old villa near the beach where Faith lived with Shane, who was a teacher at the bay's primary school and came complete with a pair of sons and an ex-wife. Faith seemed to like having a ready-made family.

Personally, Charity wasn't sure what to make of the boys. Dylan was easy enough to read. He wanted what any pre-teen boy did: to be left alone to do his thing. But Hunter, who'd recently had his fifth birthday and started school, was another story. The kid was painfully shy, except around his family, but during her stay for Christmas, he'd latched onto her like she was his long-lost best friend. Not having spent much time around children, she had no freaking clue what to do with him, and even when she'd excused herself to the spare room, she couldn't shake him.

Tourists milled around the square and in the streets leading to the waterfront. She wondered why they all looked so damned happy. Was this the universe's way of rubbing her past mistakes in her face?

With a sigh of relief, she pulled onto a quieter street. Finally she was free of the throng. The journey to Faith's home was relatively short, and she parked on the roadside and wheeled her suitcases to the front door. Two suitcases that fit everything she owned, with the exception of the few items stacked in the back seat. Using the key Faith had given her, she let herself in and paused, listening to make sure no one was around. She'd prefer not to be mistaken for a burglar on top of everything else that had gone wrong recently. All was silent. She dragged her suitcases to the guest bedroom, which Faith must have taken the time to tidy earlier because it was free of the kids' toys and discarded clothes.

She sat on the edge of the bed, opened one of her suitcases, and extracted her laptop. It was the same one she'd had since before she married Samuel because most of their shared assets had been seized by the police. These days, it was a miracle the ancient laptop worked. The death rattle it made every time she used it meant she knew it wouldn't be functioning for much longer. While it booted up, she went to the kitchen for a glass of water, then she settled down and did a Google search for businesses in the Haven Bay area. Grabbing her cell phone, she dialed the first number and asked whether they needed any new employees. She didn't want to hang her hopes on the assistant librarian role. Not when Kyle would be her boss. It was unlikely he'd even pass her resumé along. She might not, if she were in his shoes.

Two hours later, when a car pulled into the drive, she'd called every business she could find within a twenty kilometer radius and had been rejected by all of them. It seemed no one wanted to hire a con artist's ex-wife. Frankly, she couldn't blame them. Disheartened, she closed the laptop and wandered out to meet Shane and the boys. She opened the front door as they reached the porch and held it while they entered. Her brother-in-law smiled crookedly. He was handsome in an absentminded professor way, with brown hair in need of a cut, spectacles that sat askew on the end of his nose, and a rumpled button-down shirt with a vest over it.

"Hi," she said, and then nodded to Dylan, who brushed past her as he headed for his bedroom.

"Charity!" Hunter exclaimed, clamping onto her side with a fierce hug.

She patted his head awkwardly. "Hey there, tiger."

"Are you staying?" he asked, angling his face up to meet her eyes.

"For a while," she replied. "Your dad and Faith are letting me use the spare bedroom, so we'll be house-buddies. Is that okay?"

"Yeah." He nodded enthusiastically. "Will you read me a story later?"

Something twinged in the vicinity of her heart. He really was adorable. "Sure thing, kiddo." When he hurried off, she turned back to Shane. "Thanks again for letting me stay here. I'll try to keep out of your way and clear out as soon as I'm able to."

He gestured for her to precede him down the hall. "It's no problem at all. It'll be nice to have another adult around. Don't feel any pressure to move out in a hurry. Faith has been looking forward to having you."

What made Faith happy apparently pleased Shane too. Because theirs was a healthy relationship, where they wanted the best for each other, unlike what she'd had with Samuel. She sighed. At least she could recognize a good relationship these days. Perhaps eventually she'd be able to have one. A girl could dream, right? She followed Shane to the kitchen, where he set his bag on the counter and looked at a dinner plan written on a whiteboard on the fridge door.

"Faith mentioned you were asking around about jobs," he said, opening the fridge, presumably to collect whatever was needed for dinner. "Did you have any luck?"

"Nope." Leaning against the counter, she crossed her legs at the ankles. "No one wants to take a chance on me. Big surprise there."

He looked over his shoulder, expression sympathetic. "Don't take it to heart. You'll find something. This is only day one."

"Yeah, I know." But the sinking feeling in her chest told her it wouldn't get any easier. "I hope you're right."

A FEW HOURS LATER, KYLE HAD MANAGED TO PUT Charity St. John to the back of his mind as he and his good friend, Brooke Griffiths, settled onto his couch to watch the latest episode of *Star Trek: Picard*. Brooke offered him a bowl of plain popcorn she'd just finished popping, and he grabbed a handful. Tuning in to *Star Trek* was a weekly ritual for them because Brooke's fiancé, Jack, didn't have the slightest interest in sci-fi.

Kyle snuck a peek at Brooke, tamping down a twinge of guilt. Even though they didn't usually keep any secrets from each other, he hadn't mentioned Charity's visit to the library. He'd told Brooke about the other woman in the past, but today's encounter had set him on edge, and he'd rather not dwell on it. They stayed silent while the episode played, both eating the popcorn, absorbed in the show. When it finished, they turned to face each other, sitting cross-legged at opposite ends of the couch.

"We booked a venue today," Brooke said. She and Jack had decided on a spring wedding, which meant they had a little over six months to organize everything.

"That's awesome! Where?"

"The vineyard at Te Awa Tui. It backs onto the national park." She beamed. "It has everything we were looking for. An outdoors aspect, cover in case it rains, and a gorgeous backdrop for photos. I'm so excited."

"As you should be." Shifting position, he reached over to hug her. "I'm happy for you. That's one thing down."

"Only thirty-five to go," she said, grinning. Kyle was a master list-maker, and he and Kat, another of their friends—who'd actually been married—had helped Brooke compile a list of wedding-related tasks to make sure she didn't miss anything. "Speaking of." She took a deep breath and threaded her fingers through his. "How would you feel about being my brides-man?"

"Oh, hell yes." He squeezed her hand and grinned so broadly that his cheeks ached. "If by that you mean your bridesmaid who's a man?"

She nodded, and excitement thrummed through his veins. He'd just assumed she'd choose the bridal party from among her girlfriends, but apart from his brother, she was his best friend, and there was nothing he'd like more than to be involved in her big day. Especially if it meant he got to make faces at Jack when she wasn't looking. He loved to rile Brooke's fiancé, and the guy took the bait far too easily.

"This is incredible. Wait, I don't have to wear a dress, do I? I mean, for you I would, but I'd prefer a tux."

She shoved him playfully. "No dress necessary, but you'll color coordinate your tie or shirt with Kat, who's going to be my matron of honor."

"Matron." He laughed. "I hope you didn't use that phrase when you talked to her about it."

"Of course not. Technically, 'maid' means unmarried, and she is, but I feel like 'matron' is more appropriate for her situation." Brooke tucked a lock of blonde hair behind her ear. "So, you're in?"

"Absolutely. One hundred percent. I can't wait. Do I get to go dress shopping with you?" He and Brooke had been attending sci-fi and fantasy conventions together since they'd first met several years ago, so he had a lot of experience helping her choose or create impressive costumes.

"You'd better." She sighed, the tension easing from her shoulders. "I can't believe how nervous I was about asking you."

"Neither can I." It wasn't as though he'd say anything other than yes. He loved how happy Brooke was in her new life with Jack and wanted to celebrate with her however he could. In fact, her relationship—along with the timely reminder of how he'd struggled with his romantic life after Charity rejected him—had inspired him to take action. He wanted what Brooke had with Jack. And he wanted to prove that he wasn't the undatable kid Charity had proclaimed him to be. "By the way, I've decided to start looking for Miss Right."

Brooke's jaw dropped. She blinked a couple of times, and then closed her mouth. He waited, knowing this was a shock. He'd always been shy about dating and hadn't been out more than once or twice with anyone since his last breakup, over two years ago. "Oh my God, really? That's so great. What's the plan?"

He retrieved a notepad and pen from the coffee table. "I'm going to write a list, and I'd like your help."

Her brow furrowed. "A list?" She looked doubtful. "I know you like lists, Kyle, but they don't work for everything. Just take me and Jack, for example. Who would have guessed what would happen with us? But some quirk of fate brought us together."

"I know." He waved aside her concern, unsurprised she'd brought it up. "But you and Jack are outliers. Lists have always worked for me before, so why not now?"

"Okay." She scratched her chin, looking interested but a little confused. "What's going on this list? Ways to meet people? Ideas for dates?"

"The qualities I find attractive in a partner," he told her, and scrawled on the top of the notepad: *Kyle's Love List*. Just seeing the words filled him with hope and excitement for the future. He was ready to start a new chapter in his life and doing this felt like progress. The first step. As if just by committing his thoughts to paper, he was inviting the universe's good vibes to bring his soul mate closer. He honestly believed the perfect woman for him was out there. He just had to find her.

"Are we talking physical attributes, or otherwise?" Brooke asked, shuffling closer to read over his shoulder.

"Otherwise." He tapped the pen against his leg, thinking. "Attractiveness is nice, but other things are more important." Case in point: Charity St. John, who had the looks of an angel but the personality of a snake. "Number one... Loyalty." He noted it down. "What else?"

Brooke hummed thoughtfully. "Do you want someone who shares your hobbies?"

"That would be ideal." Not that there were many girls in the bay area who did. "But they don't have to."

"This is your wish list. Why not include everything you'd like? We're talking about trying to find your dream girl."

"Yeah, okay." He grinned. "When you put it like that." He added *Shares my interest in sci-fi and gaming* to the list. "She should also be intelligent. I don't want someone who has no ideas of her own."

"Good call." Brooke rested her head on the back of the sofa, her lips pursed, eyes angled toward the ceiling, then she snapped her fingers and sat upright. "Kindhearted. You need a sweet girl, not one of those ones who come by the library sometimes to ogle and harass you. They'd eat you right up and spit you out."

He nodded. "On that note, trustworthiness is important. Or is that the same as loyalty?"

Brooke ummed and aahed. "No, I don't think so. Similar, but different." He added it to the list. "Would you want a woman who likes to read?"

Kyle considered this. He did spend a reasonable amount of time with his nose in a book, but that didn't necessarily make it a prerequisite for a partner. As long as she didn't mind him reading, he'd be happy.

"Has her own hobbies," he added. "Oh, and takes care of herself."

He had enough problems convincing himself to make healthy choices some days without having a girl-friend to motivate as well. He wanted someone who'd encourage him rather than drag him down.

"What about life ambitions?" Brooke asked. "Do you want a go-getter?"

He laughed. "Considering I have no ambition beyond being a librarian or maybe owning my own bookshop, I hardly think that would be fair of me. But..." He cocked his head and stared into the distance, thinking. "Perhaps someone who's at a similar life stage to me. Who has their shit together. I mean, I've almost saved enough to buy a house, and in a few years, I want kids. I have no desire to go out clubbing or anything like that." Jotting two more items on the list, he counted the bullet points. There were nine. He raised a brow. "Should we make it an even ten?"

"Oh, I've got it!" Brooke snatched the paper from

him and wrote something at the bottom, then passed it back.

Reading it, he grimaced. "Come on, I shouldn't discount a girl just because of her baggage, should I?"

"No, but I don't want you spending all of your time trying to fix someone either," she said. "I know how you operate, Kyle. You don't quit. You're determined to make things better for people."

He shrugged, feeling a flush creep up his cheeks. He couldn't exactly deny it, but that didn't mean he completely agreed, either. He read the list from start to end.

Kyle's Love List:
1. Loyal.
2. Shares my interest in sci-fi and gaming.
3. Intelligent.
4. Kindhearted.
5. Trustworthy.
6. Has her own hobbies.
7. Takes care of herself.
8. Responsible.
9. Ready to settle down.
10. Doesn't have an insane amount of baggage.

He held up a hand and Brooke high-fived it. Tomorrow, the search for his perfect match would begin, and he could hardly wait.

3

Two days after meeting with Brooke to write the Love List, Kyle was at work when his cell phone buzzed in his pocket. When he extracted it, his boss's name flashed across the screen.

"Hamish," he said as he accepted the call, strolling behind the counter to sit at his desk. "How are you?"

"As well as I can be considering I just found out we're expecting another baby." Despite his words, there was a smile in his voice.

Kyle grinned too. "What's that make? Four?"

"Sure does. Listen, I need you to call the applicant for the assistant librarian position." He heard papers rustling on the other end of the call. "Charity St. John. Ask her to come in on a trial basis, starting next week."

A sick knot twisted in Kyle's gut. Hamish was giving her the job? She was a barista, for crying out loud. She had zero relevant experience, not to mention she might not last long if she was only looking for something to do to pass the time. Surely she had enough money left from her divorce that she didn't actually *need* to work.

"But she hasn't interviewed," he protested, smoothing his hand over a book cover to calm himself. He didn't want Charity in his space. Especially not when she looked so different from last time he'd seen her—which had been on TV, during her husband's trial. She'd seemed every inch the trophy wife. Young, blonde, elegant, and tearful. He didn't know how to reconcile that woman with the awkward, downtrodden one he'd encountered the other day. He tried to reason with Hamish. "She didn't even say why she wanted to work at a library."

Hamish sighed. "Can she read well enough to shelve books in the correct place?"

"I suppose so," he allowed.

"And do we have any other applicants?"

"No." He could see where this was going. There would be no changing Hamish's mind at this point.

"Do you need the help?"

"Yeah, I do," he admitted.

Hamish made a sound of satisfaction. "Then call her, and figure it out. Now isn't the time to be choosy."

"Okay, I'll do it." Not like he had much choice.

"Great. I'll email you a temporary contract for her to sign when she comes in next Monday."

"I'll keep an eye out for it."

"See you."

"Bye." Kyle hung up, then leaned back in his chair and groaned. Of all the libraries in all the world, why had Charity St. John walked into his? The universe had an ugly sense of humor. He hadn't seen her in person since the Hagley Scandal—as people liked to call it— and he preferred it that way. He didn't care where she'd been in the intervening time, or what she'd been doing. He certainly shouldn't be curious about what had happened to turn her into the woman she was now. Searching the papers on his desk, he found her resumé and traced a finger down it until he reached the contact details. *May as well get this over with.* He dialed the number.

"Hello?" The voice that answered was wary. "Who is this?"

"Hi, Charity," he said, determined to be polite. "It's Kyle Pride, from the library. I'm calling about the assistant librarian position."

"Oh." Was it just him, or had her tone become even more tense? "What's the verdict?"

It felt strange to hear her on the other end of the line. When was the last time he'd spoken to her directly, other than after she literally ran into him? He wracked his brain. Probably when she'd humiliated him in front of everyone at school. He'd been too embarrassed to even catch her eye after that.

Not for the first time, he sucked up his pride. "We'd like to offer you the position on a trial basis. If that goes well, we can extend it past the trial three months. Are you free to start next week?"

Please say no. Please change your mind.

"Are you serious?" The question came out on a rush of breath. "Because if you're joking, this is a mean prank."

Damn it. If he was hoping for her to turn him down, that didn't sound promising. Also, what kind of person did she think he was to joke about something like this? If anything, he was the one who should be cautious of her, not the other way around.

"I'm completely serious."

"Okay then," she said. "I just have one question. Do you actually think you can work with me after what happened back at school?"

CHARITY HELD HER BREATH. THE QUESTION WAS A FAIR one. Considering their past, Kyle probably had every intention of making her life miserable once she started at the library, but as long as he was willing to work with her, she'd suffer in silence because this seemed to be the only job on offer. Even if it was on a trial basis. She'd burned her bridges when it came to Haven Bay, and the sooner she earned money, the sooner she could get out of here. Besides, she didn't want to be a burden to Faith and Shane.

Not one to beat around the bush, she'd had to ask, but she'd clearly caught him off guard. She supposed people didn't usually question job offers. But then, most people hadn't rejected their potential boss in front of the entire senior class by demanding to know why on earth he'd ever think someone like her would want to be with someone like him.

She'd felt awful about it at the time. She'd actually liked him well enough, but she'd been having the week from hell. Her boyfriend, the captain of the rugby team, had dumped her for another girl who'd apparently been more willing to get freaky between the sheets, and Charity had been feeling insecure and vulnerable. When Kyle, an undeniable geek, had publicly asked her out, she'd feared it signaled the beginning of her fall from the top of the social totem pole. She'd been desperate to save face and she'd lashed out.

It had been shitty. No excuses.

"Look where being a bitch got you," she muttered to herself.

"Excuse me?" Kyle asked.

"Nothing," she said quickly. "So? Could you work

with me? Because if not, I don't want to waste your time."

"Honestly?" He sighed. "You wouldn't be my first choice, but I don't make the calls around here. The truth is, no one else applied and I need the help. So yeah, I see no reason why we can't get along well enough if we both just do our jobs."

"You're sure of that?" She didn't want to turn up on Monday only to have him change his mind. Then again, it wasn't as though she had anywhere else to be. She'd spent yesterday job hunting around the nearby townships and come away without any promising leads.

"I am. I'll see you on Monday?"

"Yeah," she confirmed. "Do I need to bring anything?"

"Only yourself."

"See you then."

"Goodbye, Charity."

She shivered as she ended the call. God, she loved the way he said her name. It was official: she was crazy. As if Kyle Pride, with all of his newfound muscles and hotness, would ever look twice at her when she'd made it clear what she thought of him years ago.

Ugh, she had to get out. She scanned the floor for a sweater, snatched it up and shrugged it on. She tucked *The Catcher in the Rye* under her arm—she was re-reading the classics—and grabbed a beach towel, then headed outside, locking the door behind her. A few minutes later, she was strolling along the sand. Even though it was March, and starting to cool off, the sun shone overhead and the breeze that stirred her hair was warm. People played in the water, lounged on the beach, and cruised the waves on surfboards.

Rather than join them, she walked until she'd passed the last person, then continued for another ten minutes onto an isolated stretch of beach. Out here, all she could hear was the lapping of the water on the sand. It calmed her. However much she didn't like being back in the bay, the beach had always been one of her favorite places. Whenever she'd struck a rough patch over the past few years, she'd plugged her headphones in, closed her eyes, and played audio recordings of the ocean.

Deciding she'd come far enough, she unrolled her towel and spread it on a soft patch of sand, then stretched out along it and started reading. She'd read less than a chapter when a man yelled from somewhere behind her, startling her enough that she dropped the book and lost her page.

"Hey, you!" he yelled again in an American-accented voice.

Looking around, she saw no one.

"Yeah, you. With the book. This is a private beach. Get lost!"

She used her hand to shield her eyes against the sun and looked up at the nearest house. If she squinted and tilted her head, she thought maybe she could see the outline of a man in one of the windows. A man with binoculars. Creep. She raised her middle finger, then shuffled through her book to find the right place.

"I'm serious!" he called again. "Get off my beach."

She set her book down and turned to face him. Cupping her hands around her mouth, she hollered back, "There are no private beaches in Haven Bay!"

Then, making a concerted effort to tune him out, she dived back into her story. If he had a problem with her, he could come down and say it to her face. It wasn't as if she was doing anything wrong. She wasn't making noise, wouldn't litter, and if he put his binoculars aside, he wouldn't even know she was there. A shiver ran up her spine as it occurred to her that perhaps she should be worried in case he had a temper, but she had her phone if she needed to call for help, and she could always run if he turned threatening.

The guy never came.

4

On Friday, Kyle closed the library and headed home for a quick meal. Afterward, he went to The Den, the pub owned by his brother, Logan, for their weekly poker night. He waved to his mother, who was engaged in a spirited debate with a couple of men he hadn't seen before. Tourists, probably.

Corinne Pride was an attractive woman in her fifties. She had long blonde hair, a lean figure from surfing on the weekends, and the same sea-glass eyes she'd passed on to her sons. She attracted attention from many of the men passing through. Kyle had hoped she might find a nice guy to spend her life with —his father had divorced her and moved overseas when they were young—but she didn't seem interested in replacing him.

She nodded to Kyle and jerked her thumb toward the door leading to the back area, where the stairs went up to Logan's apartment. Kyle let himself through the door and turned left, up the stairs. At the top, he knocked once on the door and entered.

"Kyle!" Logan called from the kitchen, raising his

head from where he'd been bent over the sink. His shaggy blond hair flip-flopped over his forehead. "Good to see you, man. Any chance you could grab a couple of bowls and give me a hand?"

Kyle walked over and picked up a bowl of dip and one of chips, then carried them through to the rectangular table where they played poker. His friend, Tione, and Brooke's fiancé, Jack, were already seated at the table, as were Sterling Knight and Michael Briggston, who'd both moved to the area during the past eighteen months—Sterling to be with the woman he loved, and Michael to become principal of the local primary school. Kyle liked them both, although he had more in common with Michael and they often worked out together at the gym across the square, which Michael's girlfriend, Bex, owned.

Setting the bowls down, Kyle greeted them with a smile. "I can't believe it's Friday already. It's been a crazy week."

Jack eyed him with interest. "What does 'crazy' mean for a librarian? Someone returned all their books with dog-ears?"

"Not quite." He sank into a chair at one end of the table since the other men were along the sides, reached for a beer, and cracked the top. "It means we've hired a new assistant librarian whom I'd rather not work with."

Michael studied him over the deck of cards he was shuffling. "It's not like you to dislike someone. What did they do?"

Kyle shook his head. "It's a long story."

At that moment, the door opened and the last member of their group, Shane Walker, hurried into the room. As usual, his brown hair was mussed, his glasses were crooked, and he was in the process of removing a button-down shirt to reveal the t-shirt beneath.

"You'd think having an extra adult in the house would help things move along more smoothly," he said, dragging an extra chair over and placing it next to Kyle's. "But it just adds to the insanity."

"Do you have a guest at the moment?" Sterling asked, leaning forward across the table.

"Yes and no." Shane adjusted his glasses and blinked a few times. "Faith's sister moved in with us last Sunday. She was living in Auckland but something happened there—she's been a bit tight-lipped about it, at least with me—and now she's staying with us until she's back on her feet." He scanned the group and his gaze landed on Kyle. "Thanks, by the way. For giving her the assistant librarian job. She struck out every-where else."

Four pairs of wide eyes turned toward Kyle, and he shivered. Wow, that was weird. He didn't like being the center of attention. Especially when he'd just been complaining about the fact he had to work with Char-ity, and now Shane was thanking him. Way to make a guy feel like an ass. Also, what did he mean when he said something had happened to Charity?

"Where'd all her money go?" Tione asked. "She must have had millions."

"I don't know," Shane said. "But she doesn't have it anymore."

"Who are we talking about?" Logan asked as he re-entered the room.

"Charity St. John," Jack told him, his brow furrowed in a frown. "Apparently she's back in town, living with Shane, and working with Kyle."

Logan held up a hand, his eyes flying to Kyle's. "Whoa. He can't be serious, can he?"

Pressing his lips together, Kyle nodded. "Yeah, Hamish hired her a couple of days ago. She starts on Monday."

Logan swore. "How can he expect you to work with her? Did you tell him everything?"

"Nah." Kyle shrugged. "He knows who she is, and everything else is personal, between her and me."

"And the thirty-odd people who saw shit go down," Logan muttered.

Shane looked from one brother to the other. "What am I missing?"

"Nothing." Kyle prayed that Logan would just let it go. Ancient history or not, it was still embarrassing, and none of these guys had known him during his high school years, when he was chubby and awkward. He'd rather they not know the details.

But his brother wasn't having it.

"No," Logan said firmly, "it's not nothing." He turned to Shane. "That woman was in Kyle's year at school. He asked her to the senior dance and she made a scene. Rejected him publicly, then told him all the reasons he wasn't up to her standards." His nose crinkled with distaste. "She destroyed him. I just wish I hadn't been overseas at the time."

Kyle fought the urge to roll his eyes He just wished he could forget it ever happened, and that he'd been naive enough to think a pretty and popular girl like Charity might want anything to do with him. She'd just been dumped by a guy who hadn't been worthy of her, and Kyle had thought maybe—just maybe—she'd be open to giving him a chance. He'd have treated her so much better than that idiot. But he'd made a misstep and paid for it. Not only had she crushed his tender feelings, she'd rendered him untouchable in the eyes of the other girls in their year at school. His dating life hadn't recovered until he left for university.

"I didn't know," Shane said, rapidly turning pale. "I'm sorry, Kyle. I didn't realize—"

"It's okay," Kyle assured him, even though his stomach roiled uncomfortably. "I'm over it. All things being equal, I'd rather not work with her, but we're adults now, and it was a long time ago. I'm sure we'll get along fine."

"Wait." Logan held up a hand. "You're her boss, right?"

"Officially, yeah."

Logan grinned, his eyes gleaming with mischief. "You should make things so miserable that she quits."

"No." Kyle's reaction was knee-jerk. He wasn't that kind of guy. "That's not my style. On another topic," he added, searching for an adequate distraction from the disaster that was his crush on Charity St. John, "I've decided it's time for me to find a girl."

Silence greeted his proclamation.

Then Jack pumped a fist and cheered. "Good on you, man. About time."

"Wait. Hold up." Logan's eyes narrowed. "Are you going to make me the last bachelor at this table?"

"That's the plan." Distraction: achieved. "I even have a list to make it happen." He extracted the paper from his pocket and tossed it across the table to Logan, who unfolded it and skim read the ten numbered items.

"Go on, let us hear it," Jack urged.

Logan read the list aloud, and all the men grew quiet, their expressions thoughtful. Knowing what he did about them, Kyle suspected they were mentally sorting through the women in their lives and figuring out who fit the bill.

"I've got it," Jack said, snapping his fingers. "Shane's sister. Gabrielle."

Shane straightened. "Hey, now. Leave Gabby out of this."

"No, he might be onto something," Tione mused, rubbing his bearded chin. "She's only a couple of years older than Kyle. Smart, loyal, nice to look at..."

"She's not into gaming," Shane replied.

"Hey, can I hold onto this?" Logan asked, picking up the list.

Kyle shrugged. "Go for it." He'd entered the details into his phone so he wouldn't lose them. "Michael, would you like to deal?"

Michael nodded, and with that, the poker game began.

Charity bolted upright as she woke, spotting Faith on the end of her bed looking perfectly put together. Groaning, Charity dropped her head back onto the pillow. "Shouldn't you still be in bed?"

Faith pulled a face. "There's no such thing as sleep ins with the boys around. Dylan has sports this morning and Hunter and Shane are already on their way down to Sanctuary for DIY Saturday." She smiled. "They're so adorable."

"Yeah." Charity sighed and sat up. "They are."

She'd taken to Hunter. The kid was kindhearted and already seemed to like her for some reason. Not to mention he was easy company. He didn't have any preconceived notions about who she was and he didn't require long and thoughtful conversations.

"So." Faith pressed her lips together.

"So?" Charity prodded.

"Shane found out about what happened between you and Kyle. The men were apparently discussing it at poker last night. He mentioned it before he left this morning." Her face remained neutral, but Charity wondered how she managed to suppress her disdain. Even *she* was disgusted by her past behavior. "I didn't even think about it when you said you got the job at the library." She hesitated. "How are you feeling about it?"

Charity sighed. "Are you asking how I feel about working with him, or how I feel about the fact I treated a really nice guy like shit just to make myself look better?"

Faith's face creased with sympathy, but there was no judgement in her expression. "Either option."

Charity drew the blanket up to her chest, feeling exposed. "I'd rather not work with him, but I'm lucky he's even willing to give me a three-month trial. I'm sure it'll be even harder for him than it is for me." He probably hated the sight of her. "As for the past, I'm ashamed of myself." She drew in a shuddering breath that belied her calm face. "So damn ashamed."

"You'd had your heart broken," Faith said. "You were hurting."

"That's no excuse. I knew better."

Faith shrugged. "You can't undo the past, Char."

"No," she agreed. "But I can be better in the future. Don't worry. I'll do everything I can to make sure Kyle doesn't regret his decision."

Faith scooted closer and took her hand. "It's not only Kyle I'm worried about. You know you can talk to me if you need to."

Charity squeezed her sister's hand. "I know. It means so much to have you on my side, but I'm okay. I promise." She'd be grateful for Faith's support every day for the rest of her life. Especially since she hadn't always deserved it.

Faith stared at her for a long moment, then nodded. "You'll let me know if that changes?"

"I will."

"Good." She released Charity's hand and got to her feet. "I made coffee. You want some?"

Charity smiled. "Always."

She slipped from the bed and followed Faith out of the room, her heart full despite the fact she'd landed in the last place she wanted to be and would soon be working underneath a man who had good reason to hate her. Despite everything, she could manage as long as she had Faith.

5

MONDAY CAME, AND CHARITY DRESSED FOR HER FIRST day of work at the library with care. She'd been told, via the email containing her contract, to report to Kyle at 9 a.m., so at 8:55 she parked on a side street and walked to the front entrance. She'd opted to wear a black skirt, a cream shirt, and a gray cardigan, chosen specifically to not draw attention. She was going to be exposed to the bay's residents, and she'd rather have them overlook her as much as possible. She didn't want any drama—especially when that would give Kyle a legitimate reason to get rid of her. She just wanted to do her job and get paid.

She tried the door, but it was locked, so she waited outside with a couple of retired gentlemen and kept her head low until Kyle appeared through the glass pane of the door and let them inside. She waited in the foyer while he put out a sign to show they were open.

"Hey, Charity." He flashed his dimples as he stopped beside her. "Welcome to your first day on the job. I'll show you where you can leave your bag, and then give you the grand tour." He looked her up and down, and his forehead crinkled. Charity's gut churned. Had she gotten the dress code wrong? Messed up already? But he didn't say anything, just gestured for her to follow him.

"Thank you so much for the opportunity," she said to his back. It was easier talking to his broad shoulders, a knit sweater stretched across them, than it was to meet his gorgeous eyes. "I was worried you'd change your mind."

"Of course not," he replied mildly. "You signed a contract. You're here on a probationary basis for three months, unless you do something to breach the terms of your employment."

She noticed he didn't necessarily sound happy about it. But then, why should he? It wasn't as though they were friends. Quite the contrary.

He took her to a door behind the counter and held it open for her to pass through, giving her another glance at his square-jawed face. God, she wished she'd exaggerated his hotness in her mind, but no such luck. The guy was drool-worthy, with those vivid eyes and that golden complexion. Perhaps the magic factor that made him so appealing was the way he didn't seem to realize how gorgeous he was. He had that humble small-town boy thing going on, and it was working for her more than she'd like.

Toward the back, they entered a short hall. On one side was a kitchenette with a round table and four chairs. On the other was a conference room. He preceded her into the kitchenette and opened the pantry. The bottom shelves were clear.

"You can put your things in here."

She brushed past him and caught a whiff of lemongrass as she dropped her purse and lunch bag onto the lowest shelf. She closed the pantry and then followed at a distance as he opened the door across the hall. The conference room had navy carpet and a long rectangular table down its center, with chairs lining the walls. The only natural light came from a single window at the far end.

"People reserve this room from time to time," he told her. "There's a book club who use it every week, and Councilor MacAllister often hosts community meetings here. You can check whether it's been reserved using an online system that runs through the library's email server. I'll show you later. You might get requests or questions from people about it."

"Good to know."

They returned to the publicly accessible part of the library, and he stopped beside a small desk with a computer monitor on it, books stacked over a good portion of the surface, and a layer of dust half an inch thick covering the rest.

"This is your desk. Sorry about the mess. It's been a while since I had an assistant and I've gotten used to spreading out. I'll clear the books soon, and there are wipes in the top drawer to clean it off. The computer should work fine. I updated the software last Friday."

"Thank you." Charity eyed the worn chair, which she suspected had once been navy to match the carpet, but these days was a faded blue. "Will I do much on the computer?"

"A reasonable amount." He crossed to a metal cart stacked haphazardly with books and wheeled it toward the end of the counter. From what Charity could tell, the library was still largely empty. She could see down a number of aisles, with only a few places out of view. She suspected that was intentional, so people couldn't hide in the corners and break the rules. "I want you to get comfortable with issuing and returning books before we start on anything else."

"Great." While Charity was fine with the internet, social media, and basic office software, as any good millennial would be, she didn't have much knowledge of specialized software. After all, she was a barista. She hadn't needed those skills.

"Come with me. I'll show you around."

She walked alongside Kyle as he headed for the children's section. "It doesn't look like much has changed in years."

He chuckled, the sound deep and rich. "It hasn't. I've suggested a few upgrades, but for the most part, we don't have the budget to make them happen." He turned to her, one side of his mouth hitched up. "I wouldn't have thought you'd been in here enough to have a baseline to compare it to."

Ouch. Shots fired.

Yeah, okay, maybe she hadn't been a bookworm when she was younger, and maybe he had every right to throw a few snarky comments at her, but she didn't need to have been here often to remember how it looked. She didn't say anything though. He was entitled to his opinion, and she'd certainly suffered far worse for the sake of a job.

"Anyway," he said briskly. "Children's section is there. And over here"—he led her toward a corner with a couple of brown sofas and a bean bag on the floor, the window behind one of the sofas looking out onto the side street where she'd parked—"we have the young adult section." He tipped his head toward the long desk beside the bookshelf, where a handful of computer monitors were lit up. "People can use those, but they have to get a temporary login from the front desk, and they only get access for half an hour at a time."

"Okay." She nodded. "Does that come through the booking system?"

"Not these days. It used to, but too many people were using them, so we just have a bowl of passwords on slips of paper at the end of the counter."

She nodded. That seemed easy enough to monitor.

"Over here is the nonfiction." He paused, lips pursing. "I don't suppose you know about the Dewey Decimal System?"

Charity's jaw dropped. Oh, now that was too much. "Of course I do!"

"Great." He cracked a grin, and there was a gleam in his eye that made her wonder if he'd been intentionally winding her up. "Zero is at this end, nine-nine-nine at the other. And running parallel," he directed her to the end of the aisle, where another began, "is the fiction. 'A' is at the zero end. There's also a single aisle of large print and audiobooks. I'll show you those in a moment." He turned, walking along the gap between the aisles of fiction and nonfiction books, leading her toward the wall that faced onto the town square.

"The books aren't separated by genre?" Charity asked, following on his heel.

"We don't have a large enough catalogue for that to be worthwhile," he admitted. "This is just a small library. We often have to request to borrow books from the other libraries that are part of the network. Our patrons are able to reserve books from other branches and they get shipped over once a week."

"Good to know. Does the catalogue include the books from those other libraries as well as the ones here?"

He glanced over his shoulder, brow arched, as

though surprised she'd asked a good question. "Yes, it does. There's a table beneath the book details that shows where it is and whether it's available." He came to a halt in an open space with a table in the center that could seat a dozen people. "Large print and audiobooks." He pointed behind them. "Daily newspapers are kept on the table, and there are power outlets for people to connect their laptops, tablets, or e-readers. That concludes our grand tour."

"Thanks for showing me around." Not that there was a whole lot to see. The entire library occupied less square footage than the house she'd shared with her ex-husband. But it was nice, in a quaint way, and there were far worse places to spend her time. "Where would you like me to start?"

The dimples made an appearance. "You can begin by shelving the recent returns so you get a feel for what books we have and where they go. Come on." He took her back to the cart laden with books that she'd noticed earlier. His hand rested on the metal bar at one end. "My recommendation would be to separate fiction from nonfiction and sort them alphabetically and numerically before you start." He shrugged good-naturedly. "But it's up to you how you want to go about it." He checked the clock, which hung on the wall behind their desks. "That should take you an hour or so."

Charity also checked the time. Nine fifteen. If this was a test to see how efficient she was, she wanted to pass. "I'll get to it. I'll be back in an hour, boss."

She wheeled the cart to an opening near the newspaper table and got to work sorting the books. The task was quiet and solitary—very much her speed. Perhaps there was something to be said for being an assistant librarian. She wouldn't have to deal with people who were upset because their almond-milk-decaf-vanilla-latte had the wrong type of vanilla syrup. Shelving the books didn't take long, either. But while she was busy, three separate women stopped to linger at the counter and ask for personal book recommendations from Kyle. When Charity offered to help one —a pretty blonde in her early twenties—the girl giggled and confessed that she was only interested in books when the blue-eyed hottie was the one dispensing advice. Charity rolled her eyes and got back to work. She couldn't blame the woman. Kyle Pride made shirtsleeves look good.

6

By Wednesday, Kyle still didn't know what to make of Charity. She'd settled into her new role seamlessly and had picked up the basics better than anyone else he'd worked with. They didn't converse often, and she didn't interact with their customers much, but when she did, she was quiet, polite, and efficient.

Frankly, it annoyed him. Couldn't she have the decency to be a petty, unpleasant person so he could continue thinking the worst of her? As it was, he was constantly waiting for her to pull the rug out from under him. The woman she'd become bore little resemblance to the teenager she'd been. She dressed plainly, never complained about a thing, and hardly ever raised her head.

Was she putting on an act? If so, how long could she keep it up? Charity had always been impulsive and impetuous. The opposite of what he was seeing now. Even worse, heat sizzled through him every time he caught sight of her pert ass pressed against the fabric of an ugly gray skirt. And when she brushed past him in the narrow confines of the hall in the staff-only area, giving him the faintest impression of warmth and softness, he yearned for more.

All in all, he was fed up with his own reaction to her. So when he walked into the kitchenette while she was on her lunch break and came across her sitting at the table, legs tucked beneath herself, curled around a book, enough was enough. He needed a dose of reality to dispel her from his mind.

"What are you reading?" he asked, praying it would be something frivolous.

She looked up, her hazel eyes landing on him. "*The Iliad.*"

Oh, hell. Seriously? She was reading a translation of an ancient Greek epic poem?

One side of her mouth curled. "You don't believe me?" She handed him the book. "Look."

He flipped it over. *The Iliad* was printed in small text on the cover. He gave it back. "Since when do you read epic poetry?"

She shrugged. "They're not my favorite, but they're great for expanding the mind, so I pick one up every now and then."

"What is your favorite thing to read?" *Please say magazines. Cosmo, Celebrity News, anything that isn't impressively sexy.*

"I like the classics." A bell dinged in the background and she nodded toward the door. "Sounds like someone wants you."

"Thank God," he muttered, seizing the opportunity to escape without hearing anything more about her intriguing reading habits. He entered the library and spotted Betty at the counter with a pretty brunette. Betty was the leader of the local Bridge Club, a group of retirees who supposedly played cards but actually spent more time meddling in people's lives.

"Hi, ladies," he said, coming to a stop at the counter and gifting them a smile. "What can I do for you today?"

"Kyle Pride, you're looking dapper." Betty beamed and gestured to her companion. "This is Mariana. We met down by the beach." She turned to Mariana. "This young man is the one I told you about." She lowered her voice. "The one with the list."

A chill raced down Kyle's spine. "The list?"

Betty waved a hand dismissively. "Your Love List, dear."

His insides iced over. *No, no, no.*

Betty had a copy of the list?

Panic rose within him. "Where did you get that from?"

Her gaze snapped to his, hearing something in his tone that gave her pause. "From Logan, of course. He said…" She trailed off, reassessing the situation. "That boy played us! He said you wanted help finding a girl."

Kyle closed his eyes and swiped a hand down his face. "When you say 'us,' who exactly do you mean?"

"Everyone in the Bridge Club," she replied, matter-of-factly. "He gave us all copies of your list and we set up a sweepstakes to bet on who will find your perfect match."

Kyle groaned. This was even worse than he'd thought. He'd be Haven Bay's primary source of entertainment if he didn't shut the damn thing down.

"Can you stop it?" he asked, his voice an octave higher than he'd like it to be.

"No." Betty fluffed her short, white hair. "It's too late now. Everyone is on the hunt." She giggled. "It's not the worst thing ever. You want a lady, and we want to get you one. It's a win-win situation."

He wasn't so sure of that, and he was uber-conscious of the brunette—Mariana—quietly watching them. He turned to her and fought the urge to run and hide. Every time a beautiful woman expressed interest in him, he emotionally regressed to that wounded teenaged boy who'd been snubbed by almost every pretty girl in school after the death knell Charity dealt to his reputation.

"I'm so sorry she dragged you over here," he apologized, feeling foolish as hell.

"No, that's fine." She smiled impishly. She really was cute, with a button nose and twinkling brown eyes. "I came because I was curious, and because Betty showed me a photo of you." She winked. "I'm not disappointed."

A flush heated his cheeks. Unfortunately, he blushed easily. "I'm glad. Are you visiting the bay?"

She nodded. "I'm here for another two weeks. Maybe we could catch up sometime."

If he could ever get over his embarrassment.

"That sounds nice." Off to the side, Betty was gesturing for him to get a move on, so he snatched a piece of paper from the counter and scribbled on it. "Here. That's my number. Text or call if you'd like."

She tucked it into her purse with a smile. "I will." She turned to Betty. "Come on, Bets. You promised you'd get a pastry with me."

Betty waggled her eyebrows at Kyle and mouthed, "You're welcome."

Mariana raised a hand. "I'll see you later, Kyle."

"Bye, Mariana. Nice meeting you." The moment they were out the door, he dug his phone out of his pocket and dialed Logan's number. "You gave my list to Betty?" he demanded as soon as Logan answered. "What were you thinking?"

His brother's chuckle sounded down the phone. "I

was thinking that involving the Bridge Club is the fastest way to get things done around here."

He had a point, but Kyle wasn't about to admit it. Especially not when his personal life was up for debate by the nosiest busybodies he'd ever met. "You should have asked. I don't want everyone in my business."

"How's this?" Logan asked. "If they don't find anyone you like, I'll come over and do your housework for a week, but if they do, then you're on bar duty for a couple of weekends. Don't know why, but the ladies eat you up."

Trust him to turn this around. But Kyle wasn't one to shy away from a challenge, and he genuinely hoped he would find the right woman. "You're on."

———

Charity licked sandwich crumbs from her fingers, set her book aside, and returned to work. At the counter, Kyle was on the phone, and based on his expression, she didn't want to know what the conversation was about. She skirted around him and collected the books that had been stacked on the cart for shelving. She deftly rearranged the order, then started a circuit of the library to put them away. As she went, her mind drifted, dwelling on the Trojan war—the subject of *The Iliad*—and more specifically, the role of Helen of Troy within it.

She knew the story well, having learned about it during her classical history class in high school. Helen, the wife of Menelaus, King of Sparta, and supposedly the most beautiful woman in the world, ran off to the walled city of Troy with her lover, Paris. Menelaus and his brother Agamemnon pursued them and started a siege against Troy in an effort to get her back. Personally, Charity suspected their motivations were less pure than simply claiming back their queen. The Greeks' pride had been wounded, and they sought to reestablish themselves as superior to the people of Troy. Powerful men were all about their egos.

But all of that pain might have been avoided except for the selfishness of one woman. If Helen had stayed loyal to Menelaus rather than putting her own desires first, thousands of lives could have been saved. Choosing to follow one's heart could have dire consequences. Charity would know. Just look what had happened when she'd been carried away in a whirlwind courtship with an older man holidaying in the bay. A short period of bliss, and then her life had come crashing down—along with many others.

She grabbed another book and slid it onto a shelf, the repetitive motion oddly soothing. She liked her new job. She only spoke to customers occasionally, and she was surrounded by the smell of books. Despite everything, Kyle treated her well. She'd expected him to give her the jobs he didn't want, or to rub her face in the fact that he was both her boss and an absolute hunk while she was a divorcee and a social leper. Instead he was unfailingly polite and respectful.

She loathed it.

The fact he was a nice guy only made her feel worse for rejecting him all those years ago. The hot, fluttery feeling she got whenever she caught a glimpse of his toned abdomen as he reached up to return a book to its rightful place didn't improve matters. She had no right to ogle a guy she'd been so awful to in the past.

On autopilot, she finished her task, then returned behind the counter, where a stocky older lady with short, spiky hair stood with an athletic blonde in her twenties. The blonde was leaning over the counter, her elbows resting on the wood, smiling coyly and twisting a lock of hair around her finger as she spoke to Kyle, whose face was beet red. The blonde reached for his hand, took a pen, and scribbled something on the back of it. Her number, probably. Charity rolled her eyes. Of course beautiful women gave him their number. No doubt it happened all the time. Then why did she have a bitter taste in her mouth?

Crossing to her desk, she tried not to listen to their conversation, but it was difficult to tune out when the blonde laughed uproariously at something Kyle said. Eventually, she and her elderly companion left, and Charity started smoothing protective covers onto new books and loading them into the system. She was easing a wrinkle out of book number four when the library door opened and Mavis, an old crone she remembered well, strode inside, her wrinkly face set in a bulldog-like scowl. Beside her was another lady the same age, who was petite with sweet features. A tall, slender young woman with the bored look of a model on a runway completed the unusual threesome.

The young woman's gaze scanned the interior of the library, visibly cataloging every deficiency. For a moment, her attention landed on Charity, but then she gave her head a dismissive shake and moved on. Charity's grip on the book tightened, crinkling the cover more. She knew that look. It was the look someone had when they were sure of their place and found the people around them lacking. *Ouch.* Once upon a time, Charity had studied the world that same way, and it sent an uneasy feeling sliding through her gut.

The threesome approached Kyle, who was explaining the computer system to a teenager. Mavis cleared her throat. Kyle glanced over his shoulder, and something like resignation passed across his face. "I'll be with you in a minute."

Charity stayed where she was. She could offer to help, but she suspected they weren't here for her. She felt a flicker of sympathy for Kyle. If he were the type of guy to love the attention, having all of these women swarm around him would be a dream come true, but she didn't get that vibe from him. In fact, he seemed decidedly uncomfortable about it. While the women waited, Mavis's steely eyes conducted a survey of the room, passing by Charity and then doubling back. They narrowed.

Charity ducked her head. Mavis had been vocal in speaking out against her and Samuel. The shrewd old lady never believed in keeping her thoughts to herself. She'd told anyone who'd listen that Charity deserved to go to prison right alongside Samuel because she'd married him for his blood money and should be punished for her selfish choices. While the accusation hurt, Charity hadn't blamed her. In Mavis's shoes, she'd be angry too. But when others in town started echoing the same sentiment, it was like a dagger in her back.

She kept her head down, focusing intently on the task at hand until a bell rang at the counter, indicating someone wanted service. Daring to peek up, she noted that Kyle was nowhere to be seen, and Mavis and her friend were waiting with a small stack of books. The blonde lingered by the door, waiting for them. She discreetly wiped her palms on her skirt and got to her feet. Her pulse thumped in her ears like an ominous drum beat as she approached the women.

"If it isn't the charming Mrs. Hagley," Mavis drawled, an edge to her voice. "Oh, I'm sorry. You're Miss St. John again, aren't you?"

"That's right," Charity said, reminding herself that Mavis had reason to think poorly of her.

It's not personal. She doesn't know who you are. Not inside, where it counts.

This had become her mantra over the past few years. People had all kinds of reactions when they discovered who she was, but she tried not to take them to heart, because their spiteful words were only a manifestation of their trauma, and a result of the gold-digging image the media had assigned her.

"Can I help you, ladies?" she asked.

Mavis shoved the stack of books toward her, along with a library card. The Haven Bay library wasn't modern enough to have a self-service option, so Charity dutifully began issuing the books.

"How the mighty have fallen," Mavis remarked. "How did you end up back in the last place you'd ever be welcome?"

"Karma," Charity suggested, taking the air out of her sails.

"Hmph." Mavis seemed to agree but was clearly reluctant to do so out loud.

Charity pushed the books back across the counter. "Enjoy your reading."

"Enjoy your penance, you little upstart," Mavis replied, and the women turned on their heels and left.

With a sigh, Charity slumped onto the counter. Inhaling deeply, she counted to four. When she raised her head, Kyle was standing a few feet away, watching her, his face carefully blank.

How much of that conversation had he overheard?

And why did she care so much what he thought?

7

ALL WEEK, KYLE HAD BEEN FENDING OFF WOMEN. THERE were more than a dozen new numbers in his phone, and at least half of those women had convinced him to give them his number too. Several had asked him out, but he'd managed to avoid giving any firm answers because he hadn't felt sparks with any of them.

It was completely crazy.

Why did they seem to find him irresistible? He was a librarian. A list-making, gaming librarian. Hardly a rich playboy like you'd expect to find women lining up to date. But somehow the Bridge Club seemed to have a never-ending supply of women who were interested in just such a man. He should be pleased. He'd wanted to find the love of his life, and he certainly had more options now than he had five days ago, but as smart and pleasant as they all seemed, none of them felt right. Not a single woman had stolen his breath or made him stutter like a fool—sure signs of infatuation, in his experience.

Unfortunately, rather than being excited and full of optimism, he'd deflated. Being accosted within five minutes of arriving at work this morning hadn't helped either. Now, he grabbed a stack of books that needed to be covered in a protective seal and approached Charity, who'd been reorganizing a table of books.

"Do you mind staving off my admirers for a while?" he asked, uncertain how she'd respond. It was the first time he'd directly raised the issue with her, even though she must have wondered what was going on. But perhaps not. As far as he knew, she might believe him to be a player. Maybe she thought he was always pursued by pretty girls.

Charity straightened and turned to face him, her lips twisted in a smirk. "Had enough, have you?"

He chuckled and ran a hand down the back of his neck. "Yeah, I need a bit of downtime. I'm going to take these out back and work on them in the conference room, if you're comfortable taking care of things out here."

Her gaze dipped to the books, and he noticed the one on top was a romance, with a bountiful bosom exposed and the couple in a sensual clinch. She grinned. "No problem. You go have some alone time with your books and I'll stand guard."

He hesitated, not wanting to throw her in the deep end. After all, she hadn't worked here for long, and he got the feeling she preferred not to interact with people. "You don't mind? I can stay out here if you need me."

She rolled her eyes. "I can handle myself while you wind down. Don't worry, if anyone comes looking for you, I can manage them."

"Okay, thanks." Gratitude washed over him, more overwhelming than he'd expected, and to his utter shock, he set the books down and hauled her into a hug. When she stiffened in his arms, he knew he shouldn't have done it, but he was a hugger, damn it, and sometimes he couldn't help himself.

Mmm, she smells good.

Like oranges and books. Refreshing. Delicious. Her body softened against him, and she melted into his chest. Suddenly, he was aware of her in a totally different way. Her breasts pressed into his ribs, and his hands rested at the curve of her lower spine. Flustered, he backed away, dropping his hands and nearly tripping over a book that had fallen to the floor. His cheeks heated. Oh shit, he was blushing. Again. Fortunately, Charity seemed equally rattled, her eyes unfocused and her lips parting as though she wanted to say something. They closed again, and he grabbed his stack of books, including the one from the floor, before he could do something regrettable.

"Thanks," he repeated, then spun around and strode away. He stepped into the staff only area, his back to the door, heart hammering in his throat. God, what was that about?

Shaking his head, he tried to dispel the memory of her scent, but it followed him as surely as if he'd rolled around in the source of it. The worst part was, he wasn't even sure whether he was imagining it, or if it had actually rubbed off on him. He pulled himself together, went to the conference room and dropped the books on the table, then backtracked to the kitchen, where he poured himself a glass of water and downed it all in one go.

There, that ought to lower his temperature.

Returning to the books, he set to work.

Two hours later, he'd completed the entire stack and was nearly ready to face the public. *Nearly.* He paced to the door that separated the private and public parts of the library, cracked it open, and peered through. Charity stood at the counter, her reddish-blonde hair in a bun on the back of her head. She was wearing another of what he liked to think of as her invisible outfits. The ones that were designed to make her as inconspicuous as possible. Sadly, the gray skirt concealed what he suspected was a great figure without so much as hinting at what was beneath.

Raising his eyes, he looked to see who she was talking to, and abruptly drew back. Nell, one of the Bridge Club ladies, stood side by side with a petite Asian woman who had a shy smile and wore a Marvel t-shirt. She was pretty. Looked friendly too. But he couldn't handle another well-meaning grandmother thrusting a sweet woman his way, so he waited to see what Charity would do. As he watched, she smiled and chatted, reminding him more of the girl she used to be than the woman she'd become. Somehow, within a few minutes, the duo were walking toward the exit, waving as they left.

Kyle exhaled with relief and slumped against the door. When he'd regathered himself, he eased the door further open and stepped out, his eyes darting to the entrance to make sure they were really gone.

He smiled at Charity. "Thanks so much. I needed that."

She nodded in acknowledgment. "You're welcome. It's the least I can do. You've given me a chance that no one else would." As she walked to her desk, she added, "Just let me know if you need me to run interference again."

"Will do." Kyle sat behind his computer and snuck a glance at her out of the corner of his eye. She'd done him a favor without a single complaint, and as she quietly went about her day with the efficiency of someone who'd already been here for months, he couldn't help but wonder whether she'd truly changed or if she was still the same person inside she'd always been.

Something else he couldn't stop wondering: did she kiss as well as she hugged?

AT CLOSING TIME, CHARITY BROUGHT THE SIGN IN AND locked the doors for the evening. Week one had been a success. She still had a job, and she hadn't screwed up anything important. To be honest, she was disappointed to see the week end. Now she was staring down the barrel of an entire two days with Faith and Shane and the boys. She liked the Walkers—she really did—and they were more generous than she'd ever dared to hope, but she felt like an intruder in their home. She didn't belong there, and she didn't want to put them out any more than necessary.

In an effort to delay leaving, she crossed the room to Kyle, who was tidying the display on the far side of the counter, and said, "I can finish up here if you'd like to head home."

He glanced up, his blue eyes crinkling in the corners. "I'm happy to stay." He shrugged. "I'm used to being the only one around, so I've gotten in the habit of doing it myself."

Charity pursed her lips. Was that the truth, or did he not trust her? She couldn't tell. She wouldn't blame him if he was leery of leaving her alone, but in reality, what could she do to mess anything up? It was a library, after all.

"Are you sure?" she asked. "I don't mind being late. It's peaceful here after hours. I like it."

The crinkles around his eyes softened, and her stomach fluttered in response. "So do I." He leaned against the counter and crossed his ankles. "What do you have planned for the weekend?"

"Nothing much." Trying to stay out of the way. "I'll probably help out with the housework. Maybe read a book."

"Have you finished *The Iliad*?"

"No," she admitted. "It takes a while to get through. I can't just skim it; I have to think about each line. It slows me down."

He nodded. "I can't say I've read *The Iliad*, but I'm that way with Shakespeare. But then, reading the bard always reminds me of high school English class." His nose scrunched up. "I love books, but not the crap they make you read in school."

She snorted and snapped a hand up to cover her mouth. "So, what do you like to read?"

He raised one shoulder, glancing self-consciously at the floor. "Exactly what you'd expect. Science fiction. Epic fantasy. Space opera. The occasional futuristic military thriller."

She hid her smile. "Geek."

His cheeks reddened. Why did he have to be so freaking adorable? "Yeah, and what?"

She shook her head. "Nothing to be ashamed about. I lean more toward literary fiction, poetry, and classics myself, but that's because I prefer tragedies to happy endings. They're more realistic."

His eyebrows drew together. "That's a pretty bleak outlook."

She smoothed her hands down her skirt. She'd said too much already; may as well go all the way. "When you're dragged out of bed and arrested, then find out your husband was a swindler who never loved you, and you have to testify against him in court while going through a public divorce, it tends to dampen your outlook. The public hatred doesn't help either."

He studied her, those penetrating eyes of his seeing more than she wanted them to. All of the emotions she'd tried to hide. People assumed she'd married Samuel for his money, and that she'd been complicit in his crimes, but she hadn't. She'd loved him. She'd thought him a reliable man—miles above the boyfriend who'd cast her aside when she was younger, and the other guys she'd dated afterward. It had hurt so much to realize she'd been duped and left to the wolves.

"I can see that," he said slowly. "I suppose I never really thought about it that way."

She brushed her hands together and walked back around the desk, eager to move on. She shouldn't be disappointed by his opinion of her. He had even more reason to dislike her than most. "Hardly surprising. So, what are your plans this weekend?"

"Poker night," he answered, his head tilted thoughtfully. "Logan runs a weekly game for some friends at his apartment."

"Sounds like fun." She tried not to feel wistful. It would be nice to have friends of her own to do that kind of thing with. She'd had a lot of friends, once upon a time. And then everything went to shit. "Are there many of you who play?"

He rubbed his chin. "Let's see... Me, Logan, Jack, Shane, Tione, Sterling, and Michael. So, seven, usually. If everyone is accounted for. Lately, people have been missing it more than they used to. When poker night started, we were a bunch of single guys, but five of the seven are now in committed relationships."

"Is Logan one of them?" she asked, trying to recall

what she could about his brother. She remembered a tall guy with the lean, muscled physique of a surfer, scruffy blonde hair, and a flirty smile. He wasn't around much when they were in high school because he'd been traveling the professional surfing circuit. She wondered what had brought him home. A woman perhaps, although he hadn't seemed like the type to settle down. But then, people changed.

Kyle shook his head. "Nah. He and I are the only two holdouts. He enjoys being a bachelor too much, especially when he meets all the pretty tourists between his two jobs—the bar and running the surf school. As for me..." He trailed off, gazing into the distance, then shook himself back to the present. "It doesn't matter. Tomorrow, I'll catch up with my friend, Brooke. I don't see her as much as I used to because she got engaged recently and she's busy planning the wedding."

"That's nice." Charity hoped Brooke had better luck in her marriage than she'd had in hers. "When's the big day?"

"In spring."

"Good time of year for a wedding." Charity's had happened mid-winter. In hindsight, perhaps the arctic winds and pounding rain had been a sign of things to come. She fished around for something else to say. Small talk wasn't easy for her these days because she didn't tend to do a lot of it, but she wasn't ready to finish closing and go home either.

"So, are you going out with anyone special this weekend?" she asked, immediately cursing herself for wanting to know. Wasn't it bad enough that she'd had to watch him flirt his way through the week without knowing whether he intended to follow up with any of the many beautiful women who'd paraded through the library?

He shrugged, shifting his weight like the question made him uncomfortable. "Maybe. I haven't decided yet."

Jealousy fisted in her gut, hot and tight. She tried to squelch it, but it was too late. Kyle Pride, with his sexy-as-hell body and shy smile, had become someone she liked. And all things considered, that wasn't okay.

"You should do it," she said, and forced herself to take a few steps away.

"Maybe I will."

They returned to work, quietly and quickly completing what needed to be done prior to leaving. When he locked the private staff exit and they parted ways, Charity walked toward her temporary home. She'd taken to leaving her car at Faith's place, provided the weather forecast was good, because the walk gave her a bit of time to breathe and was a much-needed source of exercise. She made her way out of the town square and turned onto the road parallel to the beach. She was a few blocks from home when her phone vibrated, and she fished it out of her purse. The words on the messaging app screen made her stop dead in her tracks.

User9108: *You'll never outrun my name, Cha-Cha. I'll find you.*

She exhaled shakily, staring at the dreadful words. Not again. She didn't know who the message had come from directly, but it had no doubt originated with Samuel. In prison. He seemed to enjoy arranging for his friends and associates to mess with her head. She'd hoped they'd leave her alone after she left Auckland, but apparently she wasn't that lucky. With a few jabs of her finger, she blocked the user and deleted the message.

"Leave me alone, you fucker," she muttered under her breath. How was she supposed to move on when he wouldn't let her go?

She continued the walk home, carrying a sense of unease that hadn't been there before.

8

ON SATURDAY, KYLE FINISHED AN EARLY MORNING GYM session, showered, and drove to the house Brooke shared with her fiancé, Jack. He knocked on the front door, because Jack didn't like it when he let himself in. After accidentally seeing his friend's ass as he thrust into Brooke, Kyle had been inclined to agree they needed some boundaries. He had no desire to see that much of Jack—or Brooke—ever again. There were some things friends didn't need to share.

"Hey, man," Jack said when he opened the door. He wore a t-shirt with his outdoor adventure business's logo on the front and his hair was a mess, as if he hadn't long been out of bed. "How are you doing?"

"Not bad." Kyle stepped inside and waited for Jack to close the door, reflecting on how glad he was that everything had worked out between his two friends. There had been a time when Jack envied Kyle's friendship with Brooke, and believed it was more than it actually was, but they'd sorted out their differences long ago. "How's the wedding planning?"

A grin spread across Jack's rugged features. "We

have the date locked in. November third. It's the first Saturday of the month."

Kyle's spirits buoyed. He was looking forward to Brooke's wedding. Maybe it made him a romantic, but he loved weddings. "That's great."

"Hi!" Brooke called, spotting him as he entered the living area. She flew across the room and launched herself into his arms.

He stumbled back a step. "Whoa, there. Slow down, Brookie."

She drew back, smiling from ear to ear. "Did Jack tell you the news?"

"If the news is that you have a date, then yes, he did. Pretty exciting, huh?"

"I know, right?" She led him to the table, where a wedding binder sat with the dividers open. He'd bought it as a gift after she came back from a trip to Mt Everest Base Camp with Jack, wearing a ring. She took the chair in front of it, and he sank onto the one beside her. Jack vanished into the kitchen. "So now that we have a venue, a date, and a bridal party, it's time to get into the nitty gritty."

"Wait." Kyle held up a hand. "Who are the groomsmen?"

Brooke raised an eyebrow. "Weren't you with the boys at poker last night? Surely they mentioned it."

"Nope."

"They must be better at keeping a secret than I thought," she replied. "Logan is the best man, and Tione is a groomsman."

"I'm amazed Logan kept that to himself."

Jack stuck his head through the door, looking sheepish. "Uh, actually, I haven't gotten around to telling Logan and Tee yet."

Brooke frowned. "But you said it was taken care of."

He shrugged. "It's not like they'll say no."

He made a strategic exit before Brooke could respond.

"Men," she scoffed and looked at Kyle. "Why can't they all be as organized as you?"

"One obsessive person in the house is enough," Jack called from the other room.

Brooke's eyes narrowed. "Anyway," she said. "I'm looking at dates to go dress shopping in Auckland. Will you come?"

"Absolutely. I want to be there for everything a bridesmaid would do. I'll sip cocktails at your bachelorette party if I'm invited."

"Nothing would make me happier. Are there any days you won't be able to come to Auckland?"

He considered this. Before Charity started, he'd only have been able to commit to being available on weekends. But now, strange as it may be, he trusted that he could leave her in charge and come back to find the place unscathed. "No, I can make anything work."

"Great." Brooke opened her laptop and keyed in a password. "I need your expertise to make a list of the shops I want to check out." She typed in a web search. "First, I thought we'd start with the boutique Megan's sister-in-law runs. I've heard really good things about her."

Kyle shuffled his chair closer. "Okay, let's do this."

A couple of hours later, they had a list of seven boutiques and a document full of copy-and-paste snippets of dresses Brooke liked. She closed both her laptop and her binder and gave a satisfied sigh.

"So," she said. "Now that's out of the way, did you meet any nice girls this week?"

His jaw dropped. Something in her expression told him she was aware of exactly how many girls had come through the library since they made their list. "Who told you?"

"Logan mentioned it to Jack. Anyway, did you? I need to hear about your romantic escapades."

He winced. "There's not much to tell. The Bridge Club have been in and out with different women all week. They seem nice, and I'm sure some of them might be a good fit, but it's kind of hard to figure that out when we're being chaperoned by nosy retirees."

Brooke burst out laughing. "I can see how that could be difficult. But you know how to fix that?" She leaned forward, eyes twinkling. "You call them and ask them on a date. Have you called any back?"

"No," he admitted. "Although I've been messaging a couple."

"Do they match up with your list?"

"I'm not sure yet."

She rolled her eyes. "Then pick the one you like most and go find out."

"Maybe I will." Although none of the girls he'd talked to leapt out as the obvious choice, and to be honest, he might have mixed a couple of them up in his mind. There had been so many, and he usually hit a wall after meeting a certain number of new people.

"Or," she added, reopening her laptop, "if none of them do it for you, we could check out internet dating sites."

"We could," he agreed, unable to summon any enthusiasm.

Frowning, Brooke studied him. "What's going on?

A week ago, you were really excited about your quest for love. Did something change?"

He buried his face in his hands. She was right. He was being weird. But much as he hated it, his thoughts were occupied by Charity. He'd reassured himself that he was only trying to figure her out, but if that were the case, why did he spend so much time dwelling on the delicacy of her features and the glossiness of her hair? Why did he worry she was unhappy, rather than being glad her life had fallen apart?

He groaned. "You're not going to believe this, but I think I'm hung up on Charity St. John."

"Oh, Kyle." She gave him a pained look. "After what she did to you?"

His shoulders hunched at the memory, but he tried to make light of it. "What can I say? I'm a forgiving guy."

"And I love you for it." Reaching over, she took his hand. "But you definitely need to call one of those girls who gave you their number because I recognize Stockholm syndrome when I see it."

He chuckled.

"Come on." She raised a brow. "A beautiful girl who you're stuck with all day? Of course you're going to feel close to her. But pretty vipers are still poisonous."

"I know." He squeezed her hand. "Thanks for the reminder. Have you met her yet?"

"Nope," she said. "And I don't need to. Now, I'm going to sit here with you until you choose a woman and organize a date."

Well, that was that. It seemed he was going on a date. When Brooke set her mind to something, she became an immovable wall of determination. Grabbing his phone, he scrolled through the contacts.

"Mariana," he said, settling on one. "Cute brunette.

Nice, funny, and going to be around for at least another week."

"There." Brooke smiled. "That wasn't so hard, was it?"

<hr>

ON SATURDAY, CHARITY VOLUNTEERED TO TAKE DYLAN to his cricket game in the nearby town of Te Awa Tui while Shane took Hunter to DIY Saturday, which was apparently a weekly tradition for them. They were building skills to improve their own home, Faith had told her as she dressed for work this morning. Charity had sat cross-legged on her bed and mused on the fact that for Faith, a pink and white striped retro dress counted as work attire. Not that her sister didn't look good in it. With plentiful curves and deep red hair, Faith looked good in almost anything. Frankly, Charity envied her. While Faith had always embraced her natural figure and hair color, Charity had spent a lot of time and energy dying her strawberry blonde locks platinum and taking spin classes like diet pills.

"Do you have everything you need?" she asked Dylan now, as she hovered in the hall outside his room. Given that he was entering his teen years, she'd decided it was best not to encroach on his space. Especially since he seemed to make a point to close the door, whether he was inside or out. That was fine by her. She'd never been one to push herself in where she wasn't wanted, and she didn't mind his particular style of antisocial because it blended nicely with her own.

"Yep. Just got to fill my water bottle." He stepped into the hall, a duffel bag over his shoulder, and she moved aside so he could pass. He returned a moment later with a bottle tucked under his arm. "Ready."

They didn't talk much during the drive. Charity found a radio station they could both tolerate, and they listened to music. When they arrived at the cricket club, Dylan took off to find his friends while she donned a cap and sunglasses. She found his team easily enough and settled onto a patch of grass to watch the game. She liked being outside. Always had. Especially when the sun was shining, as it was today, and there was a pleasant hum of conversation around her. In recent years, she'd taken to hanging out in isolated areas, but it was nice to be among people. Anonymous. That was how she preferred to be. Not like when she was younger and loved being the center of attention.

Despite not understanding the rules of cricket, she enjoyed the buzzing atmosphere and was able to follow enough to know that Dylan's team won. The coach took them aside for a debrief afterward, and she stood at a distance and waited. When the team separated, Dylan headed over with a grin.

"Nice work," she said.

"Thanks." He shrugged like it didn't matter, but she could tell he was pleased. They headed for her car.

"Does your dad come and watch often?"

"He does when the games are in the afternoon."

She unlocked the car, and he tossed his bag into the trunk. "Do you want to stop by The Shack and get an ice cream on the way home?" That was what parents did after weekend sports, wasn't it?

"Yeah, that'd be cool."

They drove back to the bay and, after a pit stop for ice cream, she dropped Dylan off at his friend's place and went to the beach with a book. She walked to the same quiet stretch of sand she'd visited last time and unrolled her blanket. She'd finished *The Iliad* and started reading *Henry VIII*, one of the lesser known Shakespearean plays. She dropped to the ground, fished the book from her bag and returned to the page she'd bookmarked. While she wasn't a fan of everything Shakespeare had written—*Romeo and Juliet*, in particular—she appreciated his way with words and talent for storytelling.

"Hey!" someone yelled from behind her.

Charity rolled her eyes. She recognized that American accent. It was the same man who'd interrupted her last time, but he hadn't done anything about it then and she doubted he would now.

"Why did you come back?" he called.

She faced the direction his voice had come from and raised a hand to shield her eyes from the sun, but she couldn't see anyone. "I like it here," she answered, loudly enough to be heard over a distance. "I won't be a nuisance."

For a moment, he didn't say anything, and she thought he might have left. But then he spoke again. "Come up here. I want to meet you."

She sighed. She'd only just gotten comfortable. "No. You can come down here if you want to talk."

"I can't." This time she heard something in his tone besides annoyance. It sounded like defeat. "I just… can't."

She shook her head and wondered why she felt sorry for this mystery man who hadn't treated her with anything other than rudeness. Reluctantly, she bundled up her blanket, tucked it under her arm, and went up the beach toward him. As she drew closer, she could make out more details of the house through the trees on the edge of the beach. Through a window, she could see a man's face. She gripped her phone and swiped onto the Call screen, typing in the emergency number in case anything went wrong.

"Hi," she said, as she got close enough to see that he was a little older than her, with a bushy beard and dark, unkempt hair. He left the window before she could get more than a faint impression of his features behind the hair, but then the door opened and he filled the space. The guy was big. Broad-shouldered and tall, with a muscular frame. She bit her lip, hoping he wouldn't be the last person to see her before she vanished off the face of the earth. But then she frowned. He was familiar. She studied him. Honey-brown eyes, full lips, and strikingly handsome once she looked past the bushman beard. An image flashed through her mind from a movie.

"Anderson Gray," she said. Hollywood heartthrob. Star of many of her teenage fantasies. He'd vanished off the face of the earth after some episode with an obsessed fan, but she couldn't quite remember the details. He looked different now—no longer a clean-shaven pretty boy—but attractive, nonetheless. What was he doing in Haven Bay?

He scowled, as though he didn't like being recognized. She understood the feeling. Perhaps he was hiding too. "Why are you on my beach?" he asked. "You can read anywhere. I'm sure there are far more comfortable places."

"I suppose there are," she acknowledged. "But I needed to get out of the house, and I'm not the most popular person in these parts, so this seemed like a good option."

"Huh." To her relief, he didn't ask anything further.

"Why do you care if I'm on the beach if you're not using it?"

He shrugged one massive shoulder. "It's my beach,

and I don't like people on it." His gaze flicked past her, and he added, somewhat defensively, "I use it sometimes, but it's too cold at the moment."

"I'm sure you do," she said. "But remember, it's a public beach, much as you may think of it as yours." She knew all about wrongly thinking of things as hers. As Samuel Hagley's wife, she'd thought of his mansion and fortune as hers. She'd been a fool.

He sighed and ran a hand over his beard. "Fine. Stay. I suppose you can come back as long as you're quiet and don't bring anyone with you."

"Thank you." She bit the inside of her lip to keep herself from pointing out that he had no right to either permit or forbid her to use the beach.

He leaned on the doorframe. "Come up and tell me next time you're here though, so I don't think you're trespassing."

She nodded. "I can do that." She took a step back toward the sand. "Nice to meet you, Anderson."

"Call me Gray," he said. "I prefer it. I didn't catch your name."

"Charity," she replied, and raised her book to show him what she was reading. "I have to go. Henry awaits."

His lips twitched. "I'd hate for you to keep him waiting. Goodbye, Charity."

"Goodbye, Gray." With a light wave, she continued down to the beach. What a strange guy.

9

KYLE SLOTTED HIS KEY INTO THE LIBRARY DOOR ON Monday morning and discovered it was already unlocked. Turning the handle, he let himself in and paced down the short hall to the kitchen. It was empty, but Charity's purse was tucked away in the pantry, and when he put his lunch in the fridge, he noticed hers was already there. He glanced at his watch. He was fifteen minutes early. He hadn't expected her here yet and she shouldn't have been able to get inside. Spidey senses tingling, he entered the library proper. Still, there was no sign of her.

"Charity," he called, hoping she hadn't wandered off and left everything unlocked. "Are you here?"

"Yeah." Her voice came from the direction of the tables, and he headed over and found her in an armchair, her feet tucked beneath her, reading as she sipped coffee from a mug. "Good morning," she said, lowering the book but keeping her place with her thumb. "Enjoy your weekend?"

"I did," he said slowly, wondering how long she'd been here. "It's early. How did you get in?"

"The janitor opened the door. I hope you don't mind." She drank from her mug again. "The Walker household drives me crazy in the morning. It's full steam ahead, so I came over for some quiet time."

"Huh." Quiet time. Not something he'd thought she'd ever want.

"I hope I didn't overstep," she added, nibbling on her lower lip and drawing his gaze to it. Her lips were pink and sensual. His hormones pinged into hyperdrive. Damn it, couldn't he have had this reaction to Mariana yesterday? But nope, there'd been nothing. She was nice, but he had no desire to see her again. Charity, on the other hand…

His heart had been racing just thinking about seeing her today. Damn.

"Not at all," he assured her, suddenly noting her concerned expression. "You work here too. I don't mind you using it as a hideout as long as you don't let anyone else in and don't trash the place."

She rolled her eyes, a glint of humor in them. "Don't worry, I won't throw a rave in the library."

"Good. You'd better not." He went to the table and dragged over one of the wooden seats to join her. There was another ten minutes before he actually needed to be productive, and he was eager to see if his reaction to her was purely physical or if there might be more to it than that. "Your book doesn't look like *The Iliad*."

"It's not." She showed him the cover. "A collection of Poe's poetry."

Poetry. The former cheerleader-cum-trophy wife was reading poetry by Edgar Allen Poe. Couldn't she just fit into the box he wanted her to stay in?

He studied her intently. Delicate nose, intelligent eyes, stubborn chin. She was as beautiful as she'd always been, but less in-your-face about it. There was a light dusting of freckles across her cheeks, which she used to hide beneath a layer of makeup. She wasn't putting on any airs or acting like she thought she was better than him. She'd changed, and he kind of wished she hadn't, because it was challenging his perception of her.

"Why can't you just be the person I thought you were?" he asked. "That would make things so much easier."

She tilted her chin up, holding his gaze. The flecks of green in her irises seemed brighter than usual. For a long moment, they stayed that way, the air thick between them, but then she blinked and broke the spell. Her lips pressed together. "For what it's worth, I'm sorry for what I did to you when we were in high school."

Wait—what?

His eyes widened.

She sighed. "I was a stupid, self-involved girl with a broken heart. I actually liked you well enough as a person, but my feelings were hurt and my ego was bruised. When you asked me to the dance, I felt like you were threatening what was left of my image, so I cut you down to try to protect myself." He sensed she wanted to look away, but she didn't. Her eyes were awash with shame and guilt. Much as he struggled to believe it, he got the impression she was telling the truth. "It was wrong of me," she continued, "and it's something I've always regretted. I know it doesn't make it better or magically fix anything, but I owe you an apology, so here it is. I'm sorry, Kyle, for being a complete bitch when you were nothing but nice to me."

"Wow." He grasped for something to say, but how

the hell was he supposed to react to a confession like that? He'd spent a lot of time and energy stewing over what she'd said to him and how she'd gone about it. She'd forced some serious self-reflection on him, and he'd never gotten over it. For a long time, he'd hated her. He wasn't one of those people who badmouthed others behind their back, but he'd simmered any time he saw her—and they'd only been halfway through the year in a small school, so he saw her a lot. He couldn't deny that the situation had pushed him toward where he was now though. He hadn't had many friends, and after their encounter, he became even more of an outcast, but he found refuge in the last place he expected: the gym. Exercise had helped take his mind off his isolation and given him something to focus on. So, in a way, he guessed he should be grateful for that.

"Kyle?" she asked, bringing him back to the present.

"Uh, yeah." He swallowed, his throat dry. "To be honest, I'm trying to figure out what to say."

She shrugged and looked away. "You can say whatever you like. I'm giving you a hall pass. Call me whatever names you want, and then we can pretend it never happened."

"No." He tried to get his thoughts in order. "The truth is, I used to hate you. But in hindsight, I only discovered my love of exercise because I needed something to keep my mind off the shitty state of my social life, so I suppose it worked out all right after all."

Her lips curved ever so slightly, and some of the dread pinching her features faded away. "So what you're saying is, I can claim responsibility for your insane level of hotness?"

His heart stuttered an awkward rhythm in his chest, and blood rushed to his face. She thought he was hot?

His insides flipped upside down, and giddiness rolled through him. Logically, he knew he shouldn't put such stock in the opinion of one person—especially not her—but when she smiled at him like that, it was kind of hard not to.

<hr>

Oh. My. God.

A flustered Kyle Pride was the cutest thing ever. His entire face was red, right to the tips of his ears, and he stammered a response she couldn't even understand.

"I… Uh… Thanks, I guess?" he added.

She laughed, feeling much lighter. Apologizing to him had really taken a load off her shoulders. Her guilt had been eating away at her ever since they started working together, and getting it into the open was like airing out an old wound. It might be exactly what they needed to heal and move on to a better working relationship in the future. Maybe even a friendship. Friends were a scarce commodity where she was concerned.

"You're welcome," she said. "Don't worry though, I'm not going to become one of those girls who stalk you. And as far as the past goes, I got what was coming to me. I fell in love with a shallow man and made the mistake of believing he loved me back, but the only person Samuel has ever been capable of loving is himself."

Kyle winced. "Is it bad if I say I can believe that?"

"Not at all." She waved a hand, dismissing his concern. "Everyone else did too. But I was convinced he loved me." Frustration welled within her at the memory of how foolish she'd been. How she hadn't seen what was right in front of her eyes. She often wondered whether she'd just been stupid, or if she'd been willfully blind because she'd wanted so badly to have a handsome, successful, mature man who adored her. Which was worse?

"I'm sorry."

She didn't look up. She could hear the pity in his voice, and if there was one thing he didn't owe her, it was that. "Don't be. It turns out I didn't love him anyway. I just liked the way he made me feel. I was young and naive." She still didn't know what romantic love truly felt like, but she knew what love was in the more general sense. It was the overwhelming affection she felt for Faith, and the knowledge that she'd do anything for her sister.

Kyle hesitated, but the hitch of his breath let her know he had something on his mind.

"What is it?" she asked.

He leaned forward. She stared at the powerful cords of his forearms, which were bare because he'd rolled up his shirtsleeves. "I think you're being overly hard on yourself."

His words startled a laugh from her. "I'm not. Trust me, I was no princess back then. But being dragged out of your house in a nightgown by the police has a way of changing a girl's perspective."

"You weren't a princess," he said, stretching his hands in a way that flexed the muscles of those delicious forearms. "But you weren't that bad either. Only in front of your friends. You were nice to me when they weren't around."

Charity wasn't sure whether that made things better, and she could hardly believe he was trying to comfort her. But still, his words flagged something in her brain. Could he be right? Was it possible that she hadn't been so bad *all* of the time? She'd certainly beaten herself up enough about her past behavior and had passed a blanket condemnation on her younger self. Had she been too harsh?

"Doesn't that make me two-faced, then?" she asked.

He exhaled softly, and she raised her head to meet eyes of the richest blue. "Aren't all teenagers, to a certain extent?"

One side of her mouth quirked up. "Did you just answer a question with a question?"

He grinned, a dimple popping in his cheek. "Did *you*?" He glanced at his watch. "I'd better get ready to open." He stood, pushed the chair back, then turned to her. "I'm glad we had this talk."

"So am I," she admitted. "It's been a long time coming."

He nodded, then sauntered toward the counter. Charity slipped a bookmark into her poetry book and made to follow him, but her phone buzzed. Extracting it from her purse, she checked the screen, and her mood took a nosedive.

User78445: *Traitor. I'm going to get out one of these days, Cha-Cha.*

Her insides trembling, she tapped out a response. It seemed that blocking the profile that had messaged her last time hadn't accomplished anything. Whoever was sending the messages had just made another.

Charity: *Leave me the fuck alone.*

Damn Samuel Hagley to the deepest pits of hell. Why couldn't he let her go?

10

AT NOON THE FOLLOWING DAY, KYLE EXCUSED HIMSELF from the library, rather than eating in the kitchenette as he often did, and set a course to The Den. He needed to escape Charity for a while. Not that she was pushing herself on him, but ever since their conversation yesterday morning, he'd been unable to think clearly around her. It was as if being in the same building fogged his thoughts, and he could sense the hopeful boy he'd once been lingering beneath the surface, wondering if maybe this time she'd say yes if he asked her out.

Worst. Idea. Ever.

Had he learned nothing? Okay, so maybe she'd apologized, and maybe she found him attractive, but there was a massive divide between liking the way someone looked and wanting to be with them. Besides, he had his list, and as he frequently reminded himself, she only met two of the criteria on it. At most. She seemed to have her own hobbies—she liked reading, after all—and she was intelligent. But as for the rest of the items on the list? Forget about it. She was a lost cause. Especially when it came to Brooke's item number ten: *Doesn't have an insane amount of baggage.* Charity St. John was the very definition of baggage.

He was a few yards from the entry to The Den when someone called his name. Glancing around, he spotted Irene from the Bridge Club powering toward him, dragging behind her a petite blonde, whose expression was horrified. His stomach plummeted. Not again. After having a quiet day yesterday, he'd thought perhaps he was safe, but apparently not.

"Kyle!" Irene called. She was a stocky woman, with spiky silver hair and a square face. "I have someone for you to meet."

Looking up at the sky, he wished he could shrink into nothingness and avoid what was sure to be another awkward conversation. Irene stopped as they reached him. She was panting slightly, her cheeks flushed from exertion.

"Am I too late? Have you already found the one?"

He wanted to lie, but it just wasn't in him to fib to an old lady. "No, I haven't."

"Oh, good. This is my granddaughter, Ellie."

He smiled weakly. "Nice to meet you."

"You too," she murmured, her face a mask of such embarrassment he suspected it was a mirror of his own. "I'm so sorry about this."

"Nonsense," Irene said. "Kyle, I see you're going to The Den. Why don't you take Ellie for lunch?"

"Oh, I've already eaten," Ellie said quickly.

"No, you haven't," Irene countered. "Come on. You've come all the way from Wellington for this."

"You did what?" he asked, appalled. Ellie had traveled for hours to meet him? He had to take her out now. What kind of jerk would he be otherwise?

"Actually," Ellie said, "I came because Nana told me

she was lonely, and I was owed some time off from work." She met his eyes, blushing ferociously. "I had no idea she'd planned this. I'm so, so sorry." She turned to Irene. "I'm not desperate enough that I need you to set me up with random guys."

Irene looked unrepentant. "Kyle isn't random. He's a very nice young man. He has a good job, is polite to everyone, and never gets into trouble."

Put like that, he sounded boring as hell.

"*Nana*," Ellie hissed. "Drop it."

Kyle's heart squeezed with empathy. Clearly this was a conversation they'd had before, and Ellie seemed nice. "You know what?" he asked. "Irene is right. I was about to have lunch. You should join me. They don't have a lot of options at The Den, but the wedges or toasted sandwiches are good."

She peeked up at him, face scrunched like she was trying to tell if he was being serious or not. "That's kind of you, but you don't have to do that."

"It's no problem at all." In fact, maybe it'd take his mind off Charity for a while. He nodded to the door. "It's the least I can do if she tricked you into coming here under false pretenses."

"Well…"

He could see her wavering.

"Okay, then."

"Great."

Irene beamed. "You kids have fun."

With a last, meaningful look at Ellie, she gave them a little wave and walked back the way they'd come.

"You seriously don't have to have lunch with me," Ellie said. "I can look at the shops for a while then head back and tell her we did."

He smiled. "You don't think she has spies planted to make sure we go through with it?"

Her eyes widened and she scanned the area. "Would she actually?"

He nodded. "Those Bridge Club ladies are sneaky, and they know everything. Trust me, someone's watching. Let's eat. It's no big deal."

They went inside. Kyle's mother was behind the bar. *Of course.* She often filled in while Logan taught surfing classes at the beach.

"Hi, honey," she said as they entered, and her eyes immediately flicked to Ellie. Fortunately, Corinne Pride knew how to be low key, and she just smiled. "Hi, there. You must be visiting."

"Yeah." Ellie fidgeted with a chain bracelet on her wrist. "I'm staying with my Nana. Irene Bertram."

"How's Irene doing these days?" Corinne asked as they crossed the room and claimed a table near the bar. Only a couple of other patrons were there, and they looked to be tourists. A good thing, since he'd like to have as little gossip spread about them as possible.

"As outrageous as ever," Ellie said. "But I love her anyway."

"Family is like that." Corinne rounded the bar and passed them each a menu.

"I'll have a toasted sandwich with cheese, pineapple, and corn," Kyle said, without checking it. "Oh, and a glass of water."

Ellie skimmed the options. "I'll get a small bowl of spicy wedges, please."

"No problem. They'll be out soon." Corinne left them, and quiet descended.

"So, what do you do for work?" Kyle asked, fishing for a safe topic.

"I'm a game designer." Some of the tension eased from her as she answered.

He stared, caught off guard. "As in, video games?"

"Exactly."

"Wow, that's so cool. I can't believe you get to do that as your job."

"I know, right?" She grinned. "It's a lot of hours, but it doesn't feel like work because I love it, so it's like I get to spend all day playing."

"What kind of games do you design?"

She hesitated, her cheeks coloring. "Uh, the type where you wear medieval outfits and battle the bad guys. Have you heard of Raider? I worked on that."

"Wow," he repeated, partly because that was absolutely awesome, and partly because he should find this sexy but couldn't seem to summon any enthusiasm whatsoever. Ellie was clearly intelligent, and she shared at least one of his hobbies. Not to mention she was pretty. He should be praising the universe for sending him his dream girl, but there was no zap of interest. She felt more like Brooke. Someone he'd like to spend time with but had no desire to undress.

"And you?" she asked. "What do you do?"

"I'm a librarian."

Her mouth dropped open. "There aren't many jobs that could make me jealous, but that's one of them. You get to spend all day surrounded by books."

"I love it," he agreed, wishing that Ellie made his hormones go into overdrive the way Charity did.

Their meals arrived, and they talked while they ate. The more they did, the more he realized how much they had in common. When they finished eating and Corinne had cleared their dishes away, he wondered how to end the lunch without hurting her feelings. But then she took matters into her own hands.

"You seem like a really nice guy," she said, and he could hear the "but" coming from a mile away. "But there's no spark, and it kind of feels like you might be emotionally unavailable, so it's probably best if we don't take this any further."

Well, that was a surprise. And what did she mean by "emotionally unavailable"? Was it obvious he was hung up on someone? Shame sat heavy in the bottom of his stomach. Had he been rude or dismissive?

"I'm sorry if you feel like I wasted your time," he said.

"Not at all." She smiled warmly. "I've enjoyed talking to you, and I got an impromptu trip to the bay from it. I didn't mean anything bad by my comment. I just get the impression you've got someone else on your mind."

"Maybe a little," he admitted. "Sorry."

"No worries." She stood and he followed her example. Together, they headed for the door. Outside, she stopped and turned to face him. "I hope you figure everything out. See you later, Kyle."

"Bye," he said, watching her back as she walked away.

Why did he get the feeling that nothing was going to go according to his plan when it came to finding love?

<hr>

"How are you doing, Char?" Faith asked, poking her head around Charity's bedroom door that evening.

"I'm good." Charity set her notepad on the bed beside her and drew her knees up to her chest. "Why don't you join me for a bit?"

"Ooh, an invitation into Charity St. John's lair." Faith's eyes sparkled mischievously. "How could I say no?"

"Easy," Charity replied, feeling snarky. "First, you

make an 'nnn' sound, and then you make an 'ooo' sound."

Faith rolled her eyes and settled on the edge of the mattress, her floral skirt swishing around her knees. "What's got you in a snit?"

Charity sighed. She'd been short-tempered since lunch, when she'd glanced outside and seen Kyle engaged in an intense conversation with a pretty blonde. The kind of girl who looked like she belonged with him. Cute, quirky, cheerful. Completely unlike Charity.

"Sorry, Faith. It's been a strange day. Hey, maybe you could fill in some gaps for me." She swallowed, afraid to ask what she really wanted to. "Is Kyle seeing anyone?"

The corners of Faith's scarlet lips lifted. "Why do you want to know? Are you interested in our resident hot librarian?" She waggled her eyebrows suggestively.

Despite herself, Charity smiled. "I'm just curious. He's good-looking, nice, smart. I saw him with a girl at lunch and wondered if she was his girlfriend."

Faith shook her head. "Doubt it. I would have heard if he'd started seeing someone. I know some of the older ladies are trying to match him up. Maybe they have a bet riding on it. But anyway, as far as I know, he hasn't dated for a couple of years. He's either very discreet, or practically a monk, but let me tell you, it's not for lack of interest."

"I bet it's not," Charity murmured, unable to help a pang of envy for the girl he'd had lunch with. Things had been different between the two of them since their heart to heart yesterday, and she liked the change.

"So..." Faith drew the word out. "Are you thinking about staying in the area for longer? Because I know you don't believe it, but you deserve a guy like Kyle, and if you like him, you should say something and see where it goes. Although considering the past, you might have an uphill battle on your hands."

Charity winced. "Uphill" would be an understatement. She doubted Kyle would ever see her in a romantic light again. "I'm not interested in pursuing a relationship, and I'm definitely not staying in the bay any longer than necessary." Even the thought of it made her break out in a cold sweat. As for her deserving a man like Kyle Pride... Dream on. Pigs would fly before she was worthy of someone as decent as him. Charity hadn't had many men in her life, but the ones she'd invited in had been rotten. The first, back in school, had dumped her for someone more willing to put out, and the second, who she'd been sure was the love of her life, had conned everyone around her and betrayed her. She'd chosen her partners poorly. Perhaps it was karma. "I'd rather be somewhere I can remain blissfully anonymous."

Faith's smile dropped away. "Is it that bad here for you?"

Charity shrugged. "It isn't great, that's for sure."

Faith cocked her head and drew in a slow breath. "Maybe it would be easier if you made some friends."

She snorted. "Yeah. Because people are clamoring at the door to be besties with the bay's most hated woman."

"Don't talk like that," Faith snapped, and Charity drew back, shocked. Her sister hardly ever raised her voice in anger. "Have you ever considered that maybe people would like you more if you gave them the chance to?"

"Um, no," she admitted. In her experience, that wasn't the way things worked.

"Well, now is your opportunity. My friends are

having a cupcakes and cocktails night at Sanctuary on Saturday. You should come."

Charity's mouth watered. It had been a long time since she treated herself to either a cupcake or a cocktail, and both sounded good. "I'd better not. I'd feel like I was intruding."

Faith's lips twisted. "It's all in your head. My girls are very welcoming."

"*All* of them?" Charity wondered if any of Faith's friends had been among the women coming and going from the library since she began working there.

"Every last one." Faith reached over and grabbed her hand. "Come on, beautiful. Do you trust me?"

Charity ignored the finger of dread curling around her spine. It was only a result of having played it safe for so many years. "I do." She squeezed Faith's hand. "You might be the only person I trust in the world."

Faith sniffed, her eyes suspiciously bright. "Then you know I wouldn't intentionally do anything to harm you. Come with me, Char. You'll have a good time, I promise."

Everything inside her rebelled at the idea, but it clearly meant a lot to Faith, and Sanctuary wasn't that far away. Only two or three miles. She could always walk home if she needed to escape.

She drew in a fortifying breath. She could do this. "Okay, I'm in."

11

"ARE YOU SURE I SHOULD BE COMING?" CHARITY ASKED on Saturday, examining her reflection in the bathroom mirror. She and Faith were due to leave for the cocktails and cupcakes night soon, and a sense of impending doom was warning her not to go. It made no sense, but as a general rule, she listened to that cautious voice in her head because it saved her from a lot of rejection and angst. "I don't want to make anyone uncomfortable or put a dampener on things."

"You won't," Faith assured her as she fixed her lipstick and blew a kiss.

"But surely they know what happened..." She trailed off as Faith narrowed her eyes.

"You're not getting out of this," her sister said. "Most of them know your past—okay, probably all of them—but they won't judge you for it. Everyone has done stupid things. They'll give you a chance. Anyway," she added, grabbing the mascara. "Cocktails go a long way toward dispersing awkwardness."

Charity laughed. "That they do." She took one final look at herself. Jeans, tank top, jacket, heeled boots.

She looked nice, but not wow. Forgettable. Exactly where she preferred to fall on the memorability spectrum these days.

Faith finished adding mascara to her eyelashes and glanced at her. "You really should wear a dress. I still have all those cute sundresses you used to love."

"You what?" Charity spun to face her and glared. "I told you to throw those out. They're not who I am anymore."

Faith didn't back down. "You changed, Char, but that doesn't mean everything about you has to change. You can still appreciate a pretty dress without slipping back into being the person you used to be."

Charity shivered. Was she that transparent? "Don't act like you know what it's like to have a bad streak, Faith. You're good, through and through."

"So are you, boo." Faith's eyes gleamed mischievously. "And you're wrong. Hangry Faith is a massive bitch, but if I keep her supplied with ice cream and cupcakes then we don't have any trouble. Now let's go, before you change your mind." She touched Charity's elbow and steered her out of the bathroom. They collected their bags from a stool beside the front door and headed out.

Faith drove them along the coast, past the school and the glamping ground, all the way to the lodge her friend Kat owned and operated. Charity hadn't met Kat, although she'd heard a lot about her and seen photographs of her in the news years earlier, before her professional rally career had ended. Charity also hadn't met the other girls who'd be there. Nor had she asked anything about them, because she was afraid the details would scare her off.

Several cars were parked in the gravel lot where they came to a stop. Charity scanned the lodge. It was an interesting building—a weatherboard villa, in the style of the early 1900s, with a large central section and a wing coming off each side. It looked like it had been freshly painted in a shade of off-white, and the window frames and eaves were cream. The sun had gone down, but she could imagine how charming the place would be during the day.

"It's nice," she said, her gaze lingering on a bicycle with a basket on its handlebars, near the door.

"Come on in. We'll be in the kitchen." Faith led her through a foyer with a massive glass window on the far wall and to the left, into a dining hall filled with rectangular tables. They passed through the hall and went to a door marked "Staff Only," where they entered a well-lit kitchen. Inside, four women turned to face them. One, whom Charity recognized as Kat Hopa, broke into a smile.

"*Kia ora*," Kat said, flashing teeth that were white against her olive-toned skin. Her inky black hair swished over her shoulders, falling midway down her back. The scar curving her cheek gave her a slightly roguish look. "You must be Charity. I'm glad you came."

"Thanks," Charity replied, offering a hesitant smile. "Faith didn't give me much choice."

At this, Kat laughed. "It's best just to go along with her. Have you met any of the others?"

Charity scanned the faces, seeing Faith's business partner, Megan, immediately. "Hey."

Megan smiled in return and tucked a lock of honey-brown hair behind her ear. She was a sweet-natured woman—something you could tell just by looking at her. "Hi, Charity."

Other than Megan, there was a blonde wearing a t-shirt that read "Sith Happens," and a mixed-race woman with the kind of lean, toned physique Charity dreamed of having.

"Brooke and Bex," Kat said, introducing them. "Ladies, this is Faith's sister, Charity. She recently moved back to town and she's working with Kyle at the library."

The athlete, Bex, studied her with narrowed eyes. "I've seen you around the square," she announced. "I run The Hideaway. It's the gym and art studio near the library."

Charity nodded. "I know the one you mean. But I have to ask, why a gym *and* an art studio? It's a strange combination."

"Yeah," Bex acknowledged with a tilt of her head. "I'm a qualified personal trainer and when I first moved to town, that's how I was primarily earning a living, but art is my biggest love. The Hideaway has enough room for both, so I figured, why not? Besides, I couldn't always take PT clients while my daughter was young, but I could usually find time to paint while she was napping."

"Makes sense."

"What kind of deliciousness did you bring for us today, Meg?" Faith asked, bustling further into the room to inspect the cupcakes on the counter.

Megan joined her and indicated a row of cakes in green cases. "These are apple martini. The ones in red are cosmos, and the white is mint julep. We have fruit, frosting, and a couple of syrups." She met Charity's eyes. "The way this works is that we decorate the cupcakes, and then sit around and eat them, with cocktails to match."

"Ooh." Charity's eyes widened. Suddenly, she was glad she'd come. This sounded like her kind of event.

"I'm down for that. Do we just grab whichever we want to start with?"

"Absolutely."

Charity waited for someone else to make the first move. It hadn't escaped her notice that Brooke had yet to say anything, and the other women were casting bemused glances at her as if this was out of character. Charity sighed. She supposed it had been too much to hope for that they'd all be friendly to her. She recalled Kyle had mentioned having a friend named Brooke and wondered if this was her. She eyed her more closely. They were probably a similar age, but she looked like the kind of girl Charity wouldn't have had much to do with when she was younger. Glasses, geeky shirt, very preppy.

Yes, probably Kyle's friend.

"So." Faith headed to the counter and grabbed a small tray, putting one of each cupcake on it. It was obvious she was trying to defuse the tension, and Charity loved her for it. "Shall we dig in?" She lifted the tray, sniffed, and proclaimed, "You've outdone yourself, beautiful."

The other women followed her lead. Charity's shoulders relaxed and she joined the group around the counter, selecting a plump cosmo cupcake to begin with. A bowl of pink-tinged frosting labeled "cranberry" sat adjacent to the cupcakes, and she scooped a pile of it into a piping bag. While she was technically a trained barista, she'd spent enough time in the food service industry to know her way around a piping bag. She piped a swirl onto the cupcake and topped it with several glacé cherries. Behind her, she could hear chatter, but she didn't try to involve herself. If someone wanted to talk, they could come to her. She wouldn't reach out and run the risk of rejection. Searching the counter, she discovered a small container of pink shimmer powder, pinched a portion between her fingers, and sprinkled it over the frosting.

"Looks good," a voice said over her shoulder.

Glancing up, she noted Bex watching her with interest. "Thanks."

"Have you done this before?"

"Ish." She shrugged. "I've worked in a lot of cafes."

Bex's dark brows drew together, a furrow forming between them. "But your new job is in the library? What's with that?"

"The cafe wouldn't hire me."

"Huh." She cocked her head. "Because you married an asshole?"

Charity exhaled, the air whistling between her teeth. "A rich asshole nearly twice my age who conned locals out of their savings. Trust me, people around here have long memories."

Bex laughed. "They do. Fortunately, I've never been on the wrong side of that, but I can see how it would be difficult."

"It sucks," she said bluntly. "But I kind of deserve it, and it is what it is."

Bex studied her, expression thoughtful. "You're honest. I respect that." She leaned over and wrapped an arm around Charity's shoulders. "Welcome back to the bay. You just do your thing and people will move on eventually." She gave a squeeze. "Hang in there."

"Thanks." The backs of Charity's eyes prickled, and she prayed she wouldn't tear up. She was tougher than that, but it had been so long since a stranger showed her genuine compassion and kindness. Her throat clogged up, and she tried to pull herself together. She couldn't start bawling in the kitchen or she'd have no dignity left. "I really appreciate that."

"No problem." Bex started to back off, but then something flickered in her expression, and she leaned in close and said quietly, "Brooke is Kyle's best friend. She's quite protective of him, and I heard you guys have some kind of history, so if you're getting weird vibes from her, that's probably why."

"Ah." So she'd been right. And if Brooke was Kyle's *best* friend then most likely she knew about what had happened back in high school. "Thanks for the tip."

"Any time." Bex sauntered away, and Charity set her cupcake aside and approached Brooke. The blonde was bent over an apple martini cupcake, arranging thin slices of candied apple across the surface. She didn't raise her head as Charity stopped beside her. Patiently, Charity waited for her to be done. Finally, Brooke straightened and adjusted her glasses, which had shifted askew on her nose.

"Hi," Charity said, figuring she needed to make the first move. "Do you have a moment? There's something I'd like to say to you."

Brooke pressed her lips together and seemed to ponder this, but then she nodded. "Go ahead."

The room had fallen silent, and Charity had no doubt that everyone there was straining to hear each word she said. Oh well, she supposed it saved her from repeating herself. "You're Kyle's friend, right?"

"Yes. I've known him for years." Brooke's chin jutted forward. "He's a good guy."

"I know."

One of Brooke's eyebrows leapt up. "Is that what you wanted to say?"

"No. I wanted to tell you that I know I wasn't good to him when I was younger. I was hurting from a breakup and I behaved poorly, but I regret it with my whole heart. I'm not sure if he's mentioned this, but I apologized to him recently." She paused, weighing her next words carefully. "I'm trying to mend bridges, not burn them to the ground, so you don't need to worry about me doing anything to hurt him again. I don't expect you to like me, but I promise, I'm not the same person I used to be."

Brooke nodded and some of the ice in her eyes thawed. The corners of her mouth softened. "Thank you for saying that. It takes a lot to be open about something you're not proud of."

Charity shrugged like it was no big deal. As if her heart wasn't thundering like she'd run up several flights of stairs. No matter how accustomed she was to facing people who'd been hurt by her actions, it never became easy. "So, do you think we could start over?"

"I guess so." Brooke offered a hand, which Charity shook firmly. "Nice to meet you, Charity. How do you like working at the library?"

Her turnaround surprised a grin out of Charity. If only everyone was so willing to issue a second chance. "Actually, it's one of the best jobs I've ever had."

"Really?" Brooke's answering grin was cheeky. "Is it because of the eye candy?"

"Not *only* that. I love books, so being surrounded by them all day is pretty great." Noise in the kitchen resumed—the others having apparently decided it was safe to continue without supervising their conversation.

"I wouldn't have guessed that," Brooke said. "I suppose it goes to show you shouldn't judge people before you know them."

"Here's to that." Charity grabbed her cupcake and raised it. Brooke did the same, and they bumped cupcakes, then each took a bite.

The rest of the night passed in a blur of delicious

food, drinks, and laughter. Once Brooke had decided to accept her, it was like the elephant had cleared out of the room and everyone felt free to have a good time. Although Charity remained wary enough to evaluate everything she said before saying it, it also was the most comfortable she'd felt among a group in years. She couldn't help wondering if maybe—just maybe—she could stay in Haven Bay for longer than she'd initially planned. With these women on her side, surely she could become part of the community at some point. People might not forget, but perhaps they could forgive.

Only time would tell.

12

"Let me know whether you enjoy it." Kyle waved to Betty as she exited the library on Monday with the latest naughty paperback he'd recommended for her. Betty had a taste for men in kilts and she was quickly working her way through their supply of Highlander romances. As he watched her leave, movement outside the window caught his attention. Charity had gone on her lunch break ten minutes earlier, and instead of curling up in the kitchen as she usually did, she'd headed out. Now, he could see the back of her head, with her reddish-blonde hair curled in a tidy twist as she spoke to someone. Her hands were moving in uncharacteristically animated gestures.

Curious, he shifted along the counter until he could see who she was deep in discussion with, and his breath caught at the back of his throat. Holy crap, it was Brooke. The two women were smiling and laughing like friends. Charity said something, and Brooke reached out and touched her arm, then they hugged, and Charity continued on her way while

Brooke entered the library. Spotting him immediately, she beelined over.

"Hey, Kyle." She grinned broadly.

Kyle's mouth opened and closed. For some reason, seeing Charity and Brooke together had really thrown him for a loop. Brooke had given every impression she hated Charity on his behalf, even though they'd never actually met, but now they were friends? When had that happened?

"Uh, what was up with that?" he asked.

Brooke cocked her head. "Do you mean with me and Charity?"

"Yeah." He nodded vigorously. "Since when is there a 'me and Charity'?"

She leaned forward, her forearms resting on the counter. "I'm sorry, did that freak you out? We met at cupcakes and cocktails night, and I have to admit, she isn't like I thought she'd be."

"She isn't like I thought she'd be either," he muttered. "That's what bothers me."

"I can stay away from her if it makes you uncomfortable."

"No, don't worry about it." He didn't want to be the ogre who got in the way of Charity making friends. It was clear she needed them. In the time she'd been here, he hadn't seen her talking to anyone for longer than strictly necessary—unless they were under the age of ten—and the only person she ever talked about spending time with outside of work was Faith. "It's just going to take me a bit of getting used to." He finally registered her baby blue dress, and the fact she was wearing makeup. "It's graduation day?"

"Sure is." She bounced on her toes, her grin expanding. "It's been a long time coming, but I'll finally have the right to make you call me 'Doctor.'"

He rounded the counter and pulled her into a hug, resting his chin on the top of her head. "I'm proud of you, Brookie. Is Jack going?"

"Yes." She drew back and touched a hand to her hair, as if to make sure it was all still in place. "He's waiting outside." She lowered her voice. "He's wearing a suit. It's the sexiest thing ever. I tried to tell him he didn't need to, but he wouldn't hear otherwise."

Kyle couldn't help laughing at the mental image of Jack in a suit. As a professional adventurer and tour guide, he rarely wore anything other than shorts and t-shirts. "I need photos, or I won't believe it."

"Done." She kissed his cheek. "We'll be away overnight. My parents are meeting us there, and we're all staying in a hotel together." Her teeth worried her lower lip. "I'm afraid Mum will corner Jack about the wedding and try to bully him into doing everything her way. We want to keep it simple."

"Nobody bullies Jack into anything. Don't worry, I'm sure they'll just be thrilled to see you graduate."

"They are pretty excited." She glanced over his shoulder, at the clock. "I'd better get going. I just wanted to drop by and see you before we left."

"Have a good trip." He gave her one last hug for good measure. "Bye, Brooke."

"See you." She waved and hustled out the door.

On Friday, Charity was reorganizing the children's shelves at the library, which were often muddled because kids tended to ignore the alphabetized shelving, when she heard the rustle of fabric as someone approached her from behind. She turned to find Shane, Hunter, and a little girl with a mass of dark hair standing behind her.

She straightened and smiled. "Hey, guys. Is school all done for the week?"

"It is," Shane confirmed. "And these guys wanted to pick up a couple of books for the weekend. Charity, have you met Izzy?"

"No." Charity bent and offered the little girl her hand. Izzy shook it, her expression serious. If memory served, Izzy was Bex's daughter and one of Hunter's best friends. "Hi, Izzy, it's nice to meet you. I'm Charity. I work here, and Faith is my sister."

"Faith is funny," Izzy declared.

"She's very funny," Charity agreed. "She makes me laugh all the time."

"Are you funny too?" Izzy asked.

Charity exchanged a glance with Shane. "Not really, but I'm good at choosing books for people. Would you like me to find one for you?"

Izzy clapped excitedly. "Yes! I like unicorns and fairies and dogs and cats."

"Let's see what we've got." Charity knelt and rifled through the books. She guessed Izzy to be about seven or so—a little older than Hunter. She stopped when she landed on one that had a girl with a cartoon puppy on the cover. She pulled it out and held it up. "What about this one?"

Izzy leaned closer to examine it. Her eyes narrowed. Finally, she nodded. "Can you read it to us?"

"Sweetie, Charity needs to work," Shane said, resting a hand on Izzy's shoulder.

Izzy scowled. "But it's better when someone else reads a story."

Charity hid her smile, amused by the precocious girl. She glanced around, noting that the library was empty except for a couple of teens on computers and an older man reading a newspaper. It wouldn't matter if she took a few minutes to read to Izzy and Hunter.

"Okay, let's do it. I have time." She sat and tucked her legs beneath her. Izzy beamed and dropped to the ground, cross-legged. Hunter hurried to mimic her, casting sideways glances to make sure he was doing it right. Clearly, Izzy was the one in charge.

"Are you sure?" Shane asked. "We can take care of ourselves."

"I'd like to," Charity replied, and to her surprise, she meant it. Even if she didn't have much experience with children, she appreciated their bluntness and the fact they treated her like anyone else. She patted the ground. "You get down here too, Daddy."

He made a face as he sank to the floor. "I'm too old for this."

Charity opened the book. She scanned the first page of text then cleared her throat and started to read. At first, she simply recited the words, but as she went, she found herself making up voices for the different characters and enjoying the children's reactions to her theatrics. The enthusiastic sounds they made encouraged her as she fell into the role of story-teller. When she finished, Izzy asked if she'd read another, but Shane told the little girl they needed to choose their books and go home before Dylan beat them there. Charity helped them select a few. When they left, she leaned against the counter and sighed. That had been a fun interlude, but it was time to get back to the status quo.

"You're good with them."

She flinched at the voice intruding on her thoughts and glanced up to see Kyle standing in front of her. "Don't sneak up on me like that."

He raised an eyebrow. "I didn't sneak. You were in another world."

"Oh." She didn't argue because he was probably right.

"Do you like kids?" he asked.

She shrugged. "I haven't had much to do with them, but Hunter is my little buddy, and Izzy makes me laugh."

He grinned. "Yeah, she's a lot of fun. It's the first time I've seen you—" He cut himself off.

"Seen me what?" Charity demanded, straightening in case she didn't like his response.

"Seen you so relaxed," he finished with a wince. "It's not that you're always uptight or anything—"

"I am," she interrupted. "Don't worry, you don't have to shelter me from it. I'm well aware of the fact."

"But you were different with them." His smile softened. "It was nice."

Charity's stomach fluttered, but she tried to tamp it down. He didn't mean anything by the comment. She shouldn't read into it. "Thanks. I'd better get back to shelving."

She flashed him a smile and walked away before he could say anything else that might give her more of those uncomfortable, tingly feelings. Fortunately, there was a lot to do, and an hour passed before a prickle at the back of her neck caught her attention. She turned warily. A balding man with a paunch stuffed into a too-tight button-up shirt stood a few feet from her.

"Can I help you?" she asked when he stared at her.

The man drew something from his pocket. A small, black handheld device that she recognized immediately as a voice recorder. She'd seen many of them after her arrest and during Samuel's trial. A chill darted up her spine.

"Charity Hagley," he said. A statement, not a question.

Uh-oh. Whatever was going on here, it wasn't good, but she couldn't escape because he stood between her and the staff only door.

"That's not my name anymore," she said quietly, trying to avoid attracting attention.

"Ah, that's right." He snapped his fingers and gave her a condescending smirk. "You go by Charity St. John these days, don't you?"

"Yes." She was getting a really bad feeling about this, and she'd learned to listen to her instincts. "If you'll excuse me, I need to get back to work." She moved to step past him.

He blocked her path. "Not so fast. Where are you off to in a hurry?"

Looking around, she wondered whether she could get away from this weirdo without making a scene. Already, several people had paused to watch. None of them made any attempt to help, and she couldn't say she was surprised.

"I'm sorry, but I have a job to do."

"So do I." Reaching into his shirt, he withdrew a lanyard that read "New Zealand Daily News." Charity's stomach bottomed out. Just fucking great. It had been months since any reporters had approached her, and she'd hoped the story had gotten old.

"Jim Curry." He offered his hand, which Charity ignored. "Tell me, how does it feel to be back in one of the places where your husband screwed over so many people?"

She spun around, her heart in her throat. Maybe if she tidied the shelves and pretended he wasn't there, he'd leave. She sensed him come closer. Shutting her eyes, she bit her lip—*hard*—and prayed she wouldn't cry. She was sick and tired of this treatment. She'd been a stupid girl and paid the price. When would karma finally stop kicking her ass?

"You think you're better than me?" the reporter persisted. "Better than everyone else? Is that the reason you married a man who could have been your father and helped him swindle hundreds of people's life savings?"

At this, a murmur swept around the library. Charity was afraid to turn. She felt several pairs of eyes on her back and the knot of dread in her gut told her that by this point, they had everyone's undivided attention.

"I wasn't involved," she said, softly but firmly.

"Is that why the police arrested you?" he demanded. "Because you weren't involved?"

"No charges were filed." He must know this. He was just goading her, hoping to get a response. Something he could use as a good headline. A slow thread of anger heated within her, and she pivoted away. "I wasn't part of his scheme."

Hold your tongue, Charity.

If she let her temper get the better of her, she'd give him exactly what he wanted. She breathed in, held onto the breath for a moment, and released it as she turned to face him.

"Please don't make a scene. This is where I work."

Their audience tittered.

Jim Curry held his arms out wide. "Who's making a scene, Ms. St. John? All I want is to ask you a few questions."

"Which I have the right not to answer."

"You do," he allowed. "But if you don't say anything, then I can play this however I like. So, let me ask again: how's it feel to be back in a place where you're infamous and everyone will always remember you as the trophy wife of a con man?"

"How do you think it feels?" she fired back. "Use your imagination. I'm sure you have plenty of experience in that field." She tried to maneuver around him, but he crowded her.

"I don't know. Do I?" He shrugged. "For all I know, you're a psychopath and don't care what anyone else thinks of you. In fact," he cocked his head, his expression growing lascivious, "your past decisions support that. Or do you just prefer to be with men who are twenty years older than you?"

Charity opened her mouth, but no words emerged. The *gall* of him. She wished she could kick him in the balls, but she'd no doubt be arrested and dragged off in cuffs for assault. Just think how many newspapers that would sell.

"Get out of my library," a voice boomed from behind the reporter. Her gaze skittered to a space over Jim Curry's shoulder, where Kyle's furious face had appeared. He bore down on the man like a warrior, coming to her rescue. Her heart thumped overtime, and she could have sworn the light formed a halo around his head. "I said, get out."

Jim blinked in shock, then returned to his senses. "Who are you?"

Kyle placed himself between Jim and Charity. "I'm the librarian in charge, and I have the authority to ask you to leave if your behavior is unacceptable. He gestured at Charity, who was watching in open-mouthed awe. "This is unacceptable. Please leave."

"Come on," Jim said in a tone that implied Kyle was being unreasonable. "Just give me two more minutes and I'll get out of your hair."

Dread pooled in Charity's gut, but she needn't have worried.

"No." Kyle folded his arms over his broad chest, emphasizing the physical difference between the two men, and her knees just about gave out. How long had it been since a man defended her? Especially one like Kyle? "If you don't remove yourself from the premises immediately, I'll call the police and have them do it."

"On what grounds?" Jim sputtered.

"Harassment," Kyle replied matter-of-factly. "I have plenty of witnesses to back me up."

Finally daring to look around, Charity noticed there were at least half a dozen people watching, enthralled. But would they stand up for her if Kyle asked them to? She doubted it. Jim didn't know that though. Kyle was bluffing, and for that, he earned her eternal gratitude. God, it felt good to have someone on her side. She swiped a hand across her eyes, hoping she didn't make a fool of herself.

"Fine," Jim snapped. "I'm leaving."

Kyle leveled him with a stare. "Don't let the door hit your ass on the way out."

The reporter shot him a hateful look and stalked off. Charity raised her eyes to Kyle's, and her lower lip wobbled.

"Thank you." Her voice was husky, and she hated that it made her sound frail.

Get your shit together, girl.

She wasn't the type to get sentimental over a simple gesture of kindness, was she?

"Don't thank me; I just did what anybody should," he said, speaking louder than necessary. Several people turned away, their cheeks flushing with embarrassment.

She nodded. "Well, thank you anyway. It means a lot."

She resumed tidying the shelves. Her throat was tight, and she sniffed when her nose threatened to drip. She reached for a book, and a hand landed on top of hers.

"Put it down, Charity." Breath whispered over her ear, and she sensed a large, warm body behind her. "Are you okay?"

Her hands trembled. How long had it been since anyone had touched her so gently?

Too long. Far too long.

"I'm fine," she whispered, because she didn't trust herself not to cry if she spoke properly. Harshness and cruel words, she could handle. Gentleness and kindness, not so much. "Don't worry about it. I can go back to work."

A hand smoothed down her back. "Come on. Let's get you a hot drink."

"No, I'm fine."

"Charity." His tone brooked no argument. "Come with me."

"Okay." She meekly followed him out of the main library and into the kitchenette. She kept her eyes downcast until they were out of view of other people. Kyle turned on the kettle and placed a mug on the counter. While it heated, he leaned against the kitchen wall. She wrung her hands, unsure what to do with them.

"Does that happen often?" he asked.

"Not really." She met his eyes and read the concern in them. Something clawed inside her chest. It didn't help her peace of mind when he looked at her like she was fragile and he was determined not to break her.

"Not anymore, anyway. There was a time when I couldn't get away from the press."

He shook his head, his mouth set in a grim line. "I'm sorry you had to go through that."

"It's in the past." She tried not to dwell on it.

He stepped closer and skimmed the backs of his fingers along her cheekbone. Her eyes fluttered shut and her entire being concentrated down to that touch. "I can tell you believe you deserve it. But you don't."

Oh, God. He was too much. And he smelled so good. Like books and clean male. Her eyes flickered open, and she stretched onto her toes and pressed her mouth to his.

13

———

Holy crap. She was kissing him. Charity St. John was kissing him. In what world did this make sense?

Kyle wanted to pinch himself. He'd been desperate to ease her pain—the pain no one else seemed to see—but he hadn't expected this.

Now her mouth was on his, and he needed to taste her. His tongue brushed over her lips. Tart, yet sweet. Like cherries. Her lips parted and her tongue darted out to meet his. A sizzle shot down his spine. Her hands fisted in his shirt and she deepened the kiss. His head swam, and his body melted into a dizzying pool of lust. He grasped onto the last threads of his control. They needed to stop. Charity was overwhelmed. She was reaching out because she needed someone and he happened to be there, but if he let things go further, he'd be taking advantage of her heightened emotional state.

Reluctantly, he drew back, his hands going to her shoulders so he could look her in the eyes. She blinked up at him, trying to reorient herself. Her gaze was open and trusting—so different from the shuttered view she usually presented to the world. He wanted to gather her in his arms and hug her tight, but that wouldn't do either of them any favors.

"Let's not get carried away," he said. "I don't want to go down a road you'll regret later."

Her eyes had refocused, and she winced, her cheeks blazing red. "Well, this is awkward."

He hated that she was embarrassed, but surely a little embarrassment was better than doing something irrevocable and having to live with it.

"Why didn't you fight back against that guy?" he asked, eager to change the subject. "Why'd you just stand there and take it?" As a victim of bullying for most of his teenage life, he couldn't stand to see people get pushed around, but the Charity he remembered would have given that asshole a piece of her mind and shown him to the door.

She shrugged and angled her face so he couldn't see her expression. "It's a karmic kick up the ass. I'm not a victim, Kyle. I earned everything I get. Probably more."

He battled the impulse to roll his eyes. She was acting like a martyr, and it was pointless. Her attitude frustrated him. But a question kept rising to the top of his mind. "If you won't fight back when people treat you poorly, why are you even here? Surely, you don't need to work, and being exposed to the public must be miserable for you."

Another shrug. "I like to keep busy."

Her tone was evasive.

"I don't believe you."

Her eyes snapped to his. "I don't care what you believe."

Despite himself, he grinned. That was the feisty girl he remembered. "I don't care that you don't care. Just tell me why you work here."

She fidgeted, as though the conversation made her uncomfortable. God. *Everything* about her made him uncomfortable. "I'm broke," she admitted.

His jaw dropped. "How?"

Samuel Hagley had been worth tens of millions of dollars, and the police had been unable to repossess a significant chunk of it.

She sighed and wound her ponytail around her hand. "Do you really want to know?"

"Yes."

"Fine." She glanced up, nibbling on her lower lip. "I used the money I got in the divorce to set up a charity for his victims."

"Wait." He held up a hand. It was common knowledge that a charity had been established to benefit the people Hagley had scammed, but a wealthy philanthropist had taken credit. A man who'd previously called Hagley a friend. "I thought Tim Mayor was behind the charity."

She shook her head, her expression cautious. "I asked Tim to be the face of the foundation because I knew no one would accept the help otherwise."

"You gave away all of it?" Her entire fortune?

"Every cent," she said with relish. "I was left with enough money for a month of rent and groceries. Then I got a job and moved on."

"Shit." She'd had more money than he was likely to see in his lifetime, and she hadn't kept any of it, which meant that his opinion of her had been based on half-truths. It was rewriting itself so rapidly he could almost see the computer code flashing through his brain, severing old connections and creating new ones. Why hadn't she told anyone? He understood her concern about people refusing to take handouts, but if she was getting flailed by the public every day, why would she accept the condemnation when she could stop a good portion of it simply by telling the truth?

"That's massive. But why keep it secret?"

"Because I didn't do it to make myself look good." Her stance shifted. Became firmer. "I did it because it was the right thing to do, and I don't need anyone patting me on the back. It was the only way I could make up for even a sliver of the pain I caused by not noticing what was going on right under my nose."

"I'm sure people would understand that. You could just tell them."

"No!" Her voice cracked, and some of the color drained from her cheeks. "And you can't tell anyone either. You don't understand the way people think when they're determined to hate someone. Trust me, I'm doing myself a favor by staying quiet. Promise you'll do the same."

"But Charity," he said helplessly, "wouldn't you like people to treat you better?"

She shook her head, and he couldn't tell whether she was disagreeing with him or if she was just frustrated. "The money shouldn't make a difference. I fucked up, and I ought to face the consequences."

He ground his teeth together. Did she have to be so exasperating? With every sentence from her mouth, it became more obvious that he had no idea who this woman was. The only thing he could see clearly was the guilt that weighed heavily on her shoulders. She held herself more accountable for her ex-husband's crimes than a court of law ever had. While it was disconcerting to realize he needed to reevaluate all that he'd thought of her, he couldn't help but wonder if that was a good thing. Maybe she was a girl who was worth his time and affection after all.

CHARITY DIDN'T KNOW WHAT TO MAKE OF THE WAY KYLE was looking at her. She'd taken him by surprise, but he seemed to be hesitating over how to respond. In the meantime, she studied the slight groove above his upper lip and the furrow between his brows that appeared when he was thinking. Her battered heart somersaulted in her chest, and she took a slow, deep breath, trying to calm it. But her efforts were futile. She was no longer just physically attracted to him. Her crush was fully formed.

He'd been wrong about her getting carried away by emotion. Sure, she was worked up, but she liked him too. Truly liked him. After how he'd come running to her rescue, she had to admit the guy was worth admiring. She couldn't switch off the part of her brain that noted every small fact about him, like the fullness of his lower lip and the way he tilted his head as if mentally examining something from every angle. A fizzing began in her stomach. Kyle was kind, smart, and insanely hot. But could he ever consider her romantically, given their past?

She'd shut him down in their senior year of high school. Publicly. Painfully. Even then, she'd felt terrible about it, but the guilt had turned into a long-simmering shame that quadrupled in size three years ago, when she learned exactly how awful public censure could be. Why would Kyle Pride ever waste his time on her? Especially when he had women literally lining up for a chance with him, while she'd only ever given her love to men who didn't deserve it.

But then, he *had* kissed her back. Only for a moment, but that gave her hope. For some reason, it had become crucial to convince this man to give her a second chance. She doubted she deserved one—she certainly didn't deserve *him*—but she'd always been selfish, so maybe she'd make a play anyway. First, though, she needed to get her head on straight. If she pursued him right now, he wouldn't take her seriously. Not when she was hyped up on adrenaline and over-whelmed by the emotions she'd been holding in for so long.

"Thank you," she said, when he didn't speak. "For being so good to me."

"Charity…"

She waited, but he didn't finish the thought. Instead, he added, "Perhaps you should wait back here for a while until the rubberneckers have cleared out."

She nodded. "I will, thanks." She didn't want to hide, but nor did she want to venture into the library when she was certain everyone was waiting to see how she'd taken the public scolding.

"Okay." He jammed his hands in his pockets. "I'll let you know when it calms down." With one last sweep of his gaze over her body, leaving tingles in its wake, he asked, "Are you sure you're okay?"

"I am." She sounded more certain than she felt. Something inside her had irreversibly changed. She'd thought she'd never want another man again, and that she'd never find one she could trust. But she hadn't counted on Kyle.

"See you soon." He headed out, and she went straight to her purse and grabbed her phone, then collapsed onto a chair. She dialed Faith's number. Her sister answered just as it was about to go to voicemail.

"Hey, beautiful. What's up?"

Charity told her what had happened with the reporter.

"What a piece of work," Faith exclaimed. "I hope you kicked him in the nuts."

"No, but Kyle got rid of him."

"As he should. I'm glad you're working with him. He's one of the good guys."

"I know." She paused for a beat. "Actually, that's what I wanted to talk to you about."

"Oh?"

"I've been trying to ignore my attraction to him, but it's kind of impossible," she admitted.

"So don't try," Faith said. "He's a genuinely great person. Easy on the eyes, too. You should go for it."

"You think? What if he's not interested in me that way? I wouldn't blame him."

"He's a forgiving person." Faith's voice was soft. "Besides, he liked you once, so maybe he will again."

Charity rolled her eyes. "Be serious, Faith. I'm not exactly a prize."

"I'm serious as can be. Look, Kyle doesn't date much, but you can be charming when you want to. Just try not to bite his head off and see how it goes." Someone called out in the background. "Sorry, I have to deal with a customer, but we'll talk more about this later. Bye, Char."

"Bye." The call ended, and Charity placed her phone on the table, pondering her sister's words. If she set her mind to it, could she persuade Kyle to go on a date with her? All she needed was one, and they could take it from there. It had been years since she'd dated though, and she was out of practice.

She picked up a book from the kitchen counter—one she assumed Kyle had left there—and read the first couple of chapters. When she finished, she pieced together her courage and headed into enemy territory. A few patrons glanced at her, and one arched an eyebrow, but most ignored her. Thank God. Kyle was at his computer, and he smiled and mouthed, "How are you doing?" She gave him a discreet thumbs-up and made her way to the book cart, where she started arranging novels in alphabetical order. As she worked, her attention kept wandering back to Kyle. Her subconscious had become hyper aware of him, and every time he moved or spoke to someone, she couldn't focus on anything else.

Shortly before closing time, a woman came by looking for him, and Charity watched as he awkwardly took her number and brushed her off. He seemed to do that to most of the women who flirted with him. He was all politeness but had this air about him as though he couldn't wait to get rid of them. She frowned. If none of the women who flirted with him were his type, then who was?

She'd seen him talking to athletic girls, preppy girls, gamer girls, and a couple who looked like they'd eat him alive. None of them seemed to have made an impact. She pursed her lips. He was a nice guy, so maybe he wanted a nice partner. A girl-next-door type. That put her firmly out of the running. But perhaps it could be a case of opposites attracting. She'd rather believe that, because it was becoming increasingly obvious she was a goner where he was concerned. Unfortunately, he didn't seem to feel the same.

14

<hr>

As he worked, Kyle kept an eye on Charity. She seemed to have bounced back well after her encounter with that slimy reporter. If he hadn't been with her immediately afterward, he might not have realized it had affected her at all, but he'd seen the pain in her eyes, and now, when he looked closely, he noticed the occasional tremor of her hand. She wasn't the soulless tough chick she liked people to think she was. Not even close.

Even *he* was shaken. That guy—he hadn't caught his name—was a bully, and Kyle detested bullies. Always had, always would. But regardless of that, he rarely came to someone's defense as fiercely as he had today. The moment he'd noticed the almost preternatural thread of tension in the air, he'd known Charity was in trouble and rushed to her side. And okay, perhaps she hadn't been in physical danger—although the douche had been a little too pushy for his liking— but every protective neuron in his body had fired.

Why?

Why was he so protective of a girl who'd left his seventeen-year-old self brokenhearted?

Because she's not that girl anymore.

When the clock struck six, he waved the last patron out, closed the doors, and found Charity in the stacks. Their stacks weren't dusty like ones in other towns tended to be, because he had a dust allergy and kept them clean so he wouldn't sneeze all over everything.

"We're done for the day," he told her.

She finished returning a book to its rightful place. "It's been a long one."

"Tell me about it."

As usual, she wasn't wearing makeup, and he could see that her eyelids were drooping with weariness.

"How you holding up?" he asked softly.

She shrugged. "Fine." The corners of her lips lifted slightly. "Don't worry. It wasn't the first time I've met someone like him, and it won't be the last. I can handle myself."

He shook his head and chuckled. He was too easy to read. "Has it always been that bad?"

"Worse." The groove between her eyebrows deepened. "I considered changing my first name for a while, immediately after the trial, but I didn't want to feel like more of a fake than I already do. I'm me, for better or worse."

She didn't seem to realize how brave that was. He wished he could take her in his arms the way he had earlier, to kiss her and reassure her. But he resisted, because it wasn't his place to comfort her.

He nodded toward the door. "I locked up. Why don't we call it a night?"

"Sounds good."

Together, they went to the kitchenette and gathered their belongings. He escorted her out and made sure the alarm was set. They said their goodbyes and then, instead of heading home, Kyle wandered over to The Hideaway for an exercise session. When he'd worked off his excess energy and his muscles were crying for a reprieve, he showered and crossed the square to The Den.

"Hey there, honey," Corinne said as he approached the bar. "Your brother is upstairs."

"Thanks, Mum." He leaned over to kiss her cheek, then made his way to Logan's apartment above the bar. The minute he entered, four faces turned his way. Logan, Jack, Shane, and Sterling were huddled around the table and appeared to have been deep in discussion.

"Dude, what happened at the library today?" Logan asked in lieu of a greeting. "I've been hearing rumors all afternoon."

Kyle's stomach soured. Of course he had. The town's gossip mill was probably in overdrive. "Some jackass reporter cornered Charity and was giving her a hard time. I kicked him out."

Logan scowled. "Why? It's exactly what she deserves."

Shane gave Logan a look, then turned back to Kyle. "Thank you for going to bat for her. She's had a hard enough time as it is."

Logan raised his palms toward the ceiling. "She's not the wounded party in this scenario. Just because she's pretty, and good with the puppy-dog eyes, doesn't make her a victim."

"Puppy-dog eyes?" Shane snorted. "You clearly haven't spent any time around her at all. She could shoot lasers from those eyes and skewer a man, but she's not the villain everyone makes her out to be." He arched a brow at Kyle. "Right?"

Kyle squirmed, uncomfortable with the way Logan was staring at him, but he'd never been one to say what was easy just for the sake of it. He also found it interesting that Shane was defending Charity, because in general, he considered Shane an excellent judge of character.

"I have to agree," he said. "She seems to have changed for the better."

Logan turned to Jack. "I can't believe what I'm hearing. Help me out here."

Jack shrugged. "I haven't met her, and I wasn't in the area when everything went down with her ex. Brooke says she's brutally honest, and that wins her points in my book."

"Seriously," Logan said. "Brooke could find something to like about a snake, even as it was taking a bite out of her."

"Whoa," Jack snapped, rising to his feet. "Don't—"

"Let's not go there," Kyle interrupted before Jack could get his hands on Logan for speaking ill of his fiancé. Jack drew in a couple of breaths and sat down. Kyle addressed his brother. "You might not agree with my assessment. You'd be one of the majority. People around here are good at holding grudges and some of them have been quite vicious toward her."

"As they should be." Logan's nostrils flared. "Tell me you're not still carrying a torch for her."

"Of course not." But his words were hollow. Even he didn't believe them. All he could think about was that damned kiss and how amazing her lips had felt against his.

It was a mistake. She was emotional and it went too far.

"You've been awfully quiet," Logan said to Sterling. "What's your take on it?"

Everyone turned toward the silent member of their group. Sterling seemed to mentally evaluate their debate. Finally, he said, "I don't know Charity, and I've never been sure how involved she was in the Hagley Scandal, but people can change. I'm living proof of that."

Logan rolled his eyes. "It's hardly the same thing."

"Maybe not, but you must admit, she spoke very convincingly at the trial."

"She what?" Kyle asked. "Are you talking about her husband's trial? She spoke on the stand?"

"Yes." Sterling regarded him with interest. "I take it you didn't know?"

"No."

"She was a witness for the prosecution," he continued. "In my opinion, she was the final nail in his coffin."

"Huh." Why hadn't she mentioned that? While most of the bay had tuned in to watch the trial every day, Kyle had been at university and hadn't bothered. "Then why does everyone hate her so much?"

"Because she threw Hagley under the bus and divorced him to get her greedy hands on what was left of his fortune," Logan said.

The fortune she donated to charity.

Kyle didn't voice the thought because she'd asked him not to. In light of this conversation, he had to query the wisdom of that decision.

"Forget Charity," Jack said impatiently. "Are we going to play cards, or what?"

"Thanks for coming with me," Charity said to Faith as they drove toward Auckland on Sunday morning. They were taking Faith's car rather than Charity's, because Charity's might die halfway there.

"Are you kidding?" Faith bounced in her seat. "My baby sister wants new clothes to impress a man. Of course I'm coming. We're going to hit every hot spot in town, and you're going to blow Kyle's mind."

"I don't need to blow his mind," Charity replied. "I'm just aiming for something that isn't totally bland and shapeless."

"Honey, you're capable of driving any man crazy. Why would you settle for less?"

"Because look where that got me last time." Charity shook her head. "No, thank you. All I want is an outfit that says 'I'm an available woman in my twenties' rather than 'I'm a divorcee with cobwebs between my thighs.'"

Faith laughed. "I thought you liked that look."

"I did, when I wasn't trying to woo the world's hottest librarian. It's very nonthreatening and flies beneath the radar, but it's time I landed myself on someone's radar."

"Good for you, sweet cheeks."

A while later, they parked at the largest mall in the city and made their way inside.

"What kind of vibe are we going for?" Faith asked as they wandered past boutiques and peered into windows. "Fun? Classy? Girl next door? Upmarket?"

Charity shivered. Upmarket was the last thing she needed, given her past. "How about girl next door meets boho chic?"

"I like it." Faith gestured at a shop with a series of floaty dresses and skirts on display. "Want to take a closer look?"

They entered the shop and smiled at a woman who was rearranging blouses.

"Hi," the woman said brightly. "Let me know if you'd like some help."

Charity nodded. "We will." She beelined for the sales rack. She wanted enough clothes to make several outfits, and there was no way she could afford that many items at full price. Frugality was just one of many things she'd learned since she gave all of her money away. Not that it had really been hers to begin with.

She chose a white shirt and a pair of denim shorts. "There's no way I could get away with wearing this to work, is there?"

Faith eyed them critically. "The shirt, yes. The shorts, no. But if you like that look, we could find you a tidy pair of jeans to go with it."

"Hmm." Charity weighed her options. "Actually, I'd like to start with a dress. I haven't worn many of those recently. At least, not ones that look nice." It was time to start wearing clothes that reflected the woman she was now rather than the girl she'd once been or the nonsexual being she'd been posing as.

Faith clasped her hands together. "A dress it is." She scanned the options and withdrew one in delicate shades of pink and white. "How about this?"

"Let's try it. This, too." Charity handed her a short dress of the palest green.

"Oh, and this one!" Faith grabbed another and slung it over her shoulder.

An hour later, they emerged from the shop with three new dresses and a pair of shoes that Faith had insisted on buying as a gift for her.

"What's next?" Faith asked.

Charity considered the options. "Pants and blouses. Just a couple each."

"Pish." Faith waved a hand. "Let me treat you. Business has been good lately, and we don't get to go shopping like this often."

A wave of guilt washed over Charity. She hadn't been the best sister, and she was well aware of it. Back when they were younger, she'd been spoiled and selfish, then the past few years she'd refused to visit the bay unless she absolutely had to.

Faith rolled her eyes. "Don't give me that look. It's in the past."

"If you say so." Personally, Charity couldn't let it go.

Faith looped their arms. "Come on. Let's do shoes first."

By the time they'd visited all of the clothing shops in the mall, Charity owned two pairs of pretty flat shoes, a pair of strappy sandals, and a pair of boots with a little heel. She also had cute shorts, several blouses, and two pairs of work pants that felt glorious against her skin.

"Time to head back?" she asked, glancing at her phone. It was mid-afternoon, and the drive would take a while.

"Shall we get our hair done first?" Faith suggested. "I haven't had a cut in ages."

Charity squirmed. "I'm all out of money."

"It's on me." Faith gave her a look that said she wasn't taking no for an answer, and they crossed the wide corridor to a hairdresser on the other side.

"No dye jobs," Charity said. "That feels like too much." She'd colored her hair blonde for years. She was done with that now. If Kyle didn't like her just because she was closer to ginger than blonde, then screw him.

"Not for me, either."

She laughed. "As if that was ever in the cards."

Faith loved her fiery hair—or if she didn't, she did a good job of hiding it.

The salon was busy, so they waited for fifteen minutes until spaces freed up, then sat side by side in chairs. Faith asked for a trim. Charity requested a more thorough cut and treatment—something she hadn't had done in far too long.

"Shane won't know what to do with himself when he sees you tonight," Charity told her sister. In addition to the haircut, Faith had also splurged on lingerie, and the glimmer in her eyes said she knew her man would love it.

"I hope so. I like to surprise him sometimes. Mix things up."

"He's a lucky guy."

"I'm the lucky one." Their eyes met in the mirror. "He's good to me, and I wanted him for so long that it's hard to believe I actually have him."

Charity swallowed, her throat constricting. She'd felt that way, once. Although, in hindsight, she realized infatuation had played a big part in her relationship with Samuel. Yes, she'd been crazy about him, but it wasn't the kind of love Faith had with Shane. Theirs was based on mutual respect and devotion. Charity had just wanted to feel special, and Samuel had given her that.

"You deserve him," Charity said. "If he ever messes it up, he'll feel my wrath."

Faith giggled. "You're sweet." She really wasn't. "I'm so happy you're looking for love again, and that you've set your sights on a guy who's actually worthy of you."

Charity gnawed on her lower lip. "Don't get your hopes up. He may be worthy of me, but I'm not worthy of him, and he has every reason to reject me."

"Has he said or done anything to make you think he holds the past against you?" Faith asked.

Charity considered this. "Not explicitly, but if I were him, I'd hold a grudge." Hell, when it came to Samuel, she was still bitter. She sighed, watching locks of hair fall to the floor. "I guess I'll find out soon enough."

15

IF ONE MORE PERSON ASKED KYLE ABOUT THE INCIDENT with the reporter at the library, he was going to scream. He'd spent the past two hours at the gym with Jack and Brooke. All he'd wanted was a quiet workout, and instead he'd been interrogated by five different people.

"Don't they know how to mind their own business?" he asked as he jogged down the stairs, heading toward the exit to the town square.

Behind him, Jack scoffed. "Around here? Dream on."

"I think they've all cast you as some white knight coming to the rescue of the wicked witch," Brooke added as she opened the door at the base of the stairs and held it for them. Outside, the natural light had started to dim. It was early evening, and the sun sat low in the sky, soon to sink beneath the water on the horizon.

"I'm not a hero, and she's not a witch," he said, exasperated.

"No, she's not." Brooke's gaze caught on something

over his shoulder. "In fact, she might be a princess in disguise."

He spun around to see what she meant. Charity and Faith were crossing the square, bags from Cafe Oasis tucked under their arms. He scarcely noticed Faith though, his attention drawn immediately to her sister. He blinked rapidly, feeling like he was seeing her for the first time. She'd always been beautiful, but since moving back, she'd hidden her beauty beneath frumpy skirts and ill-suited outfits. Not any longer. She wore a pale pink dress with a V neckline and a long floaty skirt that twisted around her slender legs as she walked. Her hair shone under the streetlights, almost luminous, and when she glanced up, a wall of heat slammed into him.

Holy shit.

He realized his jaw had dropped and he hurried to close it. As he stared, Faith noticed him and changed course, heading their way.

"Hi," Charity said as they drew near, tucking a lock of coppery hair behind her ear. He tried to form words, but his tongue wouldn't cooperate. Her smile was such a foreign thing he didn't know how to handle it. Not to mention how gorgeous she looked. "This is a nice surprise," she added.

Come on, brain. I just need one smart, flirty quip.

Nah, he had nothing.

"Hey there," Brooke said, cocking her head and giving him a "what are you doing?" look. "It's good to see you again. You two look nice."

"We had our hair done," Faith explained. "We've been shopping in Auckland. Just got back now and couldn't be bothered making dinner, so we picked up enough to feed us, and Shane and the boys as well."

"Good thinking." Brooke smiled. "We've just

finished our gym session."

"You should sign up," Jack said. "The Hideaway is the best gym around."

Faith smirked. "It's the *only* gym around."

"And what?" He grinned. "There aren't many gyms where you can watch an artist paint while you lift weights."

"Wait, hang on." Charity held up a hand. "She actually paints in the gym while people are there?"

"Yeah," Kyle said, finally managing to force a single, strangled word out. Faith smiled lopsidedly, a little too delighted for his liking. "The owner, Bex, is an artist as well as a personal trainer."

"I met her the other day, and she mentioned both sides of her business, but I didn't realize they happen simultaneously."

"She's super impressive," Brooke said.

"Sounds like it," Charity agreed.

Faith held up one of the brown paper bags. "It was great seeing you, but we'd better get home before the food gets cold." Nudging Charity's elbow, she started to edge away.

"Have a nice night," Brooke said, and bumped Kyle's foot with hers.

"I'll see you tomorrow," he added weakly.

"See you then." Charity smiled, and his insides flipped over. She and Faith continued on their way.

When they were out of earshot, Jack laughed. "What was up with that? I don't think I've ever seen you struggle for words so badly."

Kyle ducked his head. "I was surprised. She doesn't usually dress that way, and I get a little shy around women I'm interested in."

"Ha!" Brooke pointed at him. "You just admitted you like her."

Damn. He had.

His cheeks heated. "I don't know if anything will come of it. I've liked her before, and all that got me was humiliation and a broken heart." But it felt disingenuous to compare Charity to the girl she used to be when he'd seen evidence of how much she'd changed.

"If it helps, she seems nice enough, once you get beneath the prickly exterior," Brooke said. "If you're serious about her, you should act on it."

He cast a glance at Jack, embarrassed to be having this conversation in front of the other man. Jack raised one shoulder and smirked. "Don't let me stop this heart-to-heart. Things tend to work out better for men when they listen to the women in their lives."

"We kissed," he admitted to Brooke, doing his best to ignore Jack. "After the reporter left. But she was emotional, and I don't think it meant anything."

Brooke took him by the shoulders. "Kyle, you rescued her and then she kissed you. Now she's wearing new clothes and making an effort to talk to you. Trust me, she's into you."

When she put it like that, it sounded like he had cause to be optimistic. His heart rate picked up. "You think so?"

"Yes, I do." She gave him a hug. "You're awesome. Why wouldn't she be? You just need to get out of your own way and let it happen."

"Maybe." He wanted to believe her, but could he be courageous enough to put the past behind him and take a chance on the future?

Charity adjusted the shoulder of her blouse and stared at herself in the mirror. Nice clothes, lip gloss, mascara, shiny hair brushed over one shoulder. It was the start of a new work week, and she looked like a new person. A cross between the girl she was when she was twenty and the woman she'd become in the intervening years. She felt like herself. But how would people react? Would Kyle like this version of her? Would the locals cast her even deeper into the shadows because she'd dared to emerge from her shell?

Several hours later, she had her answer. With the exception of Kyle's admirers, no one seemed to care. The women who stopped by the library shot her scathing glares, especially when she smiled at Kyle or turned up her flirtatious body language. In her previous life, she'd been a terrible flirt, and it came back to her more easily than she'd expected. Not that she intended to make full use of it, but she could have a little fun.

The trouble was, Kyle hadn't noticed. He'd smiled when she arrived, and his gaze had swept over her in a cursory way, but then he'd immersed himself in work. Apparently she'd found the one man who was immune to coy glances, light touches, and warm smiles. Or at least, he was when they came from *her*. At this very minute, he was leaning over the counter, his forearms deliciously exposed, deep in conversation with a brunette. When the woman giggled and laid a hand on his forearm, Charity wanted to stomp over there and knock it away.

The brunette cocked her head and touched her neck with her free hand. Whatever she'd said brought out a pink highlight in Kyle's cheeks. Regardless of whether or not she was a decent person, Charity wanted to drag her out the door and refuse her entry into the library in the future. The brunette slipped

Kyle her number and flounced out. Charity made it her mission to find that piece of paper and tear it to shreds. But before she had a chance, Izzy appeared, hand-in-hand with an Asian girl. They beelined toward her.

"Hi," Izzy said as they drew near. "Mum said we could come over here for you to read us a story."

Charity didn't even have to force a smile. She glanced at the clock and saw she probably had a little extra time she could give them. "Do you want another puppy book?"

"Yes please!"

"Okay then." She smiled at the other girl. "What's your name, sweetie?"

"Lian."

"Nice to meet you, Lian. You two get comfy, and I'll be with you in a few minutes."

BY THE END OF THE WEEK, KYLE WAS BEGINNING TO think Brooke had been right about Charity. She was smiling at him more often and seemed to find excuses to touch him. But he wasn't sure of her motivation. Did she truly want him? If so, was it for a relationship or a fling? Because he didn't do flings. He rounded an aisle and came to an abrupt halt at the sight of her in a tight skirt, bent over while she placed a book on the lowest shelf. The fabric strained over her ass, and he felt an answering tightness in his pants. Subtly, he rearranged himself, then cleared his throat. She looked over but took her time to straighten. Was she tormenting him on purpose?

"Sorry, do you need to get past?" she asked.

Did he? He couldn't recall what he'd been doing.

"Yes." He edged around her, inhaling the scent of oranges that seemed to cling to her skin. Behind her, he caught sight of a pair of guys in board shorts who were looking her way. He narrowed his eyes at them and the blond dudebro shrugged in response.

Half an hour later, he was circling back around when he spotted the blond guy tucked away into a corner with Charity, engaged in an intimate conversation. He was getting right into her space, staring at her as though she were a snack he'd love to gobble up. Apparently he hadn't gotten the message that she was *persona non grata* in the bay. Perhaps he was a tourist who didn't know or care.

As Kyle watched, the guy reached out and brushed her hair away from her face, his hand lingering as it curved around the shell of her ear. Every caveman instinct Kyle possessed rushed to the fore. This guy had no right to touch her. He could keep his hands to himself.

"Excuse me," Kyle snapped as he approached. Both Charity and the man whipped around. "Are you harassing my staff?"

"Uh, no," the guy said, frowning as if to say *Dude, why are you cock-blocking me?* "We're just talking. Right, Charity?"

He knew her name? Kyle's teeth clenched together.

"Right," Charity said, glaring at Kyle as though he'd lost his mind. "Riley is in the area on vacation and was asking if I know the best places to surf. I was just explaining that I've never surfed in my life."

"Oh." He deflated, feeling like a prick. "Well, don't talk for too long. We've got a busy day ahead." Having cemented his position as a massive dickhead, he turned on his heel and strode away.

16

Charity glared at Kyle's retreating back. The nerve of the man. So, it was okay for him to flirt with every woman over the age of eighteen on work time, but she wasn't allowed to talk to the one male who'd shown her interest in forever? Nope. She wouldn't stand for it.

"Excuse me," she said to Riley. "I need to find out what's gotten up his ass."

"Will you be here if I come back next week?" he asked.

"Every day." She gave him a tight smile. "See you around."

"You, too."

She took off after Kyle. Wordlessly, she grabbed his arm and dragged him out back.

"What are you doing?" she demanded, hands on hips. "I know that wasn't just because I was socializing when I should have been working. You chat with customers all the time and never worry about it interfering with your ability to do your job. So, what was it?"

His gaze slid off to the side. "I'm not sure."

She growled. Actually growled. "You admit it wasn't because you thought he was harassing me?"

He shrugged. "Well, he could have been. But to be honest, that wasn't it. I'm sure you could handle yourself in that situation if needed."

"I could," she muttered, pleased he wasn't that blind. "So?" He didn't say anything, and she huffed. *Men.* Why did they have to be so frustrating? "Kyle," she said more softly. "You can't brush me off when I kiss you and then stand in the way when another guy talks to me. You either want me or you don't. It's that simple."

His expression darkened. "It's not that simple."

"It really is." She stepped closer. "So, which is it?"

"I want you." With that, he hauled her against him and claimed her mouth. His lips were firm and furious against hers. He deepened the kiss, stealing her breath, his hands journeying up her body to cup her face. Their tongues touched, and the sensation was such a relief that she sighed. This was finally happening. She hadn't imagined the connection between them, and it wasn't one-sided. That much was blatantly obvious from the bulge trying to break free from behind his zipper.

"Why do you taste so good?" He drew back and rested his forehead against hers. She stretched onto her tiptoes, going in for another kiss, but the moment their lips met, he tore away. "This can't happen." He dragged a hand down his face. "Ugh, I'm sorry. I shouldn't have done that."

And then he walked away.

He.

Walked.

Away.

He left her there, in the kitchen, a melting mess of hormones, emotions, and need. If she'd had the capacity for thought, she'd have thrown something at his back. Perhaps this was the universe's way of reminding her she didn't deserve a guy like him. It seemed like karmic justice that their relationship was always her reaching out and him walking away. But it still sucked.

With a click that seemed to echo in the space around him, Kyle locked the bathroom door. His put his back to the wall and fisted his hands at his sides, unsure what to do with them. Anger simmered inside him, but it seemed out of proportion to the situation. He wasn't even sure who he was mad at. Not Charity. He was the one who'd screwed up. He was the one running hot and cold. But he wasn't exactly mad at himself either, because he understood why he was behaving this way. He wanted Charity—he hadn't lied about that—but if he were to check his Love List, which he'd done numerous times, she ticked very few of the boxes.

She was the wrong woman for him, but his heart—and dick—weren't driven by logic. He glanced down at his erection. With all this introspection, he'd have expected it to deflate, but it was still going strong, spurred on by his recollection of how she tasted, and the way she'd sighed into his mouth.

Ah, fuck.

He yanked his zipper down and reached into his pants, palming himself. He gave a quick stroke, then another. Pleasure zapped up his spine, but then guilt and disgust churned his stomach and forced him to stop. What was he doing? He couldn't jerk off in the men's bathroom at work. Especially not after what had just gone down. Feeling sick with himself, he pulled his zipper back up and splashed cold water on his face. Then he went out to deal with the mess he'd left in his wake.

CHARITY BARELY EXCHANGED THREE WORDS WITH KYLE after their kiss in the library. He'd pretended nothing out of the ordinary had happened, but she wasn't about to give up on him. She might want to whack him over the head with a book, but he understandably had some stuff to come to terms with. The past may be over, but as Shakespeare said, it was prologue. They couldn't ever truly start fresh.

The next day, she visited The Shack to pick up a couple of cupcakes, and took them along the beach until she reached the place where Anderson Gray had yelled at her. Before she could second-guess herself, she marched up to the door and knocked.

"Go away!" he called.

She knocked again, more forcefully. A few moments later, the door swung inward and a heavily bearded face glowered at her. The glare eased as recognition dawned.

"It's you." His voice sounded rusty, as though he hadn't used it in days.

She thrust the cupcakes into his hands. "Have these."

One of his eyebrows shot up. "Why? Not that I'm complaining, mind you."

She straightened her back. "You're a man, and I need help winning a man over."

He opened the box and smiled at the cupcakes appreciatively. It was a strange expression on him. Almost foreign. Like he was exercising muscles that had been dormant for a long time. "You came to me for advice because…?"

She rolled her eyes. "It's not like I have anyone else to talk to, other than my sister, who means well but doesn't know what it's like to be inside a guy's head. You do. So, what's it going to be, Gray? Can I come in?"

He stepped aside. "It's not like I can kick you out after you've brought these."

She hid a grin. She got the feeling he wouldn't send her away even if she'd arrived empty-handed. He was a lot like her. Gruff on the outside, but lonely to the core. Even from their one face-to-face encounter, she'd picked up on that.

His home, unlike him, was tidy. Every surface gleamed, the carpet was spotless, and with the exception of a few discarded books, everything seemed to be exactly where it belonged.

"Interesting," she said. "Not what I expected."

"Dare I ask what you expected?" He settled onto a plush gray sofa and kicked up his feet. He waved a hand at the recliner opposite and she sank onto it, rapidly regretting the decision when it cushioned her body so well she wasn't sure she'd be able to get up again.

"A typical man cave, I guess," she replied. "This looks like you have a full-time housekeeper."

He snorted. "No housekeeper, just me. I'm not so Hollywood that I can't take care of my own place. Anyway, tell me about this man of yours."

Charity sighed, wondering why she felt so comfortable with this scruffy former A-lister. Perhaps because she recognized him as a kindred spirit. What-ever Anderson Gray was doing in Haven Bay, he was hiding from something. "His name is Kyle. He had a crush on me in high school and I shot him down. Publicly. I was popular, he wasn't, and I'd just been dumped so I didn't react as well as I should have. Now our situations have pretty much reversed. He's my boss, totally hot, and the nicest guy ever—except for when he's being a clueless asshat. I don't deserve him, but I've decided not to let that stop me."

"Hmm." Gray scratched his bearded chin. "Role reversal and a hint of high school drama. I'm getting some definite rom-com vibes here. Have you considered wooing him with a song, a la *10 Things I Hate About You?*"

"Uh, no. Trust me, nobody needs to hear me sing."

"How about poetry? Have you ever written a poem?"

"Yes, but no one is ever seeing them." Poetry was her secret way of venting her emotions without anybody being the wiser. The ones she'd written were dark and twisted. Definitely not romantic.

He looked disappointed. "Are you sure? Everyone likes a poem. Even if it's not the next epic, it makes people feel special to have someone go to that effort for them."

She reconsidered. But no, she didn't trust herself not to make it weird. "Next idea."

"Paintball."

She laughed. "Are all of your ideas from *10 Things I Hate About You?* I thought you'd have some real-life experience, considering your history."

He shrugged. "When you're a multi-millionaire famous for playing the hero in romances, women tend to come to you, not the other way around."

"Huh." Okay, so perhaps her logic had been off. "Fair point."

"So that's a no to the paintball?" he asked, grabbing a cupcake and taking a bite.

"Yes."

He finished his mouthful and pursed his lips, then his eyes lit up. "You said he's your boss, right? Where do you work?"

"The library." Where was he going with this?

"Is there some kind of project you can do together? Like one of those montages of couples working toward a shared goal while having fun and flirting?"

She pondered this. It wasn't a bad idea, although no particular projects came to mind. "I'll have to think about it."

"Great." He flashed his teeth, and for the briefest moment, she caught a glimpse of the smile he'd been famous for. The one that women worldwide had swooned over. "If you could try to be charming, that would help things along."

Yeah, because *that* was going to happen.

"I don't have a charming bone in my body."

He swiped frosting from his lip. "You're making this more difficult than it needs to be."

"Story of my life."

"Well, if you're determined to veto my ideas, you'll just have to *Legally Blonde* the shit out of him and woo him with your uniqueness."

Images of herself in pink suits and tortoiseshell glasses flashed into Charity's mind. She shuddered. "Thanks, but no thanks. I think I'll just keep doing what I'm doing and see how it goes." He'd kissed her, after all. Even if he'd walked away. At the very least, that meant he found her attractive, right?

Gray balled up the cupcake wrapper and shook his

head. "You simply refuse to be helped. Come back with more cupcakes and tell me how it goes."

She studied him, and he glanced away. If she was reading him right, for all his bluster, Gray wanted her company.

"Why don't you come into town and get an ice cream with me later this week?" she suggested.

"Thanks for the offer, but I'd better not. I have work to do."

Her eyes narrowed. "I didn't say when."

"I'm always working."

She scanned the living area meaningfully. If he was always working, then why did his place look like a feature for *Better Homes and Gardens*?

He ignored her.

"So, what is it you do these days?" she asked.

He reached for another cupcake. "These are fucking good. Where did you get them from? I'll have to ask my personal shopper to pick some up for me."

"The Shack. My sister's business partner makes them. Did you say 'personal shopper'?"

He nodded. "There's a kid I pay to bring my groceries over each week and run any errands I have."

"Lifestyles of the rich and famous," she muttered.

He arched a brow. "Yeah, I'm really living it up. To answer your question, I'm a screenwriter now."

"Oh, wow. What have you worked on?"

"The latest one that's out in theaters is *Love Reimagined*. Have you seen it?"

"No," she admitted.

"Then we'll have to fix that." He stood and stretched, revealing a stain on his shirt. Clearly he didn't care as well for himself as he did his home. "I have a personal cinema. Come on, I might even show you the deleted scenes."

Movies weren't really Charity's thing, but she found herself going with him because she got the impression he wanted her to stay longer, and she didn't have the heart to disappoint him. She didn't leave until hours later, and on her walk home, in the dark, with the sea breeze sending goosebumps up her arms, her phone rang. She answered without thinking.

A voice said, "Hello, this is Adrian from Waikato Correctional Facility. Have I reached Charity St. John?"

Charity tensed. "Yes."

"An inmate at our facility, Samuel Hagley, has requested permission to call you at this number. Would you like to grant permission?"

"No," she spat. "No, I'd be happy if I never spoke to that man again."

"Okay. I'll make a note of that. Sorry to have upset you."

Adrian hadn't upset her. Samuel had. How dare he reach out to her after what he'd had his friends do in Auckland?

"I have to go," she said.

"Goodbye."

Charity hung up. No, she would not like to receive a call from her bastard of an ex-husband. She only hoped he didn't know where she was. The last thing she needed was for his buddies to turn up in the bay. Things were difficult enough without adding another layer of drama.

Why can't he just leave me alone?

But she knew why. He wanted to make her pay for helping put him away. And he didn't care what collateral damage there was, as long as she was miserable.

17

All weekend, Kyle mulled over Charity's statement about how he had no right to stop her from seeing other men. She was completely correct. He either needed to suck it up or do something about it. He'd decided on the latter option. She was no longer riding the emotional rollercoaster she'd been on after the confrontation with that reporter, and she still wanted him, which meant he was free to go for it.

She flounced into work on Monday morning in a form-fitting floral dress, smelling like oranges and looking like spring. He'd wanted to pounce on her immediately, but it was important he do this properly, which was why he found himself approaching her in the stacks, out of sight of everyone else, during the quiet period before lunch.

"Charity," he said as he came up behind her. His gaze wandered over her slim form and down to her delicately rounded butt. His hands twitched, and he curled his nails into his palms to stop himself from reaching for her. "Can we talk?"

She straightened, turned to face him, and tucked a

loose lock of spun-gold hair behind her ear. "What's up?"

He took a breath and let it out. "I'm sorry for being weird on Friday. The truth is, I like you more than I'm comfortable with and I acted like a jerk because I didn't know how to handle it." He eased his thumb along the furrow in her brow. Her lips parted, and she angled her head. It looked like an invitation, but he didn't want to make any assumptions. "I want to make it up to you, and I'd like to start with a kiss. Is that okay?"

"Yeah." She nodded, her eyes glazed, but as he stepped forward to close the space between them, her hands came up to his chest. "Wait a moment. Just so nothing gets lost in translation, I don't want any kisses —no matter how good they are—unless you plan to take me on a date."

"Okay." The reply came easily and brought with it a sense of relief because she must truly be interested in something serious with him or she wouldn't be making conditions like that.

"Okay?" Her eyes focused. "It's that easy?"

He nodded. "Yes, but I get to choose what the date is." He wanted to share something with her that would make it clear who he was in no uncertain terms so she didn't harbor any illusions. He was a guy with hobbies that probably didn't align with hers, but he loved them and wasn't about to play them down or reduce that part of himself to win her affection. Nope, she'd be coming into this thing with her eyes wide open.

Charity hesitated for a second, then smiled. "You got it. A date of your choice."

Deal made, Kyle clasped her face between his palms and kissed her. Charity's hands dropped from his chest and wound around him, settling in the small of his back. She pressed closer and her hair shifted, a waft of citrus-scented shampoo enveloping them. Her lips tasted of citrus too. Fresh, sweet, and a little tart. He wondered if she'd taste the same way everywhere.

His dick stiffened, and she rubbed herself against the bulge. A groan rumbled low in his throat. Backing her into a cabinet, he cupped her ass and lifted her onto the wooden surface. She shimmied to the edge and wrapped her legs around his waist. Kyle's vision swam. He was intoxicated by the sensation of her body against his, and the urgency with which she returned his kiss. He'd never been reckless at work, but he couldn't seem to stop himself. Now that he had his hands on her, he didn't want to let go. She reached for his shirt and tugged it free from the waistband of his pants, slipping her hands beneath the hem. Her palms splayed over his abs, which tensed instinctively. Her fingers teased him, making him want to throw caution aside and drag her into the staff only area so he could strip her clothes off and finally see what she looked like naked.

A bell rang, and the sound prodded at the back of his mind.

It rang again.

Damn. The counter. Someone needed assistance.

He drew back from Charity, caught sight of her kiss-swollen lips, and couldn't resist brushing his mouth over them again.

The blasted bell rang a third time.

He grimaced, and ran a hand through his hair, smoothing it. "I'd better get that."

"Get what?" she asked, and he couldn't tell if she was joking or not. Hands on her waist, he lifted her from the cabinet and lowered her to the floor. She looked up at him and sighed. "Go. But this isn't over."

He grinned, feeling suddenly wicked. "Not by a long shot."

<hr>

CHARITY WAS IN THE STRATOSPHERE WITH NO INTENTION of coming down. She floated around the library, returning books to their shelves, her feet seeming to hover above the ground.

Kyle wanted her, and she hadn't needed to sing a song or write a poem or be anything other than herself.

"'Scuse me, miss?"

She stopped and glanced down at the little boy in front of her. He was six or seven, with a mop of dark hair and serious brown eyes. "Hi, there."

He shuffled nervously from foot to foot. "Do you have any alien books?"

Charity cocked her head, thinking about whether they had anything for his age range. Most of those books were for slightly older children. "What sort of alien book are you looking for?"

He shrugged. "I dunno. I just think aliens are cool."

She racked her brain. "Come with me." She led him to the wall of children's books and selected a couple of options. One was an illustrated book about friendly visitors and another was a short chapter book that was probably above his reading level but might not be, depending on how much he usually read. She held them up. "How about one of these?"

He nibbled his lip, glancing from one to the other. "Can I take them both?"

The question was so soft she nearly missed it.

"Do you have a library card?" she asked.

He nodded. "Mum has it."

"Is your mum here?"

He nodded again and gestured toward the adult fiction section. "She's over there."

"Great." Charity smiled. "You hold onto these, and she can get them for you when she's ready to go."

The little boy offered a hesitant smile in return, then took the books and headed for one of the child-sized seats nearby. To her surprise, he set the illustrated book aside and opened the chapter book. Charity went back to work. Soon after, a dark-haired woman approached the front counter with the little boy at her side.

"Did you find what you need?" Charity asked.

"Yes, thanks." The woman stacked several books on the counter, including the two her son had chosen. "Alec says you helped him. Thanks for doing that. He's homeschooled and loves to read, so it feels like we're always trying to find something new to keep him going."

"You're welcome. I enjoy helping kids with their books." Even though it wasn't something she'd thought much about, it was the truth. Much as she generally enjoyed her work, her favorite moments had happened while reading for the little ones. Kids were clean slates. And they were fun.

"Well, thanks again," she said as Charity issued the books and pushed them across the counter. "I'm sure we'll see you soon."

"See you." Charity waved to Alec as his mother steered him out. He tentatively lifted a hand to wave back.

She checked the time. She was due for her lunch break. She headed for the kitchen and was reading on the armchair when Kyle swept in, set her book aside, and kissed her so thoroughly she feared she'd pass out.

He swept out again as quickly as he'd arrived. When she replaced him at the counter after her break, she discreetly ran her palm over his gym-buff behind as he turned to leave. An eyebrow hiked up his forehead, and she winked, loving the splotches of red that blossomed on his cheeks. He was a blusher, and she'd never known what an attractive trait that was.

Later, he repaid her by pulling her into an unoccupied aisle and kissing her until her thoughts were muddled and she didn't know which way was up.

She smiled all day, giddy on feelings she hadn't experienced in a long time. In fact, she couldn't recall being this lighthearted since she was a girl. Even when she was married to Samuel, it hadn't all been sipping cocktails and shopping. They'd had their arguments. But this? This felt good. So good that when a petite blonde wandered in off the street, casting her eyes around in a way that made Charity think she wasn't looking for the next Nora Roberts book, Charity crossed over and whispered, "Sorry, he's off the market."

The blonde's face fell. "Are you sure?"

Charity grinned, the movement stretching her face in a way that felt unusual and unfamiliar. "Really sure. Sorry."

The blonde pouted. "Thanks for letting me know before I made a fool of myself. I'll head over to the bar. I hear the bartender is off-the-charts hot."

"Good choice." Charity knew that Logan would be only too happy to flirt with a tourist.

Whistling, she got back to work, her smile broadening when Kyle glanced between her and the departing blonde and cocked his head inquisitively.

She shrugged. "Apparently we don't have what she's looking for."

18

After a night of brainstorming, Kyle had come up with the perfect date. He even had the tickets. The only problem was, he'd booked them for himself and Brooke. Usually, they attended the annual Galaxy Con together, but Brooke knew he was interested in Charity and she'd encouraged him to pursue her, so hopefully she wouldn't mind.

"Rise and shine," Kyle said as Brooke answered his call a little after eight in the morning. "I hope I didn't wake you."

"You didn't," she assured him. "I've been up for an hour, working on a design for the wedding invitations."

"You're doing them yourself?"

"Yeah. Between being a part-time receptionist for Kat and doing Jack's paperwork, I have the time and it's nice to be creative for once. I've been working on my Rey costume for this weekend too."

Kyle winced. "Yeah, about that."

"What?" He could almost sense the way her eyes narrowed.

"I feel like a massive prick for even asking this, but is there any chance you'd let me use your ticket to take Charity?" He bowled on before she had a chance to answer, wanting to explain himself before she got offended about him ditching her for another girl. "It's just that I can't think of a better way to make sure she really wants to be with me than to take her to the Con and see how she handles it."

There was a hitch in Brooke's breath. "You asked her out? That's great!"

"Technically, she asked me out." Although he'd intended to do it anyway. "But yeah, and she agreed to do whatever I chose."

"So you want to test her mettle?" He could practically see the cogs in her brain whirring. "You're afraid she only likes you because of what you've got on the outside?"

He shrugged, forgetting she couldn't see him. "It wouldn't be the first time." Unfortunately, one of the side effects of being a late bloomer was that he could never be certain whether a girl actually liked him for his personality or not. "Please, Brookie. I promise I'll make it up to you next year. We can go as Padme and Anakin if you want." She'd been after him to do that for ages.

She giggled. "Sounds like you really want me to say yes. Go for it. I want you to find a love like Jack and I have, and if you think Charity could give you that, then I'm happy for you. Do you want to borrow one of my outfits for her?"

Kyle tilted his head and imagined Charity wearing Brooke's Khaleesi costume. But then he remembered how much Jack had liked that outfit, and how high the chances were they'd defiled it.

"No, but thanks for the offer. We'll figure out

something else. That's assuming she says yes." He didn't know for sure she would. Whatever she'd been expecting him to come up with, he doubted it was this.

"Send me photos."

He grinned. "I will. Thanks again. I have to go to work now. See you."

"Bye."

The walk to work was short since his flat was on the edge of the commercial district, and he arrived at the library with ten minutes to spare, but as he'd hoped, Charity was already there.

"Good morning," he said as he entered the kitchenette and bent to kiss her cheek. "You look nice today."

"Thank you." She smoothed a hand over the front of her pale pink dress. "So do you. But then, you always do." She rolled her eyes. "That's why half the female population turns up to flirt with you."

"Does it bother you?" he asked, not having considered it previously. As far as he knew, no one had ever been jealous over him before.

"A little," she admitted. "But it's nothing I can't handle. Besides, it's not like I've had any claim on you." She drew her lower lip between her teeth, then released it. "Although I hope I do now."

He nodded, a lightness in his chest that he'd never experienced before. "Yeah, you do." On that note, he reached into his pocket to extract one of the tickets to Galaxy Con and offered it to her. "Will you come with me to Galaxy Con for our first date?"

She scanned the ticket, her eyes alight with interest. "Of course. I already gave you *carte blanche* for our date. It's this weekend?"

"Yes." He watched her carefully for any sign of

reluctance. He'd expected her to require convincing. "You're sure you're all right with this?"

She looked up and smiled, the corners of her eyes crinkling. "Yes, Kyle. I'm fine with it."

"It'll be an overnight trip to Auckland," he felt compelled to add. "I booked a suite with two bedrooms." He and Brooke had always shared accommodation, and he hadn't given much thought to what it would mean to have Charity with him rather than Brooke. He hoped the arrangements didn't frighten her off. He didn't want her to think he assumed something would happen between them. Especially when she might set one foot inside the Con and decide she wanted nothing more to do with him. It wasn't exactly her scene.

She gave him a look that said she knew what he was doing. "An overnighter works for me. Are there any other ways you want to convince me to turn you down?"

"Nope, that about covers it."

She stepped closer and rested her cheek over his wildly hammering heart. Slowly, he encircled her with his arms. A sense of calm descended on him, and warmth burst to life inside his chest, radiating outward. It felt good to hold her like this. As if she belonged with him.

She pulled back and gazed up at him, her expression serious. "I'm not going to flake out on you."

"Good." He ducked his head and kissed her. It started out as a thank you but transformed into an exploration. They tasted, sampled, learned the contours of each other's mouths. Kyle traced the muted curves of her body, from her narrow waist to the slight flare of her hips, the softness of her bottom and the elegant length of her back and neck. In return, her palms grazed the outside of his shoulders and arms, traveled around his back and came to rest above his ass.

Pulling his lips from hers, he brushed a kiss over her temple, then shuddered when she buried her face in the juncture of his neck and shoulder and lightly bit. His insides quivered and he willed his oncoming erection to settle down.

"We need to open up," he said, grappling for self-control. "Mr. MacAllister is probably waiting to be let in."

Yes, that should do it—think of Hugh, the town council representative, who turned up every morning to read the daily news, having not mastered the internet.

Charity shook her head, and it took him a moment to realize she was trying to clear it, rather than disagreeing with him. "You're right." She drew in an uneven breath, and touched her hair, perhaps checking it was still in place.

"You don't look like you've been ravished in the stacks," he assured her, winking conspiratorially.

She laughed. "I never knew how incorrigible you were, Kyle Pride. I'll have to keep an eye on you."

"You do that, beautiful."

"Oh." She stopped him with a hand on his arm. "There's something I'd like to discuss later. An idea for the library. Just whenever you have time."

He was intrigued. "Okay, I'll find you when I'm free."

"Perfect."

It wasn't until the brief lull between lunch and 3pm that Charity and Kyle had their conversation. She was scanning through online catalogues, looking for new books they could acquire, when Kyle dragged a chair over and dropped into it.

"So, what's your idea?" he asked.

She discreetly wiped her palms on her dress, wishing she'd done more preparation. She had no experience with pitching, and no expertise or reason to think her suggestion was actually a good one. It had just come to her after talking to little Alec and his mother, and in recalling what Gray had said about her and Kyle working on a project together.

"There are a lot of children who come here," she said hesitantly.

"There are," he agreed, which gave her the confidence to continue.

"I don't know a heap about kids, so I might be off base, but they seem to like having stories read to them or chosen for them."

He nodded encouragingly. "Go on."

"I thought it might be nice to have a weekly story time." The words came out of her in a rush. "We could have different themes, and maybe the kids could dress up so they feel like they're part of the story. We could print out coloring pages or have some kind of craft. I saw a bunch of coloring pencils in storage and a few stickers and glitter pens."

Kyle pursed his lips as she trailed off. "I like it," he said. "But we don't have room in the budget for any fancy supplies."

"We won't need them," she assured him. "I can make do with whatever we've got. And I'm happy to organize it, and to do the reading... although I'm not sure whether the local parents will like that." She deflated. It hadn't occurred to her until now that people might keep their children away simply because she was involved. "Perhaps I could cover your duties while you read."

Kyle frowned. "Screw that. You're doing the reading. If they don't like it, then they're not welcome here."

Charity's lower lip trembled. Her eyes prickled with tears. She sniffed. She would *not* cry, damn it. But it had been a long time since anyone stood up for her, and now Kyle was making a habit of it. "Thank you."

"Don't thank me." He looked annoyed. "It's common human decency. It's your idea, so you get to take the lead." He reached over the desk to touch her hand. "If you can make it happen within our current budget, then you have approval from me to go ahead." His expression softened. "I think it's a brilliant idea."

Excitement bubbled in her stomach. She couldn't believe how glad she was to have a project that was solely hers. "I can't wait to get started."

As soon as Charity arrived home after work, she sprawled on her bed, perched her laptop on her knees, and started googling. She had no idea what a Galaxy Con was, but she intended to find out. She refused to let Kyle down at the first hurdle by being that clueless girl who reinforced his poor opinion of her. An hour later, after deep diving into a number of rabbit holes, she'd learned enough to have some idea of what she was in for. Hundreds, if not thousands, of people gathered together to celebrate their favorite science fiction TV shows, movies, books, and comics—and many of them would be in costume. There were several famous guests slated to appear, and they'd be giving speeches and meeting fans. Furthermore, competitions would be held for the best dressed attendees, as well as panel discussions on topics that went totally over her head.

To start with, she needed to binge as many science fiction TV shows as she could so she had some idea of who the characters were. Beyond that, she needed help. She had no doubt that Kyle would be full steam ahead with costume enthusiasm and probably had something epic to wear. Meanwhile, she didn't know where to begin. He probably didn't expect her to dress up, but she wanted to fully embrace the event and prove she could stand at his side. Besides, she had been a cheerleader. She *loved* to dress up. She just didn't often have reason to.

With only a moment of hesitation, she dialed the number Brooke gave her at the cupcakes and cocktails night. Who better to prepare her than Kyle's close friend?

"Hi, this is Brooke."

"Hey, Brooke," she said. "It's Charity here. I hope it's okay that I called."

"Sure thing." Brooke's voice brightened. "Is this about Galaxy Con?"

"Yes!" she exclaimed, relieved not to have to explain herself. "Did he tell you?"

She laughed. "You could say that. How can I help?"

Charity picked at her nails, unsure where to begin. "I want to show him that I support him and I'm on board with his hobbies, so I need to find an outfit to wear that won't make him ashamed to be seen with me."

"Aww, that's sweet."

Not something she was used to being called. "Uh, thanks?"

"Okay, okay. How much do you know about *Star Trek Enterprise*? That's his favorite."

"Nothing at all." She made a mental note to start her binge with that show.

"Well, there's this Vulcan, T'Pol—do you know what a Vulcan is?"

"Err, are they the ones with the deformed foreheads?"

"No, that's Klingons. Vulcans are a race who are purely rational. They don't do emotion. They look humanoid but have pointed ears and eyebrows that raise at the ends. Anyway, google T'Pol. That's tee apostrophe pee oh el."

Charity did as she said. "I see what you mean about the eyebrows." She pulled up a shot of a lean auburn-haired woman in a belly-baring navy shirt and military-style trousers. Studying the image, she cocked her head. "I could do that."

"I know," Brooke cried gleefully. "I've been brainstorming all day in case you called. I thought you might feel a little lost, and I hoped you'd be comfortable enough to reach out."

"Talk about sweet," Charity murmured. "Okay, I could do the eyebrows with makeup. Is there a place where I could order an outfit, or at least find something in the right ballpark?"

Brooke read her a website URL. "If you order today and ask for express shipping, it'll be here in plenty of time."

Charity entered the URL into her laptop and smiled as she flicked through the massive array of options appearing in front of her. "Thanks, I owe you."

"Just make sure Kyle enjoys himself." Brooke's tone had grown serious. "If you mess him around..."

"I don't plan to," Charity assured her. "He's one of

the good guys, and I know how lucky I am to get a second chance."

"Good."

"So…any advice?"

"Hmm." Quiet temporarily descended. "He doesn't date often, so I can't tell you what his deal-breakers are, but just be honest with him. Don't flirt with anyone else and try to relax and have fun."

Charity slumped against the wall, disappointed not to get anything meatier or more definite. "Honesty is kind of my thing these days, and I don't flirt unless there's a tip in it for me. As for relaxing, I'll do my best, but no promises. This is the first date I've been on since my separation."

"Seriously?" Brooke sounded shocked, and Charity didn't know how to take that.

"Yeah. It's hard to trust a man when the last one you loved turned out to be a pathological liar and a fraud."

"Huh. I guess I never thought of it that way."

"Nobody ever does." But she wasn't looking for people to pity her. "Anyway, I haven't found anyone I thought was worth taking a chance on until now, so I've been stubbornly single."

"Fair enough." Brooke hummed in thought. "I guess that means Kyle can be sure he's not a rebound."

"Ha! A rebound several years later. No, I think he can consider himself safe in that regard. Thanks for your help. I'll let you get back to your evening now."

"Bye," Brooke said. "And good luck. Text me a picture of whatever you decide to order."

"I will. See you later."

Charity hung up and placed her phone on the nightstand, then returned to the laptop and entered 'T'Pol' into the search bar on the cosplay website. Half an hour later, she purchased an outfit similar to the one she'd seen in Google images and sat back, satisfied with her work.

On an afterthought, she sent a quick text to Brooke.

Charity: *Please don't tell Kyle we talked. I want to surprise him.*

A reply came within minutes.

Brooke: *I won't. Fingers crossed for you!*

Yeah, Charity had her fingers crossed, too. It had been a long time since she felt a spark of attraction toward any man, and she didn't want to sabotage it before they even got off the ground. She was already worried she didn't deserve him, or that there was some hidden catch. She didn't have the best track record with choosing decent guys. But Kyle seemed like the real deal, and she so badly wanted him to be.

19

THE DAY OF THEIR DATE ARRIVED, AND KYLE'S NERVES were tangled. He and Charity had been flirting and sneaking kisses all week, but this trip would mean more one-on-one time than they'd ever had together. At 8 a.m., he parked outside Faith and Shane's house and sent her a text. He didn't want to knock on the door in case the boys were still sleeping.

A few minutes later, Charity appeared in the doorway, wearing jeans and a loose white blouse and dragging a suitcase behind her. She looked up, caught his eye through the open window, and smiled. Warmth trickled through him, like sunshine landing on his soul. Her smile was rare, but it was a thing of beauty. Hopefully it would hang around. Galaxy Con would be like a different planet to her. But planets had been bridged before. Some of the most epic fictional love affairs happened between people of different species. He had to hold out hope.

As she approached, he popped the trunk and hopped out to help her load the suitcase in.

"Morning," she chirped, looking every bit as eager

as he was nervous. "I can't wait. You must be so excited. The Con only comes around once a year, right?"

He frowned. How did she know that? Had it said so on the ticket? "Yeah, it does. Each time, as soon as it's over, I start anticipating the next one."

"I bet." She slid into the passenger seat, and he got behind the steering wheel. "You said we're dropping our stuff off at the hotel first, didn't you?"

"That's right. It means I can change into my costume without getting it rumpled on the drive over."

"Great." Her lips tugged up, and a mischievous glimmer lit her eyes. "Let's hit the road then."

During the trip to Auckland, they discussed the books they were currently reading. He told her about his favorite sci-fi and space opera novels, and in return, she shared her favorite poets and classical works. He discovered she had a dry sense of humor and could easily make him laugh—especially when it came to talking about the absurdity of stories like *Romeo and Juliet*. Even though she'd read it a number of times, she claimed she still couldn't fathom how foolish the two young lovers must have been to screw everything up so epically.

"They were barely teenagers," he argued, for the sake of seeing her nose crinkle in annoyance. He hadn't actually read the play himself, so he was operating from an area of ignorance, but she didn't seem to pick up on that. "Of course they didn't have a lot of foresight."

She shook her head, disgusted. "I'm all for the whole star-crossed lovers thing, but a little communication goes a long way. There's no way it had to end with everyone dying."

He pressed his tongue into the inside of his cheek

to stop from laughing. "You don't think that's romantic?"

"Mutual suicide?" She snorted. "No. Real romance is staying alive for each other regardless of how hard it may be and how much you might want to suffocate the other person with a pillow sometimes. Real love doesn't end in a blaze of glory, it fuels people over the course of a lifetime, growing stronger each year. It means overlooking flaws because of all the good that makes up for it, and cherishing your lover's quirks and differences."

He cocked his head and glanced at her. "It sounds like you've given this a lot of thought."

Her cheeks reddened. "I spend a lot of time alone, and I tend to overthink things."

"I like it," he assured her. "Your idea of what makes true romance is deeper and more real than most people's." It was sweet how passionate she seemed about the topic, considering she went to a lot of effort to project a prickly exterior. She didn't let her cautious nature prevent her from being honest with him, and damned if that didn't make him feel special.

"What about you?" she asked. "What does love mean to you?"

His cheeks heated, and he grasped for something to say.

She grinned and nudged his side. "Come on, Kyle. I spilled my guts, now it's your turn."

"Okay, okay." He thought quickly. "I suppose to me, love is making something work no matter how many obstacles stand in the way, and sticking with someone through hard times. It's being each other's favorite person, and sharing hopes, goals, and dreams."

She nodded. "Well put."

They came to the edge of the city, and Kyle took an

off-ramp to exit the highway. The mood in the car had become intense, and he wanted to lighten it.

"What's your favorite movie?" he asked.

"*The Godfather*," she replied, tossing her shoulders back as though daring him to comment. The corners of his mouth twitched, but he managed not to make a smart-ass remark. "And yours?"

"*Star Wars: The Empire Strikes Back*." Films were a popular topic of debate between him and Brooke, who preferred the more recent Star Wars movies.

"That's the one where the rebels are on the icy planet?" she asked.

He accidentally veered to the left of the road. Righting the car, he gaped. "You know *Star Wars*?"

She shrugged, as though she hadn't just turned everything he thought he knew on its head. "I did my research. I didn't want to turn up unprepared."

"Are you telling me you studied *Star Wars*?"

"And *Star Trek*, *Battlestar Galactica*, *Stargate*, and *Armageddon*."

"Oh, my God." Was it too early to be in love?

Scratch that. Love was definitely okay. She'd taken the time and effort to learn more about his interests. And from that list, it was obvious she'd asked Brooke what his favorites were. "Did you actually watch them, or just read about them?"

"I watched the first season of *Star Trek: Enterprise*, but I didn't have time to dig into anything else."

His heart pitter-pattered happily. She'd gone straight for his most beloved series. "What did you think of it?"

"It was interesting. Not what I'd usually watch, but I enjoyed it." She sent him a sly smile. "Plus, Trip Tucker is a hottie."

He pouted, even though he was secretly ecstatic. "What's he have that I don't?"

"A uniform," she suggested. "There's something about a guy in uniform."

"I can institute uniforms at the library," he said. "Just watch me."

"You watch yourself. Girls will be jumping all over you if you do that."

He turned into their hotel parking garage. "I trust you to fight them off."

She rolled her eyes. "Maybe I'll let them have you."

"You wouldn't." He glanced over nervously. "Would you?"

She touched a finger to her nose and winked.

He parked and they gathered their bags and headed into the hotel. Nerves swam in his stomach. Charity was talking a good talk, but how would she actually handle the Con?

At reception, they checked in and got their key cards. When they reached their suite, he waited for her to claim one bedroom and then he took the other. Opening his suitcase, he extracted his costume. A *Star Trek: Enterprise* crew uniform. He grinned. Hopefully, Charity would swallow her tongue when she saw him in it. What a coincidence that she happened to think uniforms were sexy.

A few moments later, he was fully dressed and waiting for her in the small living area. Minutes passed, and Charity didn't emerge. Where was she? He'd been the one with a costume, so what could be taking her so long? He flopped onto an armchair and rested his head against the back. Five minutes passed, then ten. Finally, he heard footsteps in the hall.

Holy shit.

Was he dreaming? Because this version of Charity,

wearing a belly-baring *Star Trek* fleet costume, with her hair unbound around her shoulders, her eyebrows carefully drawn on, and plastic Vulcan ears over her own, was pretty much his perfect woman.

She'd found a costume.

Not only that, but he'd hazard a guess she was supposed to be T'Pol, from his favorite *Star Trek* series. He'd never imagined she'd embrace their trip so fully, or that she'd go to Brooke for help—as she must have done in order to get this so right. She winked saucily, and his brain nearly exploded.

"Goddamn, you look amazing," he told her.

Her smile widened. "You like it?"

"So much that I'm not sure I want to leave the hotel room. We could just stay here. Have a romantic weekend indoors." The scary thing was, he wasn't sure he was joking. He might well ditch the Con if she seemed up for it.

She crossed to him and rested her hands on his chest. "Hey. We match."

"We could also match by being naked."

She laughed. "But then you'd miss Ira Steven Behr."

His jaw dropped, and he stared at her with wide eyes. She'd really done her research. Ira Steven Behr was the screenwriter and producer behind *Star Trek: Deep Space Nine*, and the guest he most wanted to see this year. The fact that she knew that drove him crazy.

No, he was just crazy for her. Full stop. No ifs, buts, or maybes. No more denying it or telling himself she wasn't right for him. She was more than right. She was perfect.

Stepping closer, he slid his hands around the back of her head, angled her face toward him, and lowered his lips to hers.

"Mmm," he murmured between kisses. "You. Are.

The. Best."

She giggled, and it nearly undid him. He couldn't recall the last time he'd heard her make such a carefree, joyful sound, but he loved it. She stepped away from him and twined her fingers between his. "Come on, Captain Hot-Stuff. Let's go meet some quasi-famous people."

He followed along behind her, their hands stretched between, and his eyes drifted down to the small of her back, which was exposed by the low-riding pants and crop top. There were two dimples just above her waistband, and he wanted to dip his tongue into each of them. But a moment later, they were in the hotel corridor, and the opportunity for dirty deeds had passed.

The walk to the convention center didn't take long. Kyle led the way, keeping a firm hold on Charity. He couldn't help but notice the number of men whose gazes lingered on her. He glared, pleased when most of them looked away. There were benefits to being built like he could crush them into dust even if he didn't have a violent bone in his body.

When they arrived, their tickets were checked at the door and then he steered her into the throng of bodies. The crowd in the convention center bustled to and fro, their energy palpable. He loved the atmosphere at these events. They were one of the few places he actually felt like he belonged. Not that he considered himself an outsider in general, but there was a side of him most people didn't understand. His fellow convention-goers did.

"Wow, I can't believe how elaborate some of these costumes are," Charity exclaimed, scanning the area with wide eyes. Far from disparaging it as he'd feared she might, she seemed fascinated by fandom culture.

"Like that." She pointed at a woman who was painted head to toe in blue, with her blonde hair slicked back. "Who is she supposed to be? And is she naked?"

He laughed. "Best not to figure out the answer to that second question. She's Mystique from X-Men. Tell me you know what that is."

She nodded. "I do, I just haven't watched any of the movies myself."

"You're missing out." They stepped out of the way as Mystique swept by. "We need to educate you."

"I could probably handle that." She lowered her voice. "Mystique just totally eye-fucked you."

Her comment startled a snort from him. "I'm more into sexy Vulcans. You've got nothing to worry about. Me, on the other hand…" He narrowed his eyes at a man dressed in the robes of a Jedi, who was hovering at a distance, clearly waiting for an opportunity to approach. "I have all kinds of trouble I need to keep you away from."

She rolled her eyes. "As if." She tugged him toward the stall where the *Star Trek*-related people had set up camp. "Here first?"

"Nope. First, we do a circuit of the room." During which he intended to have his hands on her as much as possible to relay the message that other men ought to steer clear. "We figure out what's where, and who we'd like to talk to. Then we decide where to go."

Her jaw set in determination, as if they were launching an enemy strike. He fought the urge to laugh. If she were trying to channel T'Pol, her features were far too expressive, but he liked them that way. He released her hand and slid an arm around her waist. God, he enjoyed touching her. He could get used to this. Hopefully, she felt the same way. If not, he was in trouble.

20

____

To her surprise, Charity was having more fun than she could remember having in a long time. For starters, the vibe at the Con was excellent. She couldn't see a single person who looked like they weren't having a blast. Secondly, Kyle obviously wanted to bang her against every available surface. She'd never known he had so much caveman in him, but as soon as they'd entered, his hands had begun wandering across her body as though he were advertising the fact she was there with him. Once, when some guy dressed in a Wookiee costume—yes, she knew what a Wookiee was, thanks to Google—took his mask off to talk to her, Kyle had magically appeared at her side to drape an arm around her shoulders with as much subtlety as a gorilla bashing his chest.

She liked it. Liked knowing he cared enough to want to keep her to himself. It only made her more certain of her feelings for him. So, too, did the glimpses of that part of himself he kept buried during everyday life. He bubbled with enthusiasm and his confidence seemed to grow the longer they were there.

When he was among people he felt comfortable with, he radiated charisma and energy. But he wasn't the only one who changed. Here, dressed as someone else, she got to play at being carefree. If anyone recognized her, they didn't say a word, and she could pretend she was just a woman who enjoyed futuristic space-themed TV shows.

There was also something to be said for getting Kyle away from the bay. She didn't have to chase off so many other women. She caught several looking at him, but they seemed to respect the fact he was there with her.

As they made their way around the center, stopping to talk to people, her spirit lightened. She squeezed Kyle's hand and he squeezed hers back. Then, without warning, he pulled her out of the stream of traffic, looped his arms around her and dipped her for a kiss. Her eyelashes fluttered closed. The kiss was nothing too steamy—they were in public, after all—but a sweet lip lock with just enough heat to let her know he wanted more.

"What was that about?" she asked when it ended.

He nuzzled the crook of her neck, sending pleasurable shivers skating over her skin. "You looked like you needed to be kissed."

"I can't disagree." She angled her head and he dropped another kiss on her lips, then, with obvious reluctance, let her go. "But we should get to the signing station for Number Six."

He gave her a strange look, then grabbed her upper arms and planted another kiss on her. She grinned. Doing her homework paid off. Perhaps she should have learned that earlier in life.

"Let's not," he said. "How would you like to get out of here?" His mouth moved against her ear as he added, "I don't want to be presumptuous, but I'd really like to get you naked. Would you be all right with that?"

"All right?" Her lips twitched. "That sounds like the best idea I've heard all day. But I don't want you to miss out."

He shook his head. "We can come back tomorrow. Right now, I really want to show you how amazing I think you are."

Her heart gave an extra thump. "I'd like that. Let's go."

KYLE HAD NEVER TRIED TO SEDUCE A GIRL ON THE FIRST date. He wasn't that kind of guy. But when it came to Charity, all of his rules went out the window. He wanted her. *Now.* Based on the way her legs ate up the length of the corridor to their room just as quickly as his, she clearly felt the same. When they reached the door, he swiped his key card and waited for her to enter first.

All of a sudden, doubts assailed him. This wasn't just any woman he'd brought back to his room. It was Charity St. John. The girl he'd crushed on in high school. The one who'd broken his heart. Should he really be doing this?

Charity whipped off her pointed ears and turned to face him. "There's a lot going on in that brain of yours right now, isn't there?"

"Yeah."

She studied him. "We don't have to do anything. We can go back, or just lie on the bed and make out." She fidgeted with the ears. "I haven't had sex since before my ex was arrested, so waiting a little longer isn't going to make me any less interested in you."

He winced, hating that she'd noticed his moment of indecision, but her calm response and the certainty in her voice made him believe her. That, more than anything, helped him decide.

"Are you kidding? I finally have you alone in a place where no one can interrupt us. I don't want to stop."

"Great." She raised her gaze to his, a smile creeping over her face. Suddenly, she froze. "Wait. Do you have condoms?"

He rubbed the back of his neck, feeling his cheeks heat. "Yeah, I do. I didn't want to assume anything, but I figured it was better to be safe than sorry."

"Definitely."

She removed her top and his eyes bugged out. Beneath it, she wore nothing but a scrap of black silk that barely covered her nipples. She shimmied out of her pants, kicked them off, and stood before him in matching underwear. He swallowed, his throat working hard as he struggled to process how quickly she'd undressed. His dick had sprung to life as soon as he got an eyeful of her satiny skin. She was strawberries and cream, and he wanted to savor every inch of her.

He leapt into action, fighting his way free of an outfit that seemed unnecessarily restrictive. The shirt came off and he noted her intake of breath with satisfaction. He spent a lot of time working out—it helped to clear his mind—and moments like this made him even more grateful for it. Ego got the better of him, and he couldn't resist tensing his abs and flexing his biceps. She caught her lip between her teeth and her eyes flitted from his stomach to his arms to his face, apparently uncertain where to settle. She looked like a kid who'd been offered an array of forbidden treats, and he loved it. He began to slowly lower his trousers, and she made an impatient noise in the back of her throat. When she tried to grab the waistband, he dodged out of reach.

"You're loving this, aren't you?" she groused.

"Just as much as you are." When he was naked, he snared her around the waist and pressed the length of his body against hers. She was just as smooth as she looked, and she melted into him, soft where he was hard and curved where he was flat. The delicious contrast made him hungry for more.

He kissed her lower lip, then her nose, then her forehead, listening as her breathing grew erratic. Her palms brushed over the planes of his back as she explored him by touch. He had the strangest urge to lean into the places her hands skimmed over. Instead, he cupped her bottom and hoisted her up. She wrapped her legs around his waist like she'd done it a million times before while he carried her into the bedroom and backed her up against the wall.

She grinned, a glint of wildness in her eyes. "Don't tell me you're one of those people who'll fuck anywhere other than a bed."

"No, but I don't see the need to skip straight to the main course, either."

"Oh." Her pupils dilated, her eyes turning dark with desire, and he claimed her mouth in a fiery kiss that had none of the playfulness of their earlier exchanges. It was all-consuming. With one hand supporting her weight, he brought the other up to cup her cheek and angle her so they could go deeper. Dirtier. Tongues met, caressed, entwined. Short gasps escaped each time they separated, and his erection throbbed hot and hard between them.

"Your body is crazy," she said, throwing her head back so he could latch onto her throat. "You're a freaking librarian. How are you so ripped?"

"The gym," he muttered, far more interested in her body, and specifically, in getting the bra and panties off it. With his free hand, he tugged her bra strap down to reveal a pink nipple. The air eased from him as he paused to appreciate the view. Then he flicked the nipple with his tongue. She moaned huskily. He removed the bra and encased her breast with his hand, marveling at how dainty she seemed compared to him. Her hips rolled, stroking over his dick, and a rumble of satisfaction worked its way up his throat. Lifting her away from the wall, he turned and deposited her on the bed, where he settled between her thighs and looked down into her clear, hazel eyes.

"Is there anything you don't like?" he asked, wanting to know the lay of the land before he put a foot wrong and messed up.

She licked her lips. "I have a feeling I'll like anything you do." She hesitated, then added, "I'll let you know if I don't."

"Good." He rolled onto his side and slipped a hand into her underwear, easing them off. She shivered. "God, you're enjoying this, aren't you? I can tell."

She nodded. "Don't stop."

Why would he? After all this time, he finally had her where he wanted. He worked one finger inside her and crooked it. Her back arched off the mattress. He repeated the movement, and watched as her eyes fluttered shut, her lashes dark against her cheeks. God, she was exquisite. All sensual motion and vulnerability —none of her usual prickliness. Raising himself up onto his elbow, he kissed her. Her eyes flew open, locking on his, and she returned the kiss, rocking into his hand and making needy little sounds in the back of her throat.

So. Damn. Sexy.

With obvious reluctance, she pushed his hand away and shifted onto her knees. She pressed him back and straddled him, rubbing her slit over his hard length, soaking him with the evidence of how much she wanted him.

Fuck. Kyle bit his lip, trying to keep his cool so he wouldn't flip her over and drive into her. He wanted to be relentless. To send her to the very edge of pleasure —to a place no one else had managed to take her. She teased him with another subtle roll of her hips.

"Slow down," he ordered. "Unless you want me inside you in the next two seconds."

Holding his gaze, her own turned wicked and she repeated the motion. "I want that."

His entire body shuddered. "Wallet."

She left him and returned a moment later wielding a foil packet. He tried to take it from her, but she held up a finger to stop him, then tore it open and unrolled it over him herself.

He groaned. "You're going to be the death of me."

"But you'll die happy."

She sank onto him, engulfing his eager dick in her warmth.

"Yes, I will," he agreed, fisting the covers so he wouldn't thrust into her too hard or too rough. She was setting the pace and he didn't want to rush her. "So good, baby."

She started riding him, and white light strobed behind his eyelids. Before he could stop himself, his fingers had sunk into the flesh of her hips and he was holding her above him while he pistoned up with too much ferocity. She didn't seem to mind. Her lips parted and a whimper escaped.

"Oh, my God. Just like that." Her eyes squeezed shut, and her head flopped forward, bringing her breasts close enough for him to lick one rosy tip. "Please, please, please."

He slowed, allowing her to resume control, her expression blissed out, her hands resting on his chest. "Please what?" he asked.

"More," she demanded, pouting at the change of pace.

"Like this?" He reached between them and fingered her clit. Her channel tightened in response. She lowered herself onto his chest and claimed his lips in a ravenous kiss. A sob caught in the back of her throat, and then she was squeezing all around him, carrying him into oblivion. With a growl, he released into her, clasping her tight to his chest, refusing any mercy from the orgasm that seemed to go on forever, decimating them both.

When it was over, she slipped from him. He disposed of the condom and flopped back onto the mattress. Charity cuddled up to his side, and Kyle stared at the ceiling, waiting for his brain to start working again, wondering one massive thing: *what had just happened?*

21

———

Hands down, that had been the best sex of Charity's life. As a bonus, Kyle didn't seem to mind the fact she was a cuddler. He wrapped an arm around her when she rested her cheek on his chest, and held her close. Her fingers wandered down to his golden happy trail. His free hand covered hers, his fingers twining between her own. When he squeezed, she angled her head to meet his eyes, wondering what he was thinking. Did he regret what they'd done? Or was he, like her, eager to do it again as soon as possible?

"What's going on behind those incredible blue eyes?" she asked.

His lips curved in an expression of pure male satisfaction, and the affection in his gaze warmed her from the inside out. "Just thinking how lucky I am."

Her nerves eased. "Tell me more about that."

He laughed, his eyes crinkling in the corners, and her heart zinged in response. His smile was so real and precious. She suddenly wished she hadn't discarded her phone, so she could snap a photo of him to bring out whenever she was feeling low.

"I'm in bed with a beautiful woman who's looking at me as though I'm personally responsible for every good thing that's ever happened in the world, and who just made me come so hard I can't think straight. What could be luckier?"

Butterflies paraded in her stomach. "You're good, Kyle Pride, I'll give you that." She smoothed a hand over his ridged abdomen and added, "But I can think of something luckier."

He'd been real with her, so she wanted to do the same in return. It had been a long time since she allowed herself to be vulnerable with someone, and her voice caught in the back of her throat. She snuggled closer and tried again. This was Kyle, after all. Sweet, protective Kyle, and even if he let her down, she knew he'd do it gently.

"I'm in danger of falling for a man who never should have given me a second glance. He's sunshine personified, and his light is starting to chase away my shadows." She blinked rapidly as wetness sprang to her eyes.

For a long moment, they just looked at each other, neither of them speaking. Then Kyle's throat bobbled.

"Damn," he said. "You're a poet. I can't beat that." He kissed her. A simple brush of lips, but it meant everything because it wasn't a rejection. She'd put herself on a limb, and he'd reached out to her.

"Since we're exchanging truths, you should know that you scare me," he admitted. "I like to be prepared for anything, but I never expected you and I'm still trying to get my head around the idea of us together."

Charity nibbled on her lip. "I hope I've been a good surprise, for the most part."

"Definitely." He stroked her hair. "I'm just taking a while to recalibrate."

"I suppose it's a lot to adapt to." A thought occurred to her. "Did it ever cross your mind that you could string me along for a while to get revenge?"

"I'm not that kind of guy."

"I know." That was just her fear getting the better of her. People had publicly scorned her for long enough that trust came hard. Especially when she considered the fact she'd only been with two men seriously and both had hurt her. Then her goddamn roommate had done the same by leading Samuel's friends straight to her. She wasn't exactly a good judge of character.

"Is that what you'd have done, in my place?" he asked.

"Honestly?" She sighed. "I have no idea what I'd have done."

"I do." He kissed her forehead. "Whatever you may think, you're a good person. I have faith in that."

That made one of them.

"Anyway…" She tried to clear the heaviness of the past few minutes. "I'm hungry. Does this place have room service?"

"Sure does." He reached over and grabbed a menu from the bedside cabinet, handing it to her. She scanned the options, waiting for her internal tremors to cease. There was no hiding around Kyle. No flying under the radar and avoiding detection. He saw far too much, and while she liked that about him, it also unsettled her.

"Want to share a lunch platter for two?" she asked, passing him the menu.

He scanned it quickly. "Sounds good."

He put a call in to the restaurant, and while they waited for the food to arrive, Charity suggested a game of Two Truths and a Lie.

Kyle rubbed the back of his neck. "I haven't played that in ages. Would you like to start, or shall I?"

"I will." She thought for a moment. "Okay, number one: I had the hugest crush on Joe Jonas when I was a teenager. Number two: I'm a published poet. Number three: I once took fencing lessons."

His brow furrowed. "We're talking fencing with a sword, not building fences, right?"

"Yes." As if she'd ever been practical enough to want to learn how to build fences.

"Number three is the lie," he said. "Every girl our age had a crush on Joe Jonas at some point, and with how much poetry you read, I can well believe you've had some published."

She shook her head. "Flattering, but no. Two is the lie. I've written poems, but I've never been brave enough to put them out there."

"And fencing?"

She shrugged. "Being married to a wealthy man who didn't want me to work could be boring at times. I tried all sorts of things."

At this, he laughed. "I bet." To his credit, he didn't make any comments about poor little rich girls. "My turn." He tilted his head and tapped his chin while he thought, drawing her attention to the squareness of his jaw. "Hmm. Number one: I once participated in a bodybuilding competition. Number two: I like cats better than dogs. Number three: during university, Brooke and I used to date."

At his last statement, her stomach seized. Had they? She didn't want to believe it, but it would account for how close they were, and this would be a nonthreatening way for him to break the news.

"Um…" Her heart raced, and she tried to swallow her nerves. "Is two the lie? You seem like a dog guy."

His expression softened. "Three is the lie. I entered a bodybuilding competition once because I figured since I was spending so much time at the gym anyway, I may as well, but I realized pretty quickly it wasn't my scene. I do prefer cats to dogs. Brooke and I never dated. There's nothing romantic between us, and there hasn't ever been. I just wanted to get that out there in case you'd wondered."

"I might have," she admitted.

They played for a while longer, during which time Charity confirmed the fact that she was the one who'd wanted a divorce, and opened up about not having any idea where her life was going. In response, Kyle admitted that he hadn't done as much travel as he'd like and envied his brother for the international experiences he'd had. He also told her how he had a difficult time believing that all of the women who showed up at the library really wanted him.

"It's a little embarrassing," he said. "But every time someone flirts with me, or asks me out, I'm scared it's part of a joke or bet."

Charity tried not to ignore the stab of guilt that came from knowing she had something to do with his hang-up. "I'm sorry that would even occur to you. You're a wonderful guy. You know what I thought when I first ran into you again?"

"What?"

"That it was just my luck I'd smack into the hottest man in the bay. Fortunately, it turns out you're also the nicest."

He touched his forehead to hers. "And you are *the* Charity St. John. Do you know how many times I dreamed about this?"

"I'm guessing you also dreamed about tossing me off a cliff. I'm hoping that one doesn't come true."

He laughed. "Don't worry. You're safe with me."

She felt it. For some reason, Kyle gave her a sense of comfort and security that had been missing.

Someone knocked at the door, interrupting her stream of thought.

"I'll get it," Kyle said, slipping from the bed and rustling up a pair of jeans and a t-shirt. "Don't go anywhere."

Charity smiled. Why on earth would she? Everything she wanted was right here.

———

CHARITY WOKE TO A SOFT SNUFFLING SOUND. HER LIPS curved. Kyle snored. How perfectly adorable. She glanced at the clock on the bedside table. Seven a.m. The expo wasn't due to start for another couple of hours, which meant they had time for a little fun.

She rolled to face him and brushed her lips over his. He mumbled something in his sleep. She kissed the tip of his nose and dropped a kiss on each eyelid. When she drew back, his eyes snapped open, hazy but alert. They focused on her mouth, and one of his arms snaked around her waist to drag her within reach. The next kiss was different from the many they'd shared yesterday. Tender and slow. Capable of melting her heart. With every gentle movement, he made her feel cherished, and she poured all of her emotions into returning the kiss, hoping to give him the same.

"What a lovely wakeup call," he murmured, pressing his erection into the V of her thighs. "I've never been a morning person, but you can get me up early any time if you promise to let me do dirty things to you." He looked so hopeful she had to giggle. "You *do* plan to let me do dirty things, right?"

"Naturally." She reached between them and stroked him. "Do you always wake up like this?"

"Only when I'm in bed with a gorgeous woman. Or if I've had a really nice dream."

She encircled him with her fingers and started pumping. His hips jerked, and he thrust into her hand.

"Fuck, that's good."

She grinned in satisfaction. She may be out of practice, but she still knew how to drive a man crazy. But then his fingers dipped into the wetness between her legs, and she gasped. She'd intended for him to lie there and enjoy her ministrations, but he seemed to want to be an active participant. His thumb rubbed over swollen flesh, and she whimpered.

"You don't have to—"

He cut her off by sliding a finger inside of her.

"Oh, God." She bit her lip. "Kyle, I—"

"Relax." His voice was soothing, and he buried his face in the crook of her neck. "One-sided fun isn't my thing." His breath tickled her skin. A second finger joined the first, and she shuddered. "Are you ready for me?"

"Yes," she moaned, hating when he withdrew from her, but knowing he'd fill her again soon. While he reached for a condom, she kept a hold of his cock, spreading moisture over the tip, enjoying the knowledge that soon he'd be claiming pleasure with her.

"Charity, I need to put the condom on."

Reluctantly, she let him go. A moment later, his body settled over hers. His blunt head notched at her entrance and she took him into her body. He swore. His jaw clenched, and his forearms braced to the sides of her head, effectively trapping her. Then he started to move.

Her eyes fluttered shut and she sighed her joy. The

delicious friction between their bodies awoke nerve endings she hadn't even known existed. He brought to life the sensual part of her that had been slumbering for years. Her hips moved in concert with his and their hearts hammered in sync. They became a pulsing mass of sameness. He was her, and she was him. They were one being. And, as one, they wrung every last drop of goodness they could from being together.

Charity sensed bliss hovering just out of reach and arched back, taking him deeper, reaching for it with everything she had. She opened her eyes as he groaned above her, the muscles of his body straining to give her the pleasure she sought. She marveled over his masculine beauty. He thrust into her powerfully, his thighs bunching, shoulders bulging, and his lips parted as rapture stole over his face.

Everything inside her liquefied. She was molten heat, mindless with abandon, and with one final motion she tumbled headlong into oblivion, shaking and trembling and whispering his name.

"Fuck," he swore, his pupils expanding to fill his eyes. "You're going to make me come."

She wrapped her legs around his hips. "Please. I want it."

His eyes closed, shutting him off from her, but then he shivered from head to toe and gasped as he found his release. He collapsed on top of her, and she automatically hugged him to her chest, affection welling within her and spilling over. She basked in a glow of contentment.

Eventually, he stirred, and shifted off her. "That is hands down the best way to start a day."

She smiled. "Plus we still have time to do everything we missed out on yesterday."

Kyle shook his head. "How did you get to be so perfect?"

A sudden fear fluttered in her chest, and she tried to suppress it. She wasn't perfect. Not by a long shot. But hopefully by the time he realized that, he'd care about her too much to let it break them up.

Please. I need him to want this second chance as much as I do.

22

After a long but awesome day at Galaxy Con—quite frankly, the best date Kyle had ever had—he and Charity sat quietly in his car for their trip back to Haven Bay. Charity had fallen silent not long after they reached the highway, and he was beginning to grow concerned.

"Are you all right?" he asked after a while.

"Yeah." She sounded distracted. "Just thinking."

"About what?" He didn't want her to internalize a bunch of doubts about their fledgling relationship.

"Nothing." She sighed, something clearly weighing on her mind.

"You want to know what I'm thinking about?" he asked, figuring he could gain the truth by being vulnerable and offering his own.

"Sure." She turned to him and he sent her a quick smile before returning his eyes to the road.

"I'm thinking that this weekend was amazing, and I want to see more of you." He swallowed and rubbed his lips together to moisten them before continuing. "I'm also thinking that I'd like to date you. Officially.

187

Openly." He glanced her way again. "What do you think?"

Her hands formed fists on her lap, the knuckles white against her navy blue costume. "I think…" She hesitated, her voice dropping so low it was difficult to hear. "That I'm afraid you'll have second thoughts about dating me when you realize exactly what comes with the territory." When he opened his mouth to reply, she held up a hand. "Hold on. Let me get this out. People hate me, Kyle. Especially in the bay. Right now, you see all the sunshine and rainbows, but at places like Galaxy Con it's easy to pretend to be someone else. When I'm me, there's no hiding from the past." Her hand journeyed over to rest on his thigh, and his throat constricted. Gently, he covered it with his own. "I don't want to get attached to you just to have you realize you don't want to deal with the fallout. I'm happy to keep our relationship under the radar until you're sure I'm worth it."

"Charity." He raised her hand to his lips and kissed it. "You're worth it."

She shrugged, and he could tell she didn't believe him. Hardly surprising, given her history. She had reason to tread carefully.

"I'm not keeping this a secret from anyone," he said. "If people can't accept us, then that's their problem."

She brought his hand to her cheek and cradled it there. Fortunately, he was comfortable driving with one hand since there wasn't much traffic to speak of. "You're sweet," she said. "I hope you still feel that way in another week or two."

"I will." He didn't doubt it. But he didn't push the matter because he could tell her fear was deeply ingrained and wouldn't vanish with a few words. He'd have to show her she could rely on him with his actions. "Now, two truths, one lie. Your turn."

She laughed and kept her hand in his. "One: I prefer chick flicks to horror films. Two: my sister is my best friend. Three: I have the hots for my boss."

"That's easy," he replied. "One. You're definitely the kind of girl who enjoys a bit of fake gore."

"Guilty." Her smile hit like a wallop to his gut—one he hadn't seen coming but couldn't possibly have avoided.

"Okay, my turn." He tried to corral his racing thoughts. "One: I used to want to be a Star Fleet admiral when I grew up. Two: I have a degree in computer science as well as library studies. Three: I'm in the local rugby team."

She hummed as she thought. "I'm torn. One is definitely true, and you can't convince me otherwise. I can imagine baby Kyle wanting to be in charge of a fleet of star ships. But two and three are equally believable. On one hand, doing two degrees is a lot of work and you seem like someone who's always known where they're going, so why bother? But on the other hand, I'm not sure you're the kind of guy who likes to roll around in the mud with other men either."

Kyle tried to hide his grin as she mulled it over. "What's the verdict?"

"Three is the lie. You don't play rugby. Or it's a trick question and you do play but not on the local team. Am I right?"

"You are. No rugby for me. I prefer solitary sports."

"Yes!" She pumped her fist. "You know what? I think we're getting to know each other a little better."

So did he, and he liked it. They continued until they reached the bay, and he pulled up outside her temporary home. He wasn't ready to end the weekend, but dusk had descended and he didn't want to make her uncomfortable by inviting her to pack a bag and come to his place. Yeah, she'd jumped into bed with him this weekend, but that was away from all the snooping locals. She might want to be more low key about things here. While he wouldn't hide their relationship, he didn't want to put her in an awkward position either.

Her phone buzzed, and she checked the screen, her cheeks turning pale.

"What is it?" he asked, concerned.

Her eyes shuttered, and she shoved the phone back into her handbag. "Nothing. Just a message I wasn't expecting."

"Is everything okay?"

"Fine." She gave a forced smile. "Nothing to worry about."

She got out of the car, and he found himself swinging his door open and walking around to meet her. He still wanted to know who had messaged her, and what it was about, but he sensed that pushing wouldn't get him anywhere. Instead, he took the bag from her hands, set it on the ground, and gathered her in his arms. She kissed him, and he clasped her tighter, reluctant to let her go. Now that they'd arrived back home, fear had settled in his gut. He couldn't help worrying that this weekend had all been a fantasy.

"I'm not going to vanish if you let me go," she murmured as though she could read his mind. "If anyone is likely to back out of this situation, it's you."

"Never," he vowed. Despite everything, Charity was the woman for him. She might be wary of him. She could even try to push him away. But he'd be waiting when she realized he was serious about her. Easing back, he captured her lips one more time and savored the taste of her, trying to imprint her essence on his memory. "I'll see you tomorrow, beautiful."

"Not if I see you first."

He got her suitcase out of the trunk, and with a little wave, she grabbed the handle and headed up the path toward the house. He watched her go and knew deep in his heart that nothing would ever be the same again.

The moment Kyle was out of sight, Charity got her phone out and checked the screen again. Thank God he hadn't seen the message.

User666: *Replacing me already?*

Attached was a photograph of she and Kyle taken at Galaxy Con. Someone must have posted it online. Her stomach churned. She didn't know what Samuel's game was, but he was clearly keeping tabs on her, and that made her nervous. She blocked the account and tried to hold onto the happiness of a weekend well spent. Unfortunately, she couldn't dispel her unease.

When Mavis and Betty strolled into the library not long after opening, Kyle smelled trouble.

"So," Mavis said, depositing a stack of previously borrowed books on the counter. "We need an update on how your search for love is going. Have you fallen for any of the girls we've brought in? We have a sweepstakes to maintain, and you're not giving us much to work with."

Kyle sighed and ran a hand through his hair. It was time to set them straight. "I'm not pursuing a relationship with any of the women you've introduced me to, and while I appreciate your help, I'd ask that you stop bringing them here because Charity and I are dating now."

Mavis's mouth fell open. "All the lovely women we brought you, and you fell for her obvious charms? I thought you were smarter than that."

"I *am* smart," he countered. "That's why I can see what most people are too blind to notice. She's not her ex. She made mistakes, but those mistakes were centered around loving somebody who didn't deserve it. She's not the person that others make her out to be."

"Maybe not," Betty allowed, her tone softer than Mavis's. "But she doesn't meet many of the criteria on your list either. Does she?"

The list.

That damned list had brought him more trouble than it was worth. Yes, he'd written it, and at the time, he'd believed it was the best way to find the perfect woman, but he'd been misguided. He and Charity were different, but that didn't really matter, did it? As Brooke had said from the start, love was more than a checklist.

But he did have to wonder: were they *too* different?

No. He shook his head. He shouldn't even entertain the thought.

"Not many," he admitted. "But I'm happy, and that's what it's really about."

Betty sighed. "You could do better than her."

"That's where you're wrong."

"I can see you're going to be stubborn about this," Mavis said. "Just don't expect any help when it blows up in your face."

"I won't." He swept their books across the counter. "Good day, ladies."

"Be smart, young man," Betty said in parting.

As they headed into the aisles to search for new books, he pondered their words and hoped he was right not to be concerned that Charity didn't score a perfect ten on his list. She had the most important values: loyalty, intelligence, and—whether she believed it or not—a kind heart. Along with their scorching chemistry, it was enough. It had to be.

———

CHARITY CAREFULLY UNBENT A DOG-EARED PAGE WITHIN a copy of the latest Nora Roberts book and returned it to its rightful place. Her mind was preoccupied with brainstorming ideas for her new Story Time sessions, so she barely noticed the two ladies hustling down the aisle as she reached for the next book on her cart. They came to a stop in front of her and she gasped in surprise. They both eyeballed her, one with a mixture of curiosity and disdain and the other with straight-up contempt. She'd become adept at reading those particular emotions over the years.

"Can I help you?" she asked, hoping this wasn't going to lead to a confrontation. Nosiness she could deal with, but she'd rather not have a screaming match with a pair of septuagenarians.

"You don't deserve him," Mavis snapped, her mouth pinched. "Have the decency to leave the poor boy alone."

It seemed Mavis was angling for a confrontation.

"What are you doing with him?" Betty demanded, puffed up like an angry poodle. "Do you enjoy toying with people?"

"No." She cringed and glanced around but couldn't

see how she could quickly make an exit. At least, not without them following her.

"It seems like it from where we stand," Mavis added.

Charity closed her eyes. She'd experienced plenty of unpleasant comments over the years and she usually let them roll off her shoulders, but if she wanted to stay with Kyle, she'd have to stand up for herself at some point. Wouldn't it be best to get it out of the way now?

Inhaling deeply, she opened her eyes and looked at Betty—the only one of the pair with genuine reason to dislike her. "I know I haven't made good choices in the past, and I also know that Kyle is amazing and I don't deserve him. But here's the thing. He's accepted me and wants to be with me, and as far as I'm concerned, no one else gets a say in our relationship. So you can hit me with as much condemnation and as many snide remarks as you like, but as long as he wants me, nothing else is important."

The women stared at her. Charity drew in a ragged breath and enjoyed the moment of silence. It had been a long time since she'd stood her ground, and she'd forgotten how good it could feel to not to let people walk all over her.

"Is there anything else?" she asked.

Mavis started a slow clap. "Congratulations, Miss St. John. It seems you found your spine." She glanced at her friend. "Let's be on our way, shall we, Betty?"

Betty frowned, looking as though she didn't know what to make of Charity. "Yes, let's."

When they were gone, Charity slumped in relief, resting her forearms on the cart handle and lowering her forehead to the cool metal. Then a noise behind her caught her attention.

"Did you mean that?"

Turning, she met Kyle's gaze. "Every word."

"Good." He swept her into a kiss that made all of her previous discomfort worth it. When he pulled away, his lips curved into a smile. "I'm glad you defended our relationship, and for the record, I think you're amazing too."

"You do?" She could get used to hearing that.

"Absolutely." He nuzzled the side of her face, then kissed her once more and released her. "Now stop flirting and get back to work."

She rolled her eyes and mock saluted. "Sir, yes, sir."

23

CHARITY CHECKED THE CRAFT SUPPLIES ONE LAST TIME. Her first Story Time session was due to begin in five minutes and she was growing anxious. But she had pipe cleaners, cotton balls, a few fabric scraps, partially blunted scissors, glue, and glitter. Everything she thought was needed for children to make their own caterpillars.

"Are you sure the scissors are okay?" she asked Kyle for the second time.

He smiled patiently. "They'll be fine. They're not sharp enough for the kids to injure themselves, and their parents will be with them anyway."

"You're right." She knew he was, but she couldn't seem to shut off her nerves. She tugged the sleeves of her outfit—a head-to-toe striped green ensemble with an orange hat and a headband with antennas attached. She was supposed to be the very hungry caterpillar, but she felt ridiculous. Especially since it was nearly 4pm and the only people here were Alec and his mother Tanya. They'd advertized the event with posters on the local noticeboards and in the library newsletter, but perhaps her fears had been right and nobody would give the initiative a chance simply because she was the one behind it.

"Do you think anyone else is coming?" she asked Kyle quietly.

"I haven't heard, sorry." He sounded sympathetic. "But don't give up. If this one doesn't work as planned, maybe the next one will be better."

She wasn't so sure of that, but she didn't want to rain all over his optimism. "Thanks."

He nodded toward the counter. "I'll be over there if you need me."

"I'll be fine." She watched him go and sighed. She might as well get on with this. She offered Alec and Tanya a tiny smile. "Why don't you have a seat? We'll get started in a moment."

"Sounds good," Tanya replied. "Alec, do you want to read along?"

Alex nodded and grabbed one of the copies of *A Very Hungry Caterpillar* from the low table. Charity picked up another and sat on the chair she'd brought over from her desk. She opened it to the first page and was about to speak when a sudden noise caught her attention.

"Wait a second!"

Charity gaped at the sight of Faith hurrying across the library toward them, a small posse of children behind her. Heading up the pack was Izzy, with her halo of dark hair. She was giggling and holding hands with Lian. Hunter followed behind them, accompanied by another boy around his age, and a red-headed girl brought up the rear, accompanied by a pair of women —one Asian and the other blonde.

Charity's heart filled to the brim. Faith had pulled through for her. The display of support choked her up, and she was grateful for a momentary reprieve while the group got settled. Hunter sat beside Alec and the girls clustered together on the floor. The other little boy picked up a ball of cotton and started playing with it.

"We're here," Faith announced rather unnecessarily, puffing as though she'd run from home. "Hope you haven't started yet."

"We were just about to," Charity said, her voice thick with emotion. She'd never stop being grateful for her sister.

"Oh, good. I brought some friends." She gestured to the two women. "This is Zhang Jing and Ann. They're Dawn and Lian's mothers." She gestured to a pair of the girls. "You know Izzy. And the little boy is Benji."

Charity smiled widely. "Nice to meet you all. I'm so pleased you've come." She met Faith's gaze and mouthed, "Thank you." Her sister winked in response. "Today we're going to read *The Very Hungry Caterpillar* by Eric Carle, and afterward, you can make your own very hungry caterpillar to take home with you."

Izzy clapped excitedly, sneaking a peek at the glitter. Charity's mood lightened. This was what she'd wanted to accomplish. Bringing joy to the local children through books. She cleared her throat and started to read.

An hour later, she waved goodbye to the last of the children and flopped back into her chair, exhausted. The kid's table was a mess of glitter, torn paper, and bits of fluff, but it brought a massive smile to her face. They'd had a blast. And all three of the moms had promised to bring their children back, although Alec had put in a request for an alien story next time. Izzy had loudly demanded unicorns, and Dawn had wanted horses.

Maybe she could really make this thing work.

"They look like a bunch of satisfied customers," Kyle said as he sauntered over, looking delicious as ever in a button-down shirt and jeans. "How did it go?"

"Really well." She grinned at him and got up to start packing the craft supplies away. "I can't believe it."

He smiled back. "You were prepared for anything. And those kids will talk to their friends. Before you know it, we'll be overrun."

"I hope so." This was the first thing she'd done in ages that felt like hers, and she wanted it to succeed. Although she loved that even when it seemed it might flop, she still got the sense Kyle would be there to support her. While he'd left her to work out the details, he'd been completely on board with the project and she knew he'd made a point to mention it to people he'd thought might be interested.

"So, what are we doing next week?" he asked, bending to help her with the tidying.

"Aliens," she said with a laugh. "Or unicorns or horses. Maybe we'll start with the horses since that seems easiest to manage."

"Good idea."

She shifted the supplies she'd been organizing into a plastic crate and moved it around so he could do the same. "Perhaps we'll avoid the glitter next time."

It seemed to have gone everywhere.

He scanned their surroundings and grimaced. "At least it won't take long to vacuum."

A ping sounded, alerting them that someone was standing at the counter.

Kyle glanced up and called, "I'll be with you in a minute."

Then he had a quick look around and leaned

forward to sneak a kiss. Charity smiled against his mouth. She'd had no idea a man could make her feel both completely comfortable and as if sparks were sizzling across her skin with every touch.

"We're nearly finished for the day," he murmured.

"Good. I can't wait to have you to myself."

———

THE WEEKS THAT FOLLOWED WERE THE HAPPIEST OF Charity's life. She and Kyle fell into a rhythm of togetherness that had her smiling constantly. Even receiving several messages from Samuel's friends didn't take the shine off her joy. They hadn't mentioned Kyle again, much to her relief, and had gone back to insulting her and making vaguely threatening remarks. She'd been keeping a low profile, so she assumed they hadn't been able to find any new information on her to fuel any interest in the new man in her life. Particularly if they were looking in Auckland, where the photograph had been taken.

She tried to put Samuel to the back of her mind and enjoy her time with Kyle. They shared meals, walked on the beach, and spent lazy Sundays in bed, snuggling and making love. On one such Sunday, at the end of May, she woke in his bed feeling well-rested. When she opened her eyes, she found Kyle smiling at her and she basked in the warmth of his gaze.

"Morning," she rasped, blinking the sleep from her eyes.

"Hey there, beautiful." He dipped his head and kissed her. His breath was minty fresh and his lips were soft against hers.

"I want to wake up like this every day," she murmured. "With you right here."

"I'm not going anywhere." He cupped the back of her head and tasted her like he had all the time in the world. She loved that about him. Her diligent, responsible librarian was a very thorough lover. But she also liked pushing him to the point where his control snapped. She pulled away and wriggled down the length of his body, her limbs still heavy from slumber. She kissed a trail from his belly button to his erection, then paused and puffed a gentle breath over it.

Slowly—ever so slowly—she dragged the tip of her tongue from the root to the tip and sucked the silky head into her mouth. Pleasure rumbled in the back of Kyle's throat and he raised his hands above his head. She teased him with her lips and tongue, keeping her eyes on his face as his eyelids drooped shut and his lashes cast shadows over his cheeks.

Before long, he reached down and dragged her up so he could fuse his mouth with hers. She kissed him eagerly. She loved being reminded of how strong he was, and how much he wanted her. She could never get enough. She melted into his arms, only coming up for air so he could sheath himself and slide inside her.

She moaned. She'd never get used to the exquisite sensation of being with him. They moved together, bodies slick, tempo unhurried, and she gave herself over into his keeping. Her orgasm came upon her gradually, and she buried her face in the juncture of his shoulder, shuddering in release. A few moments later, he groaned, thrust inside her one final time and lowered his forehead to hers. Charity stared into his beautiful blue eyes and wondered if it was too soon to be in love. Because, however hard she'd tried to guard her heart, she seemed to have handed it over to him. She prayed he'd take care of it.

"You okay?" he asked, searching her gaze.

She blinked, stealing a momentary reprieve, too afraid to admit her feelings yet. "I'm just thinking that now seems like a good time for naked breakfast."

"Oh yeah?" He grinned. "Who's serving today?"

"You. I want pancakes."

He shook his head and rolled off her. "Fine. But next weekend, I want waffles with cream."

"Deal." She sat up and ran her hand through her hair, smoothing it away from her face. "I'll make us coffee while you cook."

"Perfect."

They fixed breakfast and ate together in his living room. When they'd finished, they showered and dressed, then Charity stretched out on the couch and read *David Copperfield* while Kyle played video games. Eventually, he persuaded her to join him for one of the games, then followed along behind her to protect her from virtual enemies. It was strange how that gave her warm fuzzies. She seemed to find everything he did sweet and lovable. As he leaned over to kiss her, she wished with all her heart that they could continue like this forever.

***

By the time the last Thursday of May rolled around, Kyle knew he was in deep with Charity, and it was time to make it official by introducing her to his family as his girlfriend. So far, he'd kept them away from her because he'd worried that someone wouldn't be able to resist tossing her past in her face. They were good people, but very protective, and if they thought he was being played they wouldn't hesitate to lash out on his behalf. But he couldn't keep her away from them forever, and he didn't want her to think he was ashamed, so he grabbed his phone and dialed his mother.

"Hi, Mum," he said when Corinne answered.

"Hey, baby boy. How are you doing? I haven't seen you for a while."

He felt a twinge of guilt. He'd been preoccupied, spending every free moment with Charity. "I'm good. Better than good, actually." Regardless of his nerves, he couldn't suppress a smile. "I have someone I'd like you to meet. Can I bring her over for dinner in the weekend?"

"*Yes!*"

He yanked the phone away from his ear and stared at it. He'd never heard her so excited. Usually she was as calm as the ocean on a summer's day.

"Honey," she continued, at a more reasonable pitch. "I would love for you to bring your girlfriend to dinner on Sunday."

"How did you—"

"Logan told me," she interrupted. "He heard it from Shane. You're dating Charity St. John, right?"

"Yes…" He tried to figure out how to ask her politely to be nice to Charity. He needn't have bothered.

"Don't worry, you know what I'm like. I'll take her as I find her."

He sighed, relief lightening his shoulders. "Thanks, Mum."

"No worries. Before I go, does she have any dietary restrictions?"

"Not that I'm aware of. From what I've seen, she'll pretty much eat anything."

"Fantastic." She blew him a kiss down the phone. "I'll see you Sunday."

"Bye-bye."

He hung up and resumed eating his lunch. He'd nearly finished when his phone rang. Glancing down, he saw the number was Logan's, and tensed. His brother didn't generally call—he preferred to cross the square for a face-to-face. Something made him think this was about the conversation he'd just had with his mother.

"Hello?" he said.

"Are you sure you want to do this?" Logan asked.

Kyle's gut sank. "Do what?"

"Invite that woman over for dinner with Mum."

"Her name is Charity," he hissed, hoping like hell she was out of earshot. "And she's my girlfriend, so yes, I'm sure."

"It's a mistake," Logan warned. "This is just some temporary hookup because you're hung up on the hot girl from school. Don't bring her home and disrespect Mum that way."

"Excuse me?" Kyle couldn't believe what he was hearing. "We're *together*, and I don't plan for that to change."

Logan growled. "You're being an idiot."

"And you're being a bastard." Taking a breath, he grappled with his temper. "It would mean a lot to have your support, but Charity and I are a couple whether you like it or not."

"I don't. Just..." Logan sighed. "Do me a favor and think about it again before you introduce her to Mum, okay?"

"Fine," Kyle snapped, with no intention of doing so. "Goodbye."

With that, he hung up.

24

"Hey."

Charity looked up from the craft supplies she was arranging for her second Story Time session and met the aquamarine gaze of Logan Pride. She hadn't seen him in person for years and took a moment to compare him to Kyle. They had similar coloring, although Kyle's build was broader, his jaw squarer, and his hair shorn short while Logan's was shaggy. The guy was handsome, nobody could deny that, but Kyle was definitely the better looking of the brothers.

"How can I help?" she asked, getting to her feet.

"I've got some books to return." He held them out to her. She took them and walked to the counter, figuring he must also have something to say since he could have simply left the books there for her to get to later, rather than seeking her out. She checked the books back in while she waited for him to get to the point. They were all thrillers. No surprise there.

"All done," she said, glancing up at him as she shifted the books to a cart to reshelve later. Disdain curled his lip and he made no effort to smile. He didn't like her, that much was clear. With most people, it wouldn't bother her, but since he was Kyle's brother, she wished she could have made a better impression. Unfortunately, she doubted that seeing her face splashed across the news in connection with one of the biggest con artists of the decade had endeared her to anyone. Especially not a man who was protective of his younger brother.

"So," he finally said. "You're the one he decided to date."

"Guilty." She inwardly cringed at her word choice.

He nodded, unsurprised she knew who he was. "How long are you staying in the bay?"

She resisted the urge to roll her eyes. *Trying to get rid of me already?* "I'm not sure. The plan was to get in and out as fast as possible, but then Kyle came along and things changed. I guess your answer to that question might depend on him."

"Hmm." He sounded thoughtful. "Do your major life decisions always revolve around a man?"

Her jaw dropped in shock, and she snapped it shut. A little flicker of fire sparked within her. "No. You'll be surprised to learn that I'm a fully functioning human in my own right. It just so happens that when I care about someone, I factor them into my decision-making." She started to turn away before she could say something she'd regret. "Excuse me. I need to get back to work."

For a moment, she thought he'd refuse to leave, but after a brief hesitation, his footfalls sounded on the floor as he walked away. Charity's hands trembled as she looked around the library, wondering if Logan had intentionally timed his visit for when Kyle was on his lunch break. Was she just being paranoid? It wasn't as if he'd told her to leave Kyle alone. But she definitely got the impression he wouldn't be happy until Haven Bay—and his brother—were in her rearview mirror.

Fortunately, she didn't exist to make other people happy.

She rearranged the books atop the cart and something slipped out of one and drifted to the floor. It was a piece of paper. She snatched it up and was about to discard it when she saw the heading at the top of the page.

Kyle's Love List.

What the hell?

Her pulse spiked as she read the numbered text below.

1. Loyal.

2. Shares my interest in sci-fi and gaming.

3. Intelligent.

4. Kindhearted.

5. Trustworthy.

6. Has her own hobbies.

7. Takes care of herself.

8. Responsible.

9. Ready to settle down.

10. Doesn't have an insane amount of baggage.

She read it, and then read it again, until the words were seared into her memory. Was this what it looked like? Had Kyle written a list of the qualities he wanted in a partner? Almost subconsciously, she compared herself to them. She considered herself to be loyal, although Samuel might have a different opinion. She also liked to think of herself as intelligent, but others might disagree.

Did reading count as a hobby?

She'd been taking care of herself for years now, but she didn't think anyone would call her responsible, and until recently, settling down had been the last thing on her mind. But it was item number ten that was the real kicker. *Doesn't have an insane amount of baggage.* The baggage she came with could fill a U-Haul.

Taking the list, she returned to her seat, where she placed it on her desk and stared at it. Maybe it wasn't what it seemed. Perhaps Logan had written it and set this up to make her feel inadequate. But by now, she recognized the neat blocky style of Kyle's handwriting. Although she did notice the last point was written in a different hand. More feminine. Perhaps he'd had help with it. She pressed her fingertips to her temples. If these were his desired qualities in a girlfriend, she was a four out of ten, at best. While she'd always known she wasn't exactly what he'd wanted, seeing it laid out in black and white hurt.

Don't jump to conclusions.

Maybe the list was old. The paper was crinkled as though it had been handled a lot. Perhaps it was a hangover from months, or even years, earlier. Yes, that must be it. She chose to ignore the little voice in her head that asked what it was doing in one of Logan's books if it was a relic of the past.

She tucked the list into her bag, and for the rest of the day, she tried to put it to the back of her mind. Despite her best intentions, by the time she waved goodbye to Faith and Shane as they left for their date night, she was a nervous wreck from stewing on it. When someone knocked on the door, she leapt to her feet, eager to be distracted from her thoughts. Kyle stood on the doorstep, hands in his pockets, smile curving his lips. He looked as delectable as ever. Her stomach plunged. So much for a distraction.

"Isn't poker tonight?" she asked.

He stepped forward and dropped a kiss on her lips.

"I heard Shane was missing it to take Faith on a date so I knew you'd be here alone, and I'd rather spend my time with you."

Her heart skipped. List or no list, the fact he'd rather be with her than his friends was a good thing, right? "I'm not completely alone," she told him. "I'm watching the boys."

"Great." He smiled and extracted a plastic cartridge from his pocket. "I brought a game that Dylan has been wanting to play. I thought we could have a friendly session."

Could he be any more perfect?

"So, can I come in?" he asked, and she noticed for the first time that she was blocking the doorway.

Blushing, she stepped aside. "Sure."

Would he prefer a girlfriend who played games with him rather than reading quietly in the corner?

"Stop it," she muttered to herself, blushing when Kyle raised a brow.

Don't mention the list, she told herself. *It's none of your business. You're already with him, so it doesn't matter.*

"I found something," she blurted out.

He cocked his head. "What's that?"

She dug around in her jeans pocket for the paper and passed it to him. She bit her lip, praying like hell that he'd frown and ask what it was, or even laugh and say something along the lines of, "Where did you find this old thing?" But instead, he went pale. A knot of dread cinched tighter in her gut.

Uh-oh. I should have stayed quiet.

How could I possibly have trusted the wrong person... again?

25

OH, FUCK.

Kyle wasn't prone to swearing, but times like this called for it. Charity had his list. How had she gotten her hands on a copy? Especially this one, which he'd written himself. The answer slammed into his mind with perfect clarity: *Logan*. His brother was trying to chase her away for Kyle's own good—potentially ruining his happiness in the process. Anger flared, red hot. He wasn't a child anymore. Logan didn't need to protect him, and as soon as possible, he was going to let his brother know what he thought of his tactics.

"Where did you get this?" he asked, his voice tight.

She watched him through eyes like slits, and he got the impression that whatever he said and did next would be of vital importance to their continued relationship. "It was in a book Logan returned to the library."

Of course it was. His brother was sneaky like that.

"Yes, I wrote it," he admitted, because there was no point denying it. "But it was weeks ago, and it means nothing anymore."

"Weeks ago?" she asked, closing her eyes briefly. "Before or after we got together?"

"Before," he replied, gutted it would even cross her mind that he might have written it after. "We'd just run into each other again, but nothing had happened between us."

She nodded, her lips pressed into a firm line. "Why did Logan have it?"

Busted.

"There's more than one copy." In fact, by now, there might be a dozen, but he didn't say that because it wouldn't help his cause. "Logan took that one."

"Why?" she demanded, sucking her lower lip into her mouth. Her eyes were all squinty, like she was preparing herself for the worst, and he wished he could rewind time and reclaim the list from Logan before all of this shit went down.

He sighed. "I thought he wanted to make fun of me, but it turns out he circulated it to the Bridge Club. That's why they kept bringing women to the library. They had a sweepstakes going on about who could find the one I'd want to date."

"No wonder they're so angry with me," she muttered. "It's not just that I'm dating their favorite librarian, but I also ruined their fun." Her tone was snarky, but he could see through it. She was hurt.

"It doesn't mean anything," he said, his heart hammering violently against his ribcage as he tried to undo the damage the damned list had done to their relationship. "There's more to love than ticking things off a list. I know that now, because of you." He tore the list to pieces and let them fall to the floor. "There. It's gone, and I promise you'll never see it again." If he had to hunt down every last copy in Haven Bay, he would.

"You can't just wipe the slate clean like that." She

shook her head, the motion absentminded as though she wasn't even aware she was doing it. "I was stupid not to realize something was going on with all those girls. I mean, yeah, you're hot, but so is Logan and they weren't busting down the pub door to get to him."

He frowned. She thought Logan was hot? He really needed to have words with his brother. "I was never interested in any of them. There were no sparks. You and me…we feel right. Please don't let something that happened before we got together come between us. Are we okay?"

She looked down at her hands, still chewing her lip. The fact he was responsible for her insecurity made his gut twist with regret, and he stepped forward and pulled her into his arms. She stood stiffly, but he hugged her tight, and after a few seconds, she relaxed against him.

"We'll be okay," she murmured. "It's just hard to know where I sit on your scale of the perfect girl, but you're right. It shouldn't matter to us now, and I'll get over it. I just need time to process."

"Thank God." Time, he could give her. He was a patient guy, and if she needed to go slow while she got her thoughts in order, he could do that. But he also didn't want to leave her alone to stew on it. "Can I come in and visit for a while?"

She squeezed him once—fiercely—and drew back. "If you do, I won't be able to process. I need a night of space."

Oh. His heart sank. "Just a night though, right?"

He didn't want to leave only to discover later that in doing so, he'd allowed her to drive a wedge between them.

As if reading his mind, she said, "Don't worry, I

promise not to go nuts over this. I just have some things to work through."

"Okay." He kissed her, swift and hard. "I'm here when you're ready. Goodnight, Charity. Take care."

She blinked up at him, looking dazed. "Goodnight, Kyle."

Though it was one of the most difficult things he'd done, he turned around and left, hoping with every part of his being that things would be better in the morning.

THE FOLLOWING MORNING, CHARITY WOKE WITH A plan. She couldn't do much about not meeting the criteria on Kyle's list—and she believed him when he said he didn't care about the list anymore—but she also knew that she owed it to him to take action on the one point she could do something about. The one that had really struck home.

10. Doesn't have an insane amount of baggage.

She could never completely get rid of her baggage, but she could do something to lessen its hold on her. She needed to break free of her ex-husband once and for all. She couldn't let him mess with her, or drive her from the bay as he had from Auckland, if his men found her again. Unfortunately, Samuel had never been good at letting go. That was why, as soon as she'd dropped Dylan off at a friend's place, she drove out of the bay, heading for the Correctional Facility.

The only person who knew her plan was Gray. She'd called him early in the morning to get a second opinion. She knew he had plenty of baggage too, even if he didn't talk about it as freely as she did, so she was certain he'd understand why she needed to do this. He had, and he'd insisted on providing support, even though he couldn't—or wouldn't—come himself.

While the scenery flew by, she mentally replayed the years of her marriage, as she had a million times before, noting in hindsight the hints of criminal activity that she'd overlooked in the moment. She'd been so oblivious. Just a girl living in a dream world. She'd thought she had it made. A successful grown-ass man she adored, a big house on the beach, and whatever clothing or jewelry she desired.

She'd been a fool.

None of it had been true. Not even the love. It was a crazy infatuation with a smooth-talking older guy who, admittedly, had been great in bed, but who really ought to have known better. He hadn't loved her any more than she'd loved him. Now she wasn't sure he was capable of love, but at the time, she'd believed it with her whole heart. Now she saw his possessive behavior and the way he'd liked her to dress in skimpy designer outfits for what it was: him showing off his favorite toy. He'd wanted a younger trophy wife, and he'd chosen her for the job.

She sighed. "And you just fell neatly into his lap."

But no more. Today, she was making a clean break from Samuel Hagley so she could give her relationship with Kyle the respect it deserved.

When she arrived, she went down the long driveway, showed her ID to a man at the gate, and parked outside the prison. She got out of the car and smoothed her hands down the front of her jeans. She'd intentionally worn casual attire because she didn't want Samuel to think she'd dressed up for him.

She crossed the parking lot and nodded to the

guards as she entered the building. Just inside, she met with the man Gray had arranged to join her. A bodyguard. He was tall and solid, in his thirties or early forties, with a military-style haircut. He gave her hand a firm shake and told her his name, but the rush of her blood in her ears was so loud she couldn't hear him. She just nodded and thanked him for coming. Honestly, it was probably overkill, but it had made Gray feel better about not joining her, and it would ease her nerves to have someone at her back.

After a short wait, they passed through security and were taken to a visiting room where Charity sat at a table while her personal bodyguard stood at her shoulder and a prison guard went to find out whether Samuel would agree to see her. She rolled her eyes. Of course he would. She was right where he wanted her, except that this visit wouldn't play out the way he wanted.

A few minutes later, two burly prison guards led her ex-husband into the room, his hands cuffed in front of him. He'd aged a lot in the last few years—his hair was more gray than brown, and the crow's feet around his eyes had deepened—but his figure was still trim and fit.

He smiled as he approached. "You look beautiful as ever, my darling." He glanced at her bodyguard. "You should know you don't need hired muscle around me."

Her eyes narrowed. So he was going to play it nice. Pretend he hadn't been responsible for all of those threatening messages and for messing up her life over and over again. Fine. She could deal with that. She let his silken voice roll over her and felt nothing but revulsion.

"I wish I could say you look good too, but orange

isn't your color, old man. As for him," she gestured to the guard, "he's here to make sure you know I'm serious, and that I won't stand for any more of your intimidation tactics."

"Intimidation," he scoffed. "You're as overdramatic as always." When she didn't say anything, he sighed. "It's not as if it matters." He glanced down at himself and grimaced. "I tried to convince George and Matai to let me change into something more flattering, but they denied me the simple luxury of having you see me at my best." He sank into the chair opposite and rested his hands on the table between them. "To what do I owe the pleasure?"

Charity gritted her teeth, determined not to let him get to her with his air of innocent nonchalance. "I came here to ask you to leave me alone. No more calls or letters. No more texts from your asshole friends. Stop playing with my life."

Samuel cocked a brow, pretending to be confused. She may not have been able to read him when she was twenty, but she could now. "Texts? I'm not sure what you're talking about, darling. Is it possible you've misunderstood?"

"No," she snapped. "It isn't."

"I'm sorry if someone has been harassing you, but it isn't at my behest." He actually looked quite contrite.

She scoffed, not buying his bullshit for a second. "You expect me to believe that? Are you forgetting that you arranged for the prison to ask for permission for you to call me directly? At the very least, that means you wanted to contact me."

"So I did," he admitted. "I missed you."

She rolled her eyes. As if. "Here's the thing. I don't care what your reasons were or what you have to say for yourself. We're divorced, and you're in my past.

That's what I came here to tell you." It felt damn good. Freeing. Throughout the entire divorce process, she'd managed not to see him, and now she could say to his face that they were over and truly believe it.

His eyes flashed. "I didn't want a divorce."

She cocked a brow. "But I testified against you. Why would you want to stay married?"

He smirked. "*Because* you testified against me."

Ah, he'd wanted her to be stuck with him.

Curiosity got the better of her. "Then why didn't you fight it?"

He shrugged. "Trying to fight the conviction and challenge a divorce at the same time was too much. My lawyer advised me to choose one, and staying out of prison seemed the more pressing matter." He glanced at his jumpsuit. "Well, you can see how that worked out."

She reminded herself not to feel sorry for him. He'd done this to himself and hurt dozens of people along the way. "I'm not interested in rehashing the past. You and your friends need to leave me alone, or I'll take whatever legal action I can against you." Leaning closer, she lowered her voice. "I'm sure I can tell the police things about you that they don't already know. I've done a lot of thinking since you were arrested. A lot of *remembering*." She was bluffing, but she hoped he couldn't see it. She probably could think of something to get him put away for longer if push came to shove, but there was nothing as damning as she'd implied.

Respect glinted in his eyes. "You've changed, Cha-Cha."

"Don't call me that."

"Charity, then." He rolled his eyes and gave a beleaguered sigh. "Fine, I take your meaning, and I'll leave you alone."

"Good." Satisfaction unfurled in her gut, and for the first time in years, she felt proud of herself. She'd looked her demon square in the eye and beaten him. He wouldn't hold her back any longer. She stood. "Then we're done here. Goodbye, Samuel."

26

At noon on Saturday, Kyle walked from his place to The Den. The pub was bustling with a lunch crowd, and Corinne stood at the bar, coordinating the wait staff. Logan was nowhere to be seen. Kyle waved to his mother and headed out the back entrance into the private part of the building. He found Logan in his storeroom, a wetsuit around his waist and his chest bare.

Logan looked up from placing something on a low shelf as he entered, and his eyes widened. "Uh-oh."

"'Uh-oh' is right," Kyle said. "Why did you give Charity that list? What the hell were you thinking?"

Logan straightened. "Calm down, hothead. I was thinking that she's all wrong for you and it's about time one of you realized that. If it's not going to be you, then it needs to be her."

For God's sake. Did everyone in this town have to intrude on his relationship?

"She's not, though." He folded his arms over his chest and dared his brother to disagree. "She's perfect for me."

Logan huffed in exasperation. "Don't you remember how much she hurt you? Because I do. Even from overseas, it was obvious you were a wreck."

Heat raced to Kyle's cheeks. "I haven't forgotten," he said, with as much calm as he could muster. "But she's been through a lot and it changed her. She's not the same person she used to be, and I forgave her. We're happy now. Or at least, we would have been, if you hadn't interfered."

"So it worked?"

"If your intention was to mess with the first relationship I've had in years and threaten my future happiness, then yes, it worked."

He grimaced. "You may not see it now, but you'll thank me for it one day."

"No, I won't. Because Charity and I will get over this. I have faith in that." He couldn't help but be disappointed that Logan didn't see the error of his ways. His brother seemed completely unrepentant. Did he really hate Charity that much? It didn't bode well for the future.

To his surprise, Logan laughed. "Do you know where your girlfriend is right now?"

Kyle lifted one shoulder. "I don't need to know. I trust her."

"Well, I don't, and with good reason. I've had someone keeping tabs on her, and at this very moment, she's visiting her ex-husband in prison."

Kyle's jaw dropped. Surely he hadn't heard that right. "What?"

"Charity is canoodling with her ex."

"No. You're wrong." He took a step back, his hands clenching at his sides. "There must be another explanation."

"Ask her," Logan prompted. "See what she says. If you trust her so much, that shouldn't be a problem."

"I will." He swallowed, feeling like a golf ball was lodged in his throat. "What makes you think she's at the prison?"

"I can't reveal my sources."

Kyle leveled him with a look, and he held up his hands defensively.

"Betty. Don't ask me how she knows, but she does. That lady knows everything." He hesitated, then added, "She had another man with her too. I'm not sure how he figures into things."

Kyle stepped back again. He needed to get out of here, to find someplace quiet to think. "I have to go. I'll see you…when I see you."

"Bye, little brother. Let me know what she has to say for herself."

Kyle didn't acknowledge the request. As he left via the back entrance, his mind was consumed by possibilities. If what Logan said was true, and Charity was visiting her ex, what reasonable explanation could she have for doing so in secret? He didn't want to question her loyalty, but she'd told him she hated Samuel Hagley, so why would she want to see him? Worse, why would she take someone else rather than talking to him about it?

***

"Hey, Kyle." Charity beamed when he opened his front door. She'd come straight here after returning from the prison, excited to see him now that she'd done something about her damned baggage. She went up onto her toes to kiss him, frowning when he returned the kiss with only the faintest pressure. She dropped back onto the soles of her feet. He didn't smile and he didn't stand aside so she could come in.

"Can I?" she asked, gesturing past him.

"Oh, yeah." He sounded surprised, as though he hadn't noticed he was blocking the path.

"How was your day?" she asked, heading down the hall and into the living room.

"Same old."

She turned and found him hovering in the doorway, his eyebrows knitted together. "Are you all right?"

He seemed to mentally shake himself, and ran a hand through his hair. "Yeah, I'm fine." He gave a strained smile. "How about you? Do anything exciting?"

Charity didn't answer, watching him with concern. Something was off. "What's going on?" she asked. "And don't tell me nothing, because something is bothering you."

He sighed. "Did you go to the prison today?"

Her stomach rolled over. "I did. I was just about to tell you about it, but now I'm curious. How did you know?" An awful possibility occurred to her. "Have you been following me?"

"No!" He looked horrified by the thought. "Absolutely not. I promise, I'd never do that."

She stood by the sofa, too unsettled to sit. "So, how?"

He closed his eyes and seemed to summon his courage. This was going to be bad. "Logan told me. Apparently he's been keeping tabs on you."

"Oh, my God." She swallowed hard. "Your brother hates me so much he's spying on me?"

She had a hard time picturing the floppy-haired

surfer going to the trouble of stalking her, and that surely said how strongly he didn't want her in Kyle's life. A cold fist squeezed her heart. What would it be like to be with a man whose family would prefer her to leave town and never return? She'd experienced enough of that attitude without getting it from the people closest to her.

"He doesn't hate you," Kyle said, but he didn't sound like he believed his own words. "He just doesn't trust you."

She closed her eyes and tried to get a hold of herself. She'd been dancing on air when she arrived, which made the crash back to reality that much more painful. Thoughts bombarded her from every angle, but she focused on one: if Logan disliked her enough to try to find whatever dirty tidbits he could to break them up, how must Kyle's mum feel about her?

Suddenly, the family dinner tomorrow seemed like a bad idea.

In fact, this whole relationship had disaster written all over it. She'd been in denial because she loved him and wanted to pretend she was normal for once in her adult life. But she wasn't normal, and it was time she accepted that. She didn't deserve a man like Kyle. She deserved jackasses like Samuel and her fickle high school boyfriend. That's just the way things were.

"He must hate me," she countered. "Otherwise he wouldn't be feeding you information to try and separate us." Burying her face in her hands, she muffled a groan. "Everyone in your life—everyone in this goddamn town—hates me, and I'm not sure I can deal with that." She sighed and dropped her hands. "Even *you* don't trust me."

He flinched but didn't disagree. "I want to," he said.

"Just tell me what you were doing at the prison today. And who did you take with you?"

His question tore her heart out. He truly didn't trust her. The anguish on his face told her that the situation was bothering him as much as it did her, but however much he might want to trust her, he *didn't*, and that fucking hurt. She'd been nothing but honest with him since she moved back to town.

An angry tear slipped out of the corner of her eye and she swiped it away. "I'd have told you anyway. That's what I came here for."

"Oh."

"Yeah, 'oh.'" The snarky, prickly part of herself that she'd cultivated during the most difficult times of her life rushed to the fore, and she didn't have the willpower to hold it off. "But you know what? It actually doesn't matter why, because you don't trust me, your family and friends hate me, and this relationship was doomed from the start."

He made a sound of protest and took a step forward. "Don't be like that. We write our own stories. What they think is irrelevant."

She scoffed. "Clearly not, or we wouldn't be having this conversation."

"It's one little snag. We're bound to have them."

"This isn't a snag, it's a sign from the universe."

He reached for her but she darted out of the way. If he touched her now, her soul would crack open, and she couldn't bear to be vulnerable. She'd tried that, and look how it had worked out.

His jaw firmed. "Please, just sit down. Let's talk this through."

"What's there to talk about?" She circled him so he was no longer between her and the exit. "I went to the prison to tell Samuel to leave me alone because he and

I are in the past." She picked at the hem of her sweater, afraid to meet his eyes in case she didn't like what she saw in them. "He has trouble letting go and he's been harassing me for a while, but I finally decided to make a stand and let him know that if he ever contacts me again, there will be consequences." She raised her eyes to his, forcing herself not to look away. "I wanted to get rid of some of my baggage for you, because you're worth it."

"He's been harassing you?" Kyle asked, apparently caught up on that one detail. "Why didn't you say something? I could have helped."

She shrugged. "It was just his way of making sure I didn't forget him. It hasn't been so bad since I moved to the bay, but back in Auckland..." Her expression darkened. "His friends found out where I lived and worked. My roommate sold me out to them. Because, apparently, I always trust the wrong people. They messed with my head so badly I ended up losing my job, and I knew that I couldn't stay there or it would continue. That's why I came here. The last place he'd ever expect to find me." Her shoulders slumped. "When I saw you explicitly didn't want someone with baggage, I knew I couldn't ignore it anymore. I needed to do something."

He cursed. "That was Brooke's addition to the list, not mine, and she changed her mind. She approves of you. But if what you're saying is true, then who was the man you took with you?"

Charity shook her head, exasperated. This was all too much to process, but one thing was painfully obvious: whether he wanted to or not, Kyle didn't trust her, and she was done with that. She'd made mistakes, but she'd tried to rectify them, and she deserved more.

"I don't even know his name. He's just some guy

that a friend arranged to go with me in case I needed protection."

A muscle ticked in Kyle's jaw. "Someone else knew about this?"

"Bits and pieces." She crossed her arms defensively. "My friend understands what it's like to have a troubled past so I wanted to run my idea past him. We talked earlier today."

"Why didn't you come to me?" he asked. "Since it was my fault you felt like you had to confront him, I should have been the one standing at your side."

She winced. Yeah, okay, maybe she'd messed up on that front. "I'm sorry. I wanted to be able to do something for you. It's my mess, and I didn't want to drag you into it. The whole point was to manage it so that you wouldn't have to be involved in the dumpster fire of my divorce."

"That's not how being a couple works. We should do things together. Especially things like that."

"We should also trust each other," she snapped. "But we clearly don't." She dragged her hand down her face and groaned, defeat weighing heavily on her shoulders. "What are we even doing here? There's no way we can work out long term. We're fooling ourselves." She shook her head sadly. "Unfortunately, that hasn't stopped me from falling in love with you." She walked to the doorway, ignoring whatever words were coming from his mouth—she couldn't make sense of them anyway. "Don't bother calling. I think it's for the best."

As she tried to leave, his hand landed on her shoulder, but she shook him off and ran, discarding the last of her dignity on the way.

He didn't chase her. At this point, she wasn't sure whether she even wanted him to.

She drove home, slunk in the back while the Walkers were busy in the living room, and locked herself in the bedroom. Finally, the fountain of tears she'd been holding back burst free.

27

What was lower than dirt?

That's how Kyle felt.

He'd caused that wounded animal look in Charity's eyes. He'd been the reason that betrayal flashed across her face. And worse, he was responsible for making her run. What else was she supposed to do when he badgered her for an answer, proving in the process that he didn't trust her—and that she'd rather turn to someone else for help instead of him?

He'd screwed up. But he hadn't realized either of them would take it so hard. If he had, he might have tried to swallow his questions, but once Logan's news had started niggling at his subconscious, it had poked at a bunch of emotional scabs he'd thought were healed. Then, when she told him she should have known they couldn't work...

He'd rather have taken a slap to the face.

So, now what?

He needed to talk to someone. Grabbing his phone, he called Brooke. The irony that he was turning to a friend when he'd just been upset at

Charity for doing a similar thing was not lost on him.

"Hi, Kyle," Brooke answered brightly. "How are you?"

"Not great," he admitted, running a hand over his short hair. "Could you come over?"

"Of course." She sounded concerned. "What's going on?"

"I'll explain when you get here."

"Okay. See you in five."

"Bye." He hung up and resisted the urge to send Logan a furious text message. This wasn't Logan's fault. It was his own stupid fault for listening to his brother and allowing doubt to creep in. He sat on the sofa and wallowed in regret until Brooke arrived. When he opened the door, she launched herself into his arms and wrapped him in a hug. He squeezed her back, grateful for the comfort.

"What happened?" she asked.

"Come and sit. It's a long story." He paced back to the living room and took the sofa while she perched on the edge of an oversized armchair.

"Spill the beans," she said.

He took a deep breath and told her everything. When he finished, she was frowning.

"I can see how Logan thought he was looking out for you," she said after a moment. "And I understand why it bothered you that she went to the prison without mentioning it."

"But?" he asked, sensing one coming.

"But," she said, "try to view this from Charity's perspective. Everyone sees Samuel Hagley as this awful con man, but to her, he was the man she loved and trusted. Then it all blew up spectacularly in her face. Now, when she's trying to move on, her past keeps dragging her down, and it's kind of a double-whammy of ouches because she's probably scared of trusting the wrong person, and you and Logan haven't helped matters on that front."

"Hmm." Put that way, he felt like a prick. He'd known Charity was gun-shy when it came to relationships, and everything she said about visiting Hagley to officially cut ties had rung true. She'd also mentioned the guy had been harassing her—presumably for months, if he'd driven her from Auckland. Why hadn't she told him that earlier? He could have helped.

"Let me ask you something." Brooke propped her chin on her hand, her glasses perched on the end of her nose. "Has she ever been dishonest with you?"

"Not that I know of." He was starting to get a bad feeling. "I got it wrong."

Her nose crinkled sympathetically. "Yeah, you kinda did."

"Any idea how to fix it?"

"Apologizing would be a good start, and perhaps you want to talk to Logan about boundaries."

"Yeah." He raked a hand through his hair. "I'm not looking forward to that conversation."

"Then maybe you shouldn't have listened to him in the first place," Brooke said tartly.

He scowled. "Aren't you supposed to be on my side?"

"Yes." Her smile was gentle. "As your friend, I'm giving you what you most need: the truth."

"I know, I know." He got to his feet and yanked her into a hug. "Thanks, Brookie."

"No problem, idiot." When he released her, she stepped back. "Now go and fix things."

"I'm on it."

"Bye, Kyle."

"See you." As she went out the door, he was already scrolling through his phone for Charity's number. He brought it up and hit the call button. When she didn't answer, he left a message.

"Hi, this is Kyle. I'm so sorry. I should have trusted you. Can we talk?"

After he hung up, he sent a text message to the same effect. He considered driving over to see her, but he didn't want to come on too strong when she might need time to regroup. Hours later, she responded.

Charity: *I get it. In your place, I wouldn't trust me either.*

He immediately tapped out a reply.

Kyle: *Please call me. We need to clear the air.*

She didn't call.

IF FEELING SORRY FOR HERSELF WAS AN OLYMPIC SPORT, Charity would have won gold. Even though she intellectually understood why Kyle hadn't trusted her, and couldn't fault him for it, that didn't translate to a mature emotional response during which she agreed to meet with him and discuss her feelings like an adult.

Oh, no. That would be far too forward-thinking. Instead, she spent the rest of the weekend holed up in her bedroom, crying over 200-year-old poetry and stuffing her face with Oreos. She only left the room when absolutely necessary. Faith knocked every few hours to check on her. She assured her sister she was okay—if okay meant resentful of the world.

On Sunday, she received three texts from Kyle asking if she was all right, and missed two calls. On Monday, she woke early, when she knew he'd still be asleep, and left a message on his voicemail that she'd be taking a day of sick leave. Yes, it was wimpy and irresponsible, but wasn't that pretty much the story of her life?

At a little past eight in the morning, Faith bustled in and stood over her, hands on hips. Her cat's-eye makeup added dramatic effect as she narrowed her eyes at Charity.

"I'm calling an end to your sulk," she announced. "If you don't get out of bed in the next ten minutes and leave the house, I'll be forced to take drastic action."

Charity raised a brow. "Such as?"

Faith matched her expression. "I'll empty a glass of water all over you. Then, if that doesn't do the trick, I'll call Mum."

Charity's brow arched higher. "You wouldn't."

The last thing she needed was her well-meaning but overbearing mother getting wind of this.

"Want to test me?"

Charity grumbled and dragged herself out of bed. "I can see you're going to play hardball."

"I am." Faith's lips pressed into a smug smile. "And it's working." Faith tossed her a pair of jeans. "I don't care where you go, just get some fresh air."

"Fine."

That's how, ten minutes later, she found herself stomping along the beach. An early winter breeze chilled the air and she wrapped her arms around herself to stay warm. She'd intended to be gone for long enough to get Faith off her back and no more, but somehow she ended up outside Gray's house. She frowned at the door. Why the hell not? She walked over and knocked.

When Gray opened it, his forehead crinkled with surprise. "Charity. How'd it go at the prison? You never returned my call."

"Long story." She glanced over his shoulder, wondering if he'd invite her in.

He stepped aside. "Do you want a coffee?"

"Sure." Her shoulders relaxed. She kicked her shoes off as she entered. Everything was in the exact same place as it was last time she'd visited. He really was a neat freak. "Do you mind if I mope on your couch? My sister has kicked me out of their place for the moment."

He pursed his lips. "Why the moping?"

She headed to his massive sofa and flopped onto it. "Kyle's brother somehow found out I'd gone to prison to visit Samuel, and told Kyle, who didn't trust my reasons for going. I was about to come clean about everything but he beat me to the punch."

"Huh." Gray lowered himself into a massive armchair and stretched out, his hands behind his head. "That's not ideal. Did he understand when you explained? And did the visit itself go well?"

"As well as it could." She sighed. "As for Kyle, I think he got it, to a point. But he was still upset, and I hate that he immediately thought the worst."

Gray cocked his shaggy head. "Given your past, can you really blame him for being cautious?"

"Yes," she said, just to be contrary. But then she buried her face in her hands and growled. "Ugh. No. But can't you just let me wallow? I didn't come here for therapy." She dropped her hands from her face to give him the evil eye.

He grinned, displaying a flash of the charm he'd been famous for. The expression changed his appearance so much it caught her off guard. For a brief moment, she could see exactly why he'd been one of Hollywood's most sought-after bachelors. When he smiled, his features came alive.

"Maybe not," he said. "But I get the sense I'm your only friend in town, and if you want to stay on that nice, comfy sofa, you'll have to indulge me."

"Fine." He had a point. He was the friendliest face she'd find outside of home. "No, I suppose I can't blame him."

"Especially when the news came from his brother, who you've told me he's close to. It would be fair to say that he trusts Logan, right?"

"Yeah." More than he did her, apparently. "Look, Gray, I can see where you're going with this, but it doesn't change how much it hurt to know he doubted me. It doesn't alter the fact that Logan—and everyone else in this town—will never accept us as a couple."

"Mmm," Gray mused, stroking his beard. "What have you done to change that?"

Charity blinked and opened her mouth, then closed it again. She rubbed her temples. "Excuse me?"

"You heard me." He gave her a meaningful look. "Have you actually done anything to change people's opinion of you? Because *I* know that you testified against your ex in court and donated all of his money to a charity for his victims, because you told me, but does anyone else? Have you tried to explain to the locals that you've been living a quiet life and scraping to get by? For all they know, you could've been vacationing on a tropical island and sipping mimosas while they struggled to clean up the financial mess your asshole ex left behind."

Charity swallowed, unable to speak. He was right. She'd silently taken steps to fix things as much as she was able, and congratulated herself for not seeking recognition. She'd figured that keeping her actions quiet made them more meaningful, but what if she'd shot herself in the foot? And what if she hadn't held back out of moral righteousness, but because she was afraid to put herself out there and risk being publicly slaughtered again? That didn't make her gesture better. It made her cowardly. And yes, perhaps she'd made a start at becoming part of the community with her Story Time sessions, but that wasn't much in the grand scheme of things.

"Oh, my God." She closed her eyes. "I can't believe I didn't see how it looked from the outside."

"So," he prompted. "What are you going to do about it?"

A ball of terror unfurled in her gut, but tangled within it were a few strands of steely determination. If exposing herself to the masses and being vulnerable was what she needed to do to move forward with her life, then she could manage it. After all, it couldn't possibly be worse than the last time her name was plastered across newspapers and the internet. All this time, she'd been waiting for her notoriety to magically fade away, but that wouldn't happen unless she did something.

"I'm not sure." She thought for a moment. "Will you help me?"

The edges of his grin curled up and excitement gleamed in his eyes. "This calls for a *Never Been Kissed* style reveal."

Charity sighed, but nodded. For once, she agreed with him.

28

K YLE HAD JUST RETURNED FROM HIS LUNCH BREAK ON Monday when Logan sauntered into the library, wearing jeans and a jacket. Kyle's eyes narrowed, and resentment simmered in his belly, but he tried to keep a lid on it. He hadn't spoken to Logan since Saturday because he knew he'd say something he'd regret.

Logan came to a stop at the counter and rested his forearms on the surface. "I came to apologize for butting into your business."

Kyle jammed his hands in his pockets, his back stiff. "It's a bit late for that."

Logan winced, not used to hearing harsh words from his brother. "Yeah, I'm sorry you canceled the dinner on Sunday. Mum was disappointed. When she found out I'd interfered, she really let me have it."

"Good." He didn't say anything more.

Logan sighed and tugged a hand through his hair. "Look, can you just rebook the dinner? I'll try to be more supportive if Charity really is who you want to be with."

"Like I said, it's too late for that." Kyle forced his

jaw to unclench. "I asked her about what she was doing at the prison and she got upset about me spying on her. Understandably so."

"Did she have an explanation?"

"Yes. A good one."

"Oh." Logan raised a brow. "So what's the problem, then?"

Kyle willed himself to remain calm. "She believes I don't trust her, and that my family all hate her. She won't answer my calls and when I went to see her, Faith sent me away."

"I'm sorry." Logan's expression was somber, but Kyle thought he saw a flash of something in his eyes that resembled relief. "I didn't mean for that to happen. I was trying to have your back."

"I know." Which was the only reason he hadn't totally lost his shit. "But frankly, it's going to take some time before I want to be around you. Can you please just go?"

Logan gaped at him. "You're kicking me out of the library?"

"No, I'm asking you to respect my wishes."

"Fine." Logan swung away, his expression darkening. "Next time I'll let you make your own mistakes."

"You do that," Kyle called after his retreating back.

THE NEXT DAY, CHARITY WOKE WITH A MISSION. A completely terrifying mission that made her insides quiver with discomfort, but in her heart, she knew she had to do it. She called in sick again, feeling a little guilty, but she'd make it up to Kyle later. She'd taken Gray's idea of a tell-all in the style of *Never Been Kissed*, a chick flick about a journalist who goes undercover in a high school, and ran with it. She was going to put every one of her sordid secrets into print for the world to see. But first, she needed a journalist she could trust. Certainly not one like that asshole who'd accosted her at the library.

That's where Aria Simons came in. When Charity's life fell apart, the friendly reporter from *The Press* was the only one who'd portrayed her in a sympathetic light. She hadn't stripped Charity of her dignity. She was, perhaps, the only person in the media whom Charity trusted not to twist her words and make the story into something ugly for the sake of selling more copies of the paper.

As it happened, tracking Aria Simons down wasn't easy. Charity sat in bed, blankets bunched around her waist, as she called the inquiries number for *The Press* and was informed that Aria Simons no longer worked there and hadn't for some time. Frustrated, but not deterred, she got up to make herself a coffee and cereal, and then returned to bed. After an hour of research, she found Aria Simons's byline in a small community newspaper. She searched for the newspaper's contact details and dialed the number.

"*South Canterbury Chronicle*, this is Tash speaking."

"Hi." Charity's stomach roiled with anxiety as doubt assailed her. Was she about to make a dreadful mistake? Her chest seized, and she realized she'd forgotten to breathe.

"Can I help you?" Tash asked.

"Yes." She forced herself to be firm. Pretended to be in control. "I'm looking for Aria Simons."

"Hmm…" Tash paused for a moment. "Do you mean Aria Lockwood? She's the only 'Aria' we have on staff. She's married, so her maiden name might have been Simons."

"Hold on a moment." Charity googled Aria Lockwood and dozens of photos of a very pregnant brunette in a wedding dress filled the screen. In nearly all of the pictures, a handsome dark-haired man stood at her side. Charity peered closer. "Yes, that's her."

Go, Aria. She'd scored herself a hottie.

"Great. I'll transfer you through to her line."

"Thanks." Charity waited while hold music played.

"Hello, this is Aria."

Charity squeezed her eyes shut and took the plunge. "Aria, this is Charity St. John—previously Charity Hagley. Do you have a moment to talk?"

"Yes, of course." There was a bustle of sound on the other end, and then it quietened. "Sorry, I thought it was best to move somewhere private. I never expected to hear from you."

"Yeah, well, I'd planned to avoid reporters for the rest of my life, but that hasn't really worked out."

"Oh?" Aria sounded curious. "What would you like to talk about? Is there something I can help you with?"

Charity prayed to whatever god was listening that she wasn't about to screw up her life beyond redemption. "I want to publish a tell-all interview, and you're the only person I trust to do it."

An eternity passed without a response.

Then Aria asked, "Why?"

"Because I'm tired of living in the shadow of the past. It's time to move on, and I can't do that until I tell my side of the story. Trying to act like it never happened hasn't gotten me anywhere."

"Good for you."

"There's a condition though. I don't want it only published in your community newspaper. I want it everywhere. Can you do that?"

Aria hesitated. "My husband has connections. If

you want to share your story in every corner of the country, I can make it happen."

"Thank you. I'd like that written into an agreement." She may trust Aria to tell her story, but she wasn't taking any chances.

"Sure. I'll send something through tonight, and we can do the interview tomorrow, if you'd like."

Charity finally dared to open her eyes. She'd taken the first step and it hadn't killed her. "Thank you. My laptop has a video connection so we can do it that way. You set a time and I'll be there." She could do this. She was strong enough.

"How's 2pm?"

"Perfect."

"Great." Aria hesitated for a moment before ending the call. "Thank you for choosing me, Charity. I'll talk to you tomorrow."

"Goodbye." Charity hung up, grabbed a notepad, and started writing about the day she met Samuel Hagley.

On Wednesday afternoon, Charity sat in Anderson Gray's living room, her laptop on the desk while she waited for her virtual interview to begin. She'd enlisted Gray's help since he was the only person she knew locally who'd been subject to public scrutiny. He'd briefed her on how best to respond to questions, and then he'd snapped several photographs of her to accompany the article. Now, he sat across from her, his laptop on his knee, editing the photos. She'd refused to wear makeup because if this was going to be a tell-all reveal, she needed to let every imperfection show. It was time to be real. That said, if Gray wanted to choose the best lighting and angles, who was she to argue?

A box popped up, informing her that Aria Lockwood had opened their virtual meeting room. She clicked a button to enter it.

"Good luck," Gray whispered.

She smiled at him. He'd been a better friend than she probably deserved, and when this was over she intended to return the favor, although she didn't know how yet.

"Hi, Charity." Aria's face appeared on the screen. Her hair was tied back, and she wore a faint smile. "Do you mind if I record an audio of this interview in case I need to replay it later to check details?"

"No, that's fine." Following her chat with Gray, she'd expected as much. "You can record the video too, if you'd like."

"Great." Aria glanced down at a notepad on the desk in front of her. "I'm starting the recording now." She paused for a moment before continuing. "Can you begin by telling me how you first met Samuel Hagley?"

"We met during one of his trips to the bay," Charity replied. "He owned a holiday home here." Over the next ten minutes, she gave Aria a rundown of her whirlwind romance, which included a big wedding Samuel financed because her parents refused to help. They'd thought she was moving too quickly and were worried about the age gap. They didn't understand that Samuel's age and supposed maturity level had been half the appeal. She went on to explain how Samuel had liked to show her off, and how she'd lapped up the attention.

"In hindsight, I think I was just another pretty possession to make him feel good about himself. I mean, what better badge of honor for a man than to have a wife half his age who's crazy about him?"

Aria nodded. "But you didn't see it that way at the time?"

"No, I saw what I wanted to see: the man who loved me so much he simply had to marry me, and who did everything in his power to give me whatever I wanted." She laughed wryly. "In case you haven't realized, I was a self-centered brat, and completely blind."

"Let's get to the question everyone really wants to know the answer to," Aria said, leaning toward the camera. "Did you know that your husband was a con man?"

Charity swallowed. "No, I didn't."

"You had no inkling?" Aria asked. "Even though you lived with him and helped spend his money?"

"Honestly, no." She knew the population had been divided over whether she was an air-headed fool or a scheming devil. She'd never wanted to be either, but she supposed it was better to own up to being a fool than to be thought a devil for the rest of her life. "He told me he was in real estate, and based on the visitors we had and the photos around the house, I had no reason to doubt that." She sighed. "I didn't really care. I thought his work was boring so I never asked too many questions. As long as it left me free to do as I liked, I was happy."

"And how do you feel about that now?"

Charity caught Gray's eyes over the laptop and saw the sympathy reflected in them. "I was a selfish idiot, and I regret it every day."

"So you're saying you never had any idea that Samuel Hagley was involved in illegal activities?" Aria persisted.

"The first clue I had that something was wrong was

when the police turned up on our doorstep in the middle of the night and handcuffed me. He was nowhere to be seen." The memory still turned her cold. "I was a fool, but I wasn't his accomplice."

"Okay." Aria jotted a note. "Thank you for clarifying. What did you do when the police arrested you?"

Charity cringed. "At first, I screamed at them. Told them they'd made a terrible mistake. It took a day or so for me to calm down enough to realize that Samuel had truly done what they said."

"And then?"

"I helped them track him down."

"Really?" One of Aria's eyebrows flew up. "How did you do that?"

Charity wondered how best to phrase this. "Here's the thing. After everything I've told you, I probably sound like an idiot, but I'm actually not. I knew where Samuel's personal properties were, and I was present during a lot of his dinner meetings. Even if I didn't know what they were talking about, I picked up bits and pieces. I helped the police prioritize places to search."

"What happened next?"

"He was arrested. The police dropped the charges against me and I testified in court for the prosecution."

"Let's just pause there. You testified for the prosecution. Did they coerce you into that?"

"No." Charity smiled, feeling like the conversation was finally swinging her way. "They wouldn't be able to. You can't force a wife to testify against her husband, or vice versa. I volunteered. I wanted him to get the harshest sentence possible."

"Because he broke your heart?"

"Partly," she admitted. "But mostly because I realized what a monster he was, and I wanted to do whatever I could to stop him from hurting anyone else."

Aria nodded, and rested her chin on her palm. "When was it that you divorced him?"

"During the trial. He signed the paperwork without any fuss, which surprised me, but I recently learned that his lawyer told him to do it so he wouldn't have to split his focus between the divorce and the trial."

"Once the divorce was final, did you get half of his remaining assets after the police seized everything they could?"

"Yes."

"What did you do with them?"

Heart rate picking up, Charity grabbed the glass of water beside the laptop and took a sip. "I liquefied his assets and set up a charity for the victims."

Aria cocked her head. "The trust for Samuel Hagley's victims—that was you?"

"It was," she confirmed. "But I asked Tom Mayor to administer it."

"Why keep that quiet?"

Charity shrugged. "Because if I'd told people what I was doing, they'd assume it was a media ploy to make myself look good. I'd had enough of the spotlight. Besides, I thought I deserved to live with everyone's hatred. I was trying to fix things as best I could, not make myself look better."

"How much did you donate to the trust?" Aria asked.

"Everything I had."

A moment of silence followed the statement.

"Everything?" Aria sounded dubious. "So, where did you live?"

"I got a job as a barista and moved into a crappy

apartment, which I shared with three stoners who didn't give a shit who I was."

"You moved on."

"I tried to," Charity corrected her. "But it didn't really work."

"So why now?" Aria's pen hovered above her notepad. "Why have you decided to do this interview after so much time, and without any cash incentive? I know you were offered big money to do an exposé after he was sentenced."

"Back then, I just wanted to escape the cameras. But now…" She trailed off, forcing herself to pry open one last emotional vault. "I'm back in my hometown. I never thought I'd live here again considering how many people from the area Samuel ripped off, but it's a wonderful community and I want to be a part of it. To contribute positively and make up for some of the harm I inadvertently caused." She smiled. "Since I moved back, I've fallen in love both with a local man and with Haven Bay itself. It's time to air out my old baggage and hope they accept me."

"That's lovely." Aria returned her smile softly. "Who's the lucky guy?"

Charity shook her head. "I've decided not to name him. I don't want to drag him into my mess. But he's amazing. A thousand times better than Samuel Hagley. A *million* times better. He's kind and clever and, frankly, out of my league, but for whatever reason, he sees something in me that I don't see in myself."

"I wish you the best of luck," Aria said. "Is there anything else you'd like to share?"

Charity looked straight at the camera. "Just that I'm sorry for everyone hurt by my ex-husband. I'm sorry I was oblivious, and I wish I could go back in time and fix it."

"Thank you for your honesty." Aria set her notepad aside and pushed a button. "Recording ended. You know that this is going to kickstart another wave of controversy about you?"

"Yeah." The thought of it sat uncomfortably in her stomach. "But it's what I need to do. Thank you for making it happen."

"Any time. Goodbye, Charity, and good luck."

"Goodbye." The meeting ended, and Charity flopped into her seat and groaned.

"You did good," Gray said.

She closed her eyes. "Thanks. I hope it's enough."

On Thursday morning, Kyle carted the "Open" sign through the library door and dropped it out front, then paused and looked around. The town square was nearly empty. A couple of people stood outside Cafe Oasis with coffees, but other than that, nobody was around. He supposed that since they were coming into winter, there wasn't much reason for tourists to visit.

He started to head back inside, his heart weighing him down. Charity had been away all week and while she'd returned his messages to let him know she was alive, he hadn't made any progress with her. Thankfully she'd promised she'd be back tomorrow, so he knew he'd at least see her then. The library wasn't the same without her. In fact, he'd been missing her so badly, and was so eager to get back on the right foot, that he'd taken advantage of her absence to create a corner alcove in the children's section to serve as the permanent setting for Story Time.

Though in its infancy, the concept had proved increasingly popular among the locals—despite the set who disliked it on principle because of Charity's involvement.

"Kyle!"

He stiffened at the sound of Logan's voice but kept walking.

"Kyle, wait up!"

He came to a halt. "What?"

He and Logan hadn't spoken since their conversation on Monday, and he needed a bit more time to figure out his next steps before making amends.

Logan came to a halt in front of him, panting. His hair was unbrushed, and he wore trackpants and a t-shirt that he wouldn't usually leave the apartment in. "I made a huge mistake."

Kyle raised a brow. "Which one, specifically?"

"Interfering between you and Charity. I was wrong about her."

"What's brought on this sudden epiphany?"

Logan held up his phone to show Kyle the screen. At the top was a photograph of Charity staring out at the sea, and a headline beneath it read: *Hagley's Ex-Wife Tells All.*

Kyle snatched the phone and started reading.

For the first time since the Hagley scandal broke, Charity St. John—previously Charity Hagley—has given an exclusive interview.

"What is this?" he asked, desperate to keep reading but afraid of what he might find.

Logan raked a hand through his hair. "It's all over social media and on the front page of the newspapers. Dude, she loves you."

"Did she actually say that?" He struggled to believe she'd expose herself so completely to the world, especially when she was convinced everyone wished her nothing but misery.

"She says that she fell in love with Haven Bay and with a local man—three guesses who that is." He waved the phone again. "She did this for you. I was a prick. I'm so fucking sorry."

"Okay, okay." Kyle's thoughts were racing. He needed to call Charity, but first, he needed to read the article in its entirety. "Thanks for letting me know."

"You're going to call her?"

"I will," he confirmed. "Soon."

"Do you need me to apologize to her directly?" Logan asked. "Because I will. I owe her that much."

"It's up to you," Kyle said. "But I've got to go."

"Let me know what happens," Logan called after him as he hurried inside.

He headed straight for the pile of newspapers he'd collected from the doorstep earlier and turned over the one on top. There was the picture of Charity. Hands shaking, he sank into a chair and started reading. By the time he finished, all of the love he hadn't gotten to express had swelled within him and he was desperate to see her face and hear her voice. He couldn't believe she'd laid everything on the line. She'd put herself in the public eye for his sake, so the people he cared about would accept her.

He loved her for it. Damn, he loved her anyway.

She must have been terrified. God, she was amazing. He took his phone from his pocket, scrolled to her number, and called. It went to voicemail.

"It's Kyle here. I just saw the article. We need to talk. I… I love you. Please, call me."

Then he sent her a text message.

I saw the article. Can we talk?

He wished he didn't have to be here. That he could simply shut the doors and go after her. But considering this place paid both their bills, he wouldn't be doing them any favors if he ran out on his duties. Perhaps he could call and ask Hamish to send someone to cover for him. If Hamish had seen the news then his request would look dodgy as hell, but he couldn't really say no given Kyle had only ever taken a couple of sick days.

He'd just made up his mind when the doorbell sounded and half a dozen members of the Bridge Club swept in, with Betty in the lead. She beelined toward him, Mavis at her right shoulder and Nell at her left. He gulped. Usually he got on well with Betty, but something about the look in her eyes made him nervous.

"What on earth are you still doing here?" she demanded, her hands going to her hips. "Why aren't you with Charity?"

He glanced around. "Because I'm working."

"Oh, pish." She waved a hand. "The girls and I can take care of everything. You need to go after her."

His brows drew together. "What brought on the change of heart?"

"I judged her too harshly." Betty looked around at her friends. "We all did."

Mavis snorted. "I still think she's a temperamental little tart, but I'll admit I didn't know all the details."

"I feel so bad," Nell said, wringing her hands.

Behind her, Irene nodded in agreement. "We weren't very pleasant to her."

"Which is why we're trying to make up for it now," Betty concluded. "So we'll take care of things and you go get your girl."

"But you don't know how to work the computer system," he pointed out.

Her eyes narrowed. "Are you saying we're not up to

the job, Kyle Pride? Need I remind you that I've seen you in diapers?"

He held his hands up. "I'm not going to look a gift horse in the mouth." Not when there were more important things to do. "Thank you. I'll be back before closing."

"If you're not, don't worry," Nell said. "We know what it's like. We were young once."

His cheeks flushed. He didn't want to think about a young Nell fooling around. He stood and kissed each woman on their cheeks. "Thanks, ladies. Wish me luck."

"You won't need it," Mavis said.

He jogged home to collect his car. As he moved, thoughts swirled rapidly in and out of his mind. What if some people had reacted poorly to her interview and confronted her?

What if he was too late?

What if he wasn't?

What if this was the start of the rest of his life, with her at his side, as blissfully happy as his friends were with their partners?

He smiled. Yeah, that was more like it. He wanted forever with Charity, and he wouldn't accept anything less.

CHARITY RESTED HER CHEEK ON THE COUCH CUSHION AS she read *The Luminaries* by Eleanor Catton. She'd dived into the book as soon as she returned from giving the interview at Gray's place earlier in the week, and had barely put it down since. At 850 pages long, she trusted it would keep her occupied until the weekend was over. In the meantime, she'd switched off her phone in case she was bombarded by hateful messages. She'd taken a mammoth step, and now she figured it was her right to hide for a while until the hubbub died down. If Kyle understood what she'd been trying to accomplish and wanted to see her, then he could come to her. Hopefully he wouldn't be mad that she'd dragged him into the spotlight. While she hadn't mentioned him by name, everyone in the area would know who she'd been talking about.

She was a third of the way through the book when she heard a vehicle rumble up the drive. Nerves knotted in her stomach, and she set the book aside and headed for the front door. If it was Kyle, she hoped he'd see what she'd done in the spirit she'd meant it, rather than misinterpreting her actions.

Pulse pounding in her throat, she yanked the door open, and came face to face with a breathless Kyle, whose fist was raised to knock. It dropped to his side and he hurried into the house, gathering her in his arms. All of a sudden, she had a faceful of Kyle's broad chest, and she couldn't be happier.

"I can't believe you did that," he murmured into her hair. "You are so brave."

She sank into his embrace, closed her eyes, and enjoyed his clean masculine scent. He gave the best hugs. She could stay here forever. But then he drew back, keeping a hold of her upper arms, and studied her face. He opened his mouth as if to say something, then closed it and shook his head.

"What is it?" she asked.

"It's just... I can't wrap my head around you making such a big, crazy gesture for me." A teasing smile pulled at his lips. "It was for *me*, right?"

She rolled her eyes. "Yes, you idiot. But it was for me too."

"Why?" His gaze searched hers. "I'm the one who owed you an apology or a grand gesture. I'm the one who screwed up, and when you called in sick several days in a row, I thought for sure you were done with me."

She wriggled out of his embrace and took his hand, threading her fingers through his. "Come and sit."

She led him to the living room. The house was empty this time of day because Shane and Faith were both at work, and Hunter and Dylan were at school. She sat on the couch and drew him down beside her. When they were seated, she spoke.

"I was mad, but I only partly blamed you. Most of all, I blamed myself for the bad decisions I've made. I might have also blamed all of the people who couldn't see how much I've changed. But when I talked to a friend, he pointed out that I hadn't done enough to make anyone believe I'm a decent person. For the most part, I just hid away and accepted the crap everyone slung at me." She sighed. "I hadn't seen it that way before. It was eye-opening. Regardless of who was at fault, I had to do something about it." Hesitantly, she smiled. "You're here, so something good came of it, right?"

He slid an arm beneath her knees and another around her back, then dragged her into his lap. "I love you, Charity St. John, and I'm sorry for ever doubting you."

"You're forgiven." She snuggled closer, her heart screaming at her to do or say something to acknowledge his confession, but she didn't want to disturb the beautiful moment. "I made it easy to think the worst."

"I should have trusted you more." He kissed the top of her head. "I hope you meant it when you said in the interview that you'd fallen in love, because I can't imagine my world without you in it. I hope you'll give me a chance to be better and to stand by you in the future."

"I will." She tilted her head back and met his eyes. Emotion swum in their crystal depths, and she could have stared into them forever. Everything she felt was reflected back at her. Every hope, fear, and desire. And love. So much love that her chest constricted. "I did mean it. I love you, Kyle. But you'd better be all in, because I aired my dirty laundry and put everything on the line. I'm not sure I can do it again."

"You have me, one hundred percent." He brushed his lips over hers. Her eyes fluttered closed, the whisper of skin on skin achingly perfect. She wanted more. More pressure, more kisses, more touching. Instead, he pulled back. "I'm not the only one who feels bad for misjudging you. Logan wants to apologize, and so does Betty. I bet there are plenty of others who are willing to put the past behind them too."

"You think so?" She'd hoped, but she'd been afraid to leave the house and find out for sure.

"I do." He smiled the kind of goofy, endearing grin she absolutely adored. "You took a chance, and it paid off."

"Thank you," she whispered. "But I'm still not leaving the house today. I can face them tomorrow."

"Fine by me. We can do it together." He grabbed his phone and dialed the library number, putting it on speaker.

Betty picked up after several rings. "The hot librarian is unavailable, sorry."

Kyle covered his face with his hand and groaned. "Are you answering every phone call like that?"

Betty chuckled. "After the amount of calls I've fielded, yes. How did things go with your girl?"

"Good." He smiled at Charity, who cocked her head curiously. "So good that I'm officially handing responsibility for the library over to you for the rest of the day. You can lock up and leave if you'd like, but I trust you to keep an eye on the place."

"Of course you do," she preened. "Everything will be just fine, don't you worry."

"Thanks, Betty. See you later."

"Goodbye—and use protection. Have fun!"

Cringing at that last comment, he hung up.

"I can't believe you've entrusted her with the library," Charity said.

He shrugged. "What's the worst she can do?"

Charity grinned as though she had a few worrisome thoughts, but didn't voice them. "I can hardly believe we ended up here. I mean, the odds were pretty stacked against us."

"I'm not surprised," he told her. "Obstacles don't matter when love is involved. I've seen it again and again, and I finally get to experience it for myself."

Her heart felt so full it might burst. "I'm glad you get to experience it with *me*." She leaned closer and ran her mouth up the side of his neck. "I think you should take me to the bedroom and make Betty proud."

"Oh, God." He shuddered. "Can we please not talk about her at a time like this?"

"Suit yourself." Her lips curved up mischievously. "I just want to get your clothes off."

He hefted her up, holding her securely against his chest. "I think that can be arranged."

30

Kyle rolled over and nuzzled the side of Charity's neck, rousing her from sleep. After several hours curled around each other in her bed yesterday, they'd come back to his place before the Walker family returned home. They spent the rest of the day talking and touching and weaving a web around them to hold back the outside world. Then they'd held each other all night. But now, that was over. It was time to venture out.

He eased from the bed, yanked on a t-shirt, and padded barefoot to the kitchen, where he fixed them each a mug of instant coffee. He returned to the bedroom and placed the mugs on a cabinet, then bent over and brushed Charity's hair off her forehead. She mumbled, and angled her face toward him. His heart warmed. In sleep, she was more peaceful than she ever seemed awake. There weren't any shadows under her eyes, and she was missing the weight that seemed to settle onto her shoulders each time she regained consciousness.

Or perhaps it was the courageous step she'd taken

that had erased those shadows and removed the weight. He wanted to believe so. But whatever the case, he couldn't let her sleep for any longer. He was due at work in an hour, and he was determined not to go without her. Having one day to hide from the world was fine, but she needed to see firsthand the changes that her actions had caused before she became too scared to take the next step.

"Charity," he murmured, pressing a kiss to her temple. "Wake up, baby."

She scrunched her eyes more tightly shut. "Don't wanna."

"Come on," he coaxed, kissing the tip of her nose. "I made coffee."

One eye opened. "Good coffee?"

"Black coffee."

Her nose crinkled. "It's instant, isn't it?"

He pretended to be hurt. "It's the coffee I made for you with love in my heart."

She sat up. "Okay, fine. Bring me your coffee." He handed her the mug, and she sipped, watching him above the rim. "Well played, Pride."

He settled onto the side of the bed and winked at her as he drank his own. "You're coming to the library with me today."

"I am?" Her hair flopped across her face, and she scowled and tossed it over her shoulder.

"Yes, and don't even try to avoid it or I'll—"

"Okay."

He broke off. He'd expected resistance. "Excuse me?"

She shrugged. "I'll come. I already told you I'd be there on Friday. You've been way too lenient with me over the whole work situation and being back out in public will do me good."

Well, damn. She'd stolen his argument.

He eyed her carefully. "No protests?"

"Not today." She grinned like she knew she'd caught him off guard. "I wouldn't have gone public with my story if I wasn't willing to put myself out there eventually. I just needed a little time for us to be in a bubble."

"Great." He leaned over to kiss her once more. "Then let's go show everyone what we're made of."

By the time they arrived at the library, there was a line outside. Kyle frowned. What the hell was going on? It wasn't unusual for a few people to be waiting, but this many? Unheard of. Beside him, Charity stiffened. He followed her line of sight and spotted Betty at the head of the queue, with several of her friends in tow. Hugh MacAllister, the town council representative, stood behind them, followed by Lana McQueen from Cafe Oasis. A group of women lingered off to the side. Kyle recognized several of them from the Story Time sessions. Logan brought up the rear and waved as they approached.

"Are you sure you're ready for this?" Kyle asked Charity under his breath.

Her spine straightened. "Born ready."

That was his girl. Taking her hand, he led her toward the gathered people.

"Hi, Charity," Logan called.

"Hi," she replied hesitantly.

"Shouldn't you be teaching kids to surf?" Kyle asked.

Logan shook his head. "Canceled classes today. Had somewhere more important to be."

"Here?" Charity sounded skeptical.

"That's right." It looked like he was doing his best to smile but coming up short. "I need to say how sorry I am for misjudging you. I suppose people can change after all."

"That's your apology?" Kyle sighed, but Charity squeezed his hand and gave him a look.

"Thank you," she said. "I know I have a lot of ground to make up, and I'm not deluding myself that everything will magically be all right, but I hope you'll give me a chance."

Logan's smile grew more genuine. "I think I can manage that."

"Then I'm sure we'll get along fine."

Logan raised his eyes to Kyle's. "You and Charity are invited over for dinner tonight, and Mum won't take no for an answer."

Kyle glanced at Charity. "What do you say?"

She nodded. "Let's do it. I'm on a roll."

"That's the spirit." He pulled her closer and kissed her. The old ladies gave a collective "aww."

Logan looked to his left. "I'll leave you to these guys. See you tonight."

"Bye."

He strode back to The Den. One of the women stepped forward. She was petite and Asian, with a friendly smile.

"Hi, Charity," she said, flashing her teeth. "I just wanted to come and say how brave I think you are for doing what you did. I for one am glad we have you as part of our community, and I've brought some more mums to introduce to you. They're interested in bringing their kids to the next Story Time. Will there be one on Wednesday?"

Charity looked dumbfounded. She nodded. "That's so kind of you, Zhang Jing. Thank you."

Kyle's chest puffed with pride. Just wait until they all saw the surprise he had in store. He waited while

Charity greeted each woman individually, and then the group moved away so he and Charity could speak to the next person in line.

"Lana," Charity said stiffly.

To his utter shock, Lana McQueen—one of the best grudge-holders he knew—opened her arms and enfolded Charity into a hug. Charity squeaked in surprise.

"What's this about?" she asked when Lana let her go.

Lana sniffled. "I've been so awful to you, and I'm sorry. I never knew you'd tried to make it right. The trust you set up was the only reason I managed to keep my cafe. Without it, I'd have been bankrupt. You saved me."

"No, I didn't." Charity's brows furrowed. "I just returned a portion of what was taken. It wasn't even the whole amount because some of it was confiscated by the police or disappeared to God knows where."

"But you could have kept it," Lana said. "If you were the person I thought you were, you would have. Instead, you gave it back to us."

Kyle got the distinct impression Charity was uncomfortable with the gratitude.

"It belonged to you," she said. "It wasn't mine."

"Thank you," Lana said. "If you ever need a job, I have an opening for a barista."

At this, Charity laughed. "Thanks for the offer, but I'm actually happy where I am." She smiled at Kyle, and his insides warmed at the love he saw in her gaze.

"Right." Lana looked from her to him and back again. "You hooked the bay's hottest bookworm. Of course you don't want to move."

"I got unbelievably lucky."

"Yes, well." Lana cleared her throat. "Don't be afraid to stop by. I won't kick you out."

"Good to know. Thanks, Lana."

"Have a nice day." Lana dropped her hand, nodded once, and walked in the direction of Cafe Oasis.

Charity and Kyle turned to Hugh MacAllister simultaneously. The older gentleman smiled, his eyes kind, and offered Charity his hand.

"It's a pleasure to see you again, Miss St. John. I'm sorry I didn't get around to welcoming you back to town sooner. I've been remiss in my duties."

She smirked, probably thinking the exact same thing Kyle was: Councilor MacAllister didn't make mistakes. He hadn't spoken to her because he hadn't wanted to. Until now. Kyle met Charity's eyes and wondered whether she'd call him on it, but she only gave a tight smile.

"Thank you. It's nice to be back."

He tipped his hat to her. "I'd best be getting along. Lots to do. I'll see you around."

"See you soon." To Kyle, she murmured, "No point being snarky about it. The fact he came here at all bodes well."

It did. He couldn't deny that.

"Hello, ladies." He greeted Betty and the Bridge Club with a warning in his eyes. They'd better play nice, or else.

"We're here to make peace," Betty declared, bringing a smile from Nell. "Do you think we could call a truce, Charity? We all love the library and your handsome man-friend. It would be a shame to have bad feelings between us."

Charity stuck out her hand. "If you can forgive the past, so can I."

Betty ignored the outstretched hand, closed the

distance between them, and patted Charity's cheek. Charity stood very still, and he wondered whether she was waiting for Betty to lash out. But then the older lady simply stepped back.

"Do you plan to let us in?" Mavis asked, ending the moment.

Kyle chuckled and unlocked the front door. After they entered, he grabbed Charity's hand and drew her aside, into the staff only area. He wrapped her in his arms and kissed her, and she returned the kiss eagerly. When they separated, she rested her head on his shoulder.

"I think everything is going to be all right," she said.

Kyle smiled, his heart somehow light and full at the same time. "Everything is going to be much, much better than all right. I love you, Charity St. John."

"I love you too, Kyle Pride."

He stepped away and tugged her hand. "Let me show you what I did with the children's section."

She raised an eyebrow. "What did you do?"

He smirked. "Just come see."

She let him lead her to the children's section, where he'd created an alcove for Story Time and added an elaborately decorated chair for her to sit on while she read.

Charity put a hand to her mouth when she saw it and looked to him, her eyes shining. "Is that for me?"

"And the kids. You've got something special going with them and I wanted to let you know that I see it and I think you're incredible."

"Thank you." Her lower lip trembled, and she swiped at her eyes. "Damn. I nearly made it through the first ten minutes without crying." She gave a watery laugh and swatted his shoulder. "This is amazing, Kyle."

He grinned, beyond grateful that she liked it. "You're the amazing one."

She rolled her eyes and laughed again. "Cheesy, Pride. But thanks. It means a lot."

He wrapped an arm around her shoulders and breathed her in, feeling the rightness of everything that had happened this morning, and knowing in his heart that he'd never doubt their relationship again.

Even if she drove him crazy at times.

31

Charity checked her reflection in the mirror. The knee-length navy dress seemed appropriate, but she wasn't certain. She wanted to make a good impression on Kyle's mother, who had no good reason to like her. The bedroom door opened, and Faith entered.

"Checking yourself out?"

"Do you think this says, 'I'm mostly a decent person who has good intentions toward your son'?" she asked.

Faith's lips twitched with mirth. "I think it says, 'I'm a naughty librarian who wants to corrupt your son in the stacks.'"

Charity rolled her eyes. "I'm being serious."

Faith quietened. "It's perfect, Char. Really."

For the first time, Charity noticed Faith's own dress, which was green and pinstriped. "What are you dressed up for?"

Faith winked behind her spectacles. "I'm coming with you." The door swung further inward, and Hunter rushed up behind Faith and wrapped his arms around one of her legs. "Or perhaps I should say 'we're coming.'"

Charity's heart kicked up a gear. "What do you mean? I was told it was just Kyle's family, and I don't want his mum to feel bad if she doesn't have enough food for everyone."

"Relax, gorgeous. It was Kyle's idea."

Charity's hands went to her hips. "Excuse me?"

"He called to invite us this afternoon. He didn't want you to feel outnumbered, so he figured he'd make it a 'meet the family' event on both sides."

"Seriously?" That had to be the sweetest thing she'd ever heard. "He did not."

"Did so," Faith tossed back. "All four of us will be there to make sure Corinne knows what a jewel her future daughter-in-law is."

"Oh, my God." Charity flung her arms around her sister. "I love you guys, but not as much as I love Kyle."

"Yeah, you got yourself a good one."

Shane stuck his head around the door. "Ready to go, ladies?"

His gaze lingered on Faith, reminding Charity of how she used to envy what they had. Now, she just felt grateful that her sister had Shane in her life. She crossed the room and hugged him, laughing as his eyes widened.

"Whoa, what's that about?"

"Thank you," she said, letting him go. "For loving Faith, and for being my family."

His expression softened, and he kissed her cheek. "Faith's family is my family."

Faith gave him a look that said she wanted to peel his clothes off and do dirty things to him. Shane winked, and Charity shook her head. They were insatiable.

"It's time to go!" Dylan called from somewhere

down the hall. "We're gonna be late if you don't get a move on."

Faith smiled. "We can always count on Dylan to make sure things happen when they're supposed to. Come on, shall we?"

Charity grabbed a jacket and followed her out. They piled into Shane's car and drove to a pretty stone house near the back of town. Kyle had parked out front, and she was relieved to know he was already here. She took a moment to collect herself under the pretense of checking out the house. She hadn't talked to Corinne Pride since she was thirteen or fourteen, but she had no doubt that Kyle's mum knew as much about her baggage as anyone else. Probably more. Would Corinne hate her?

Don't think that way, she reminded herself. *She invited you here. She told Logan off for messing with you.*

Hopefully Corinne tended more toward Kyle's open and forgiving nature than Logan's ability to hold grudges.

"Char, you coming?"

Here goes nothing.

She followed Faith down the paved path to the doorstep. Dylan knocked and a few seconds later, an attractive blonde woman in her fifties appeared in the frame. She smiled, revealing white teeth that stood out against the healthy tan of her skin. Seeing her now, Charity knew exactly where her sons' good looks originated.

"Hi, Ms. Pride," Dylan said.

"It's great to see you, Dylan." The corners of her eyes crinkled as her smile widened. "Come in, come in. Don't worry about taking off your shoes, we're very casual here." She bent to Hunter's height. "Hi, cutie.

Would you like a hot chocolate? I hear you love the ones with little marshmallows."

He nodded shyly, and some of Charity's fears eased. Such a warm and welcoming woman wouldn't hold her past against her.

"Shane, Faith, thanks so much for coming," Corinne said after the boys disappeared into the house. Her attention shifted to Charity. "I've heard so much about you."

Charity winced. "It's lovely to meet you again, Ms. Pride."

Damn, she should have brought a gift. That's what people usually did at dinners like this. She was out of practice.

"Please, call me Corinne." She stepped aside and ushered them in, then followed closely behind. At the end of the foyer, Charity found herself in an open-plan living area. Kyle, Logan, and the boys were already seated at a glass table.

Kyle rose when he spotted her and came to kiss her cheek. "Hi, beautiful."

"I can't believe you organized this," she murmured. "Thank you."

He threaded his fingers through hers and guided her to the seat beside his. "I wanted to make you as comfortable as possible. I figured having Faith here might help."

"It does." She raised her eyes and immediately noticed Corinne grinning with what could only be termed glee. Blushing, she dropped Kyle's hand.

When the room was quiet, Corinne spoke. "Thank you all for coming. It's lovely to have you here. I want to start the evening by heading off any concerns you might have." She looked directly at Charity. "I know about everything, and I don't care. If Kyle is happy, I'm happy. It's about time he had a special someone in his life."

Kyle squirmed. "*Mum.*"

Corinne just shrugged. "Well, it's true. It's not as if you've been playing the field." With this remark, she leveled her stare on her other son. "Unlike another man I've raised." One side of Logan's mouth hitched into an unapologetic smirk. "Anyway," she continued. "That's that. Dinner is in the kitchen; everybody help yourself."

For the rest of the evening, the two families chatted easily. Charity discovered that Corinne was even friendlier than her son. She asked about Charity's plans for the future and told her stories about when Kyle was young. For once, Charity felt welcome.

At the end of the night, instead of going home with her family, she rode with Kyle. By the time he pulled up at his flat, she was buzzing with excitement. He wrapped an arm around her waist as he escorted her to the door.

"That went well," he said, slotting the key into the lock.

"It seemed to," she agreed. "Your mum is nice."

His teeth flashed in the dark. "Every man over the age of forty-five in the bay area would agree."

Charity laughed. "She's popular with the men? I can see that. She's got a lot going for her."

He sighed. "Unfortunately, she never gives them a chance." He pushed the door open and let her enter first. She switched on the light in the hall and blinked rapidly as her eyes adjusted. By the time she'd oriented herself, Kyle had backed her against the wall. "You were great tonight." His lips drifted down her neck, skimming the surface of her skin, and she shivered. "I missed having my hands on you though. Being on my best behavior was hard."

Her hands roved over his torso and disappeared beneath the hem of his shirt, her fingers smoothing over firm abs that flexed with every breath he drew. "You can make up for it now," she suggested.

He nuzzled the crook of her neck. "I plan to give it my best shot."

"Then by all means—" She broke off when he swept her legs out from under her and swung her into his arms. "What are you—?"

He claimed her mouth in a heated kiss. When he broke away, the stark need in his expression reflected her own. "I love you," he said, carrying her toward the bedroom. "Is this okay?"

"I love you too," she replied, then sucked a cord of his neck—the only thing she could reach from her position. "But if you're not inside me within five minutes, I might have to reconsider."

He winked. "Challenge accepted."

EPILOGUE—ONE YEAR LATER

Was it too much?

No, she decided. Kyle would love it. She adjusted the skirt of the sexy Darth Vader costume—*who even knew they existed?*—and slid the celebratory cake Megan had baked onto a platter. She carried it into the living room and sat on the couch to wait. Right on cue, Kyle rumbled up the drive. He'd been at poker night with the boys, giving her the perfect opportunity to organize her surprise.

She switched off the light, immersing herself in darkness, and waited for him to enter. She wanted to catch him completely off guard. A couple of minutes passed and then she heard footsteps on the porch. The door creaked open and he stepped inside. She hardly dared to breathe, her innards a bundle of nerves and excitement, intertwined until she couldn't tell one from the other.

The light came on, revealing him in all of his gorgeousness. Broad shoulders, strong jaw, brilliant eyes. She positively melted. It took a moment for his vision to focus on her and for him to notice she was wearing a skimpy outfit. A banner above her read "Baby, I am your father." He gasped, his gaze flying straight to her stomach. "Is it…" he started, then swallowed, and started again. "You're pregnant?"

She nodded. "Six weeks, give or take."

"Oh, my God." He took a step forward, then another. "I'm going to be a dad."

She waited, nibbling her lip, to see what his reaction would be. They hadn't technically been trying to get pregnant, but they'd made the decision to stop her birth control and see what happened. Apparently, they were a fertile combination.

A broad smile creased his features and he swooped in for a kiss that left her knees trembling. Then he ran a hand over her belly.

"My baby." His touch was gentle, as though he was afraid of hurting her or their unborn child. He dropped to his knees and pressed his lips against the flat surface. "I'm going to love you like crazy."

Affection filled Charity's heart to bursting. But as she started to run a hand through his hair, Kyle drew back and reached into his pocket, withdrawing a small purple box.

"Erm, what's that?" she asked as the evening took a turn she hadn't expected. Still on his knees, he popped the box open. A diamond ring glittered when the light hit it. Her heart beat a staccato rhythm. "Kyle, what's going on?"

He took a breath, his chest rising and falling. "I've been carrying this around for a while—basically since Brooke and Jack's wedding—waiting for the perfect opportunity to propose. I don't think it's going to get much better than this, so here goes. I haven't prepared a speech. You'll have to bear with me."

She nodded, and gestured for him to go on, spellbound by the sparkly ring in his hand but not yet daring to reach for it.

"Charity St. John, I love you with my whole heart. No one has ever gotten to me the way you do, and no one has ever made Darth Vader look so damn sexy. Will you marry me, and officially take me off the market?"

"Yes!" she exclaimed, then swatted his arm. "You haven't been on the market for the past year. You're already mine, and don't you forget it."

Grinning, he took her hand and slid the ring onto her finger. "I wouldn't dream of it. Love you always."

Charity pulled him up and threw her arms around his neck. For the longest time, she didn't let go. Tears prickled her eyes, but they were happy tears. A year ago, her life had been in ruins, but now she was blessed with all the goodness she'd never believed she deserved. Samuel had paid attention to her warning and kept his distance, leaving her free to enjoy her fresh start. She had a fiancé, a baby on the way, a job she loved, and she was on her way to becoming a qualified librarian. Not to mention that other thing...

"Oh, and by the way," she added. "You're going to be an uncle."

He pulled back and cocked his head. "Faith's pregnant?"

She nodded. "She's breaking the news to Shane tonight too."

They'd made a pact to do it at the same time and then report back to each other.

"Brilliant!" He spun her in his arms. "Best night ever."

Charity laughed, knowing deep inside that every night from now on would be the best night ever, because each day she loved him more than the one before, and when they had a baby in their family, that love could only grow exponentially.

This wasn't the end of her happily ever after. It was only the beginning.

THE END

LET ME LOVE YOU EXCERPT

Mikayla Talbot hung up the phone and glared at where her computer monitor sat on the desk of her well-appointed inner-city office. It seemed the computer would be the only company she'd have tonight. She'd had to cancel Friday evening plans with her friends *again* because her boss, Price Marshall, the chief executive of New Zealand's most successful hydroelectric company—and in her opinion, the sexiest man alive—had asked her to stay late. It wasn't the first time she'd had to ditch her friends because of him, but her sacrifices would be worth it when he finally realized he couldn't live without her. Meanwhile, she'd just be here, doing everything he asked, as hopelessly in love with him as she'd been for the last couple of years.

She opened the email on her screen and reread Price's request. The task he'd asked her to do was something he should be doing himself, but he'd said he had an important dinner he couldn't miss. Perhaps he was meeting with one of the company's shareholders or the director of the board. And yes, perhaps it should have irked her that he expected her to drop everything for him, but considering she'd made a habit of doing just that ever since she'd been employed as his chief operations officer, she couldn't blame him. His instructions weren't particularly clear though. He needed her to follow up with the manager of one of the smaller operations bases, but she didn't know exactly what needed to be said.

Standing up, she grabbed a notepad and pen and headed down the corridor to his office. Through the glass wall facing onto the hall, she could see Price sitting at his desk, presumably finishing up for the day. He ran his hand through his dark hair, tousling it in a way that made her stomach flip over. Price was, without a doubt, gorgeous. It used to kill Mikayla to see him date other women, but she'd learned by now that none of them lasted. One day, he'd wake up and see what was right in front of him. After all, he and Mikayla were perfect for each other. He was great at the big picture, while she was a details person. He was all affability and charm, whereas she could be a human bulldozer when the need arose. They complemented each other, and he was too intelligent to overlook that for much longer.

"Hey, Mik," he said as she breezed through the door and into the office. A single strand of hair fell across his forehead, tempting her to smooth it back into place. "Did you get my email?"

"I did." She flashed a smile at Price. "I just need to clarify something." She started to round the desk so she could stand at his shoulder and point out the part of the email she was confused about, when he held up a hand to stop her.

"It can wait for a moment. I have something I need to talk to you about. It's important."

"Um, okay," she said, caught off-guard. "Is it about your meeting tonight?"

"Kind of." He stood up and cupped a hand around her elbow, guiding her around the desk to the chair he kept at the side of the room. "Here. Sit. I prefer talking face-to-face than having you hovering over me."

She nodded, pressing her lips together, nerves and excitement churning in her gut. She considered herself an expert on Price Marshall, and he was acting unusually. What was going on?

He dragged his chair around and angled it so they were facing each other.

"I've been doing a lot of thinking lately," he said. "I'm thirty-six. I'm not getting any younger. I've prioritized my career for years now, and I don't regret that, but it's time to let some light shine on my personal life."

Mikayla nodded encouragingly, hope flaring in her heart. This didn't sound like a work conversation—unless he was quitting, which she doubted. Could it be that he'd finally seen her in the way she'd always wanted him to?

"I've been afraid of committing to a woman because of my work schedule," he continued. "But I want a wife and family, so I need to stop being scared of messing up and put my heart on the line."

A smile spread over her face. "That sounds like a really good idea."

His white teeth peeked out from between full lips. "I'm glad you agree. I've always valued your opinion." He leaned closer, and she caught a whiff of expensive cologne. "You're an incredible woman. Smart, ambitious, determined. I'd like to think we're friends, of a sort."

"Yes, of course." Friends, colleagues, and hopefully,

one day soon, lovers. She barely managed not to bounce on the spot.

"To that end, I'd like to ask you something really important."

Mikayla sat forward, desperate to hear the next words out of his mouth. But then he pulled a small black box from his pocket and flipped the lid open to reveal a dazzling diamond solitaire ring.

Oh my God.

He had a ring. *A ring.* The man of her dreams was sitting in front of her, expression serious, holding out an engagement ring.

Tears blurred her vision. All her waiting had been worth it. Her dreams were finally coming true.

Her mouth was dry, and her heart hammered a rapid rhythm. This was a proposal. Price wanted to marry her. She touched a palm to her chest.

"Mikayla, will you t—"

"Yes," she interrupted. "Yes, yes, yes!"

He chuckled. "I'm glad you're enthusiastic. I was worried you might be concerned about your job with everything the change may mean in terms of a shift in your duties."

"Of course not." She waved a hand dismissively. "We'll work that out."

"We will?" He looked bemused.

"Absolutely." She reached across the space between them and took his free hand in hers. "I've been waiting for this moment for such a long time."

"Well, good." A smile curled at the edges of his lips. "I can't say it's been the same for me, but I've finally gotten there, and I couldn't be happier."

A rogue tear slipped out. Her heart was brimming with joy. She couldn't wait to finally kiss him. To be held in his strong arms and know how it felt to be his.

And sure, proposing like this, out of the blue, wasn't his usual style, but it felt right.

"I love you," she whispered, closing the space between them.

"Whoa!" He stopped her with a hand to her chest, and a sudden coldness washed over her. "What the hell do you mean, you love me?"

She shook her head, which suddenly felt foggy. "What do you mean, 'what do *I* mean'? Didn't you just propose?"

"No." He cocked his head, his eyes wide. "I'm going to. Later. To Alison. My *girlfriend*." He stood up and dragged the chair back behind his desk, not taking his eyes off her, his expression cautious, as though she might attack. "I think we've had a miscommunication."

"Alison," she repeated, feeling sick. "But you just...."

She clapped a hand to her mouth, their conversation racing through her mind. He'd never actually said anything about marrying her. He'd held out the ring and started to ask something, but she hadn't let him finish. She'd thought it had been self-evident. What if he'd actually been asking for her opinion on the ring? And that reference to her change in duties could be if she had to do more as a result of him spending time at home with Alison.

Her stomach rolled. She wished the floor would open up and swallow her.

He'd been trying to tell her of his impending engagement, and she'd jumped the gun and told him she loved him.

Oh no.

"I was asking what you thought of the ring." His voice was tight. "Because I put a lot of stock in your opinion. Why would you think I was proposing to you?"

She jolted to her feet, her throat so tight, it was nearly impossible to speak. "You wouldn't be. Of course you wouldn't. That would be ridiculous." She tried to rally. She could still save face. "What I meant was...." Her usually razor-sharp mind deserted her, offering up no viable suggestions. Her cheeks flamed. "I, um...."

"Mik." Price sounded troubled. "Are you really in love with me?"

"No. I meant I love you in a platonic sense. You're, uh, a good boss."

Weak, Mikayla. So weak.

"Because if I've done something to lead you on, I—"

"You haven't," she snapped. Oh God, this was mortifying. She'd outed herself. How was she supposed to continue working with him now when it was clear he knew exactly what she'd meant? Price was oblivious, but not stupid. She swallowed past a lump in her throat. Not to mention the fact that all of her patience had been for nothing and she'd have to be around him every day, knowing he was out of reach. A dull pain throbbed in her chest.

She gathered herself. "I'm sorry for any misunderstanding. I wish you the best for the proposal. It's a beautiful ring, and she's a lucky woman."

Alison was getting everything Mikayla had always wanted, and she could hardly even summon an image of the woman to her mind from the few times they'd met. She'd dismissed her, as she had all the others, because Price tired of them all eventually. Or so she'd thought.

"Mikayla...."

"I've got to go. I'm afraid I can't stay late after all."

She turned and bolted from the office. She couldn't let him see her cry. She made it to the bathroom before breaking down. She sank to the floor, tears streaming down her cheeks, no doubt ruining her perfectly applied makeup. She drew her knees to her chest, not caring if it revealed her underwear because who the hell was going to see? The floor was empty, other than her and Price.

She buried her face in her knees. How was she supposed to face him again after this?

"Stupid, stupid, stupid," she muttered to herself. She'd ruined everything.

<hr>

AFTER TAKING A TAXI HOME AND DRINKING THE BETTER part of a bottle of wine, Mikayla was soaking in her bathtub, pondering her life choices and debating what to do now that she'd spectacularly humiliated herself, when her phone rang. Her immediate inclination was to ignore the call, but it could be a work emergency, and habit won out. She answered.

"Mikayla Talbot speaking."

"Hi, Mikayla." It was a woman with a soft, cultured accent. "This is Alison."

Great. Just great.

"Are congratulations in order?" she asked, sounding as bitter as she felt.

"I'm sorry." Alison's tone was heavy with pity. "Price told me what happened, and I can't imagine how difficult that must have been for you."

Mikayla grabbed her glass of wine and downed the rest of it. Of course Price had told her. They'd probably laughed over it while they ate dinner. Was Alison calling to warn her to back off?

"You don't have to worry about me doing anything inappropriate." Her words slurred a little at the end, the combination of heat and too much wine inter-fering with her ability to speak properly.

Forget inappropriate—she didn't even know if she'd be able to face him on Monday.

"I'm not worried about that. I wanted to check and see how you are. Price can be so clueless. I could see you cared about him the first time we met, so I know it must have hit you hard."

Mikayla sniffed, experiencing a fresh wave of embarrassment. How much of a fool had she made of herself over Price? Did everyone know she loved him? And was Alison really calling to make sure she was okay, or was this an underhanded way of gloating?

"I'm an idiot," she said bluntly. "But I'm not going to hurt myself or do something stupid. You don't have to worry about that."

"Yes, but…."

"But what?"

The other woman hesitated, as if figuring out how best to phrase what she wanted to say.

"What?" Mikayla insisted with the silence dragged out.

A sigh came down the line. "So, I was thinking—and I could be overstepping here—but you must be dreading going back into the office."

Mikayla frowned. Where was she going with this?

"Maybe you should tell Price you need a break." Alison had lowered her voice. "You have a heap of leave owed, right?"

"Yeah." She never took time off because she hated to leave Price in the lurch. He needed her. She'd been so stupid. Letting a man dictate her decisions in the hopes he would one day fall for her. She'd been certain they were good for each other, and she was used to being right. This time, she'd been so, so wrong.

"Why don't you take advantage of that? My aunt has a holiday home by the beach in Haven Bay. She only uses it once or twice a year, and I'm sure she wouldn't mind if you went to stay there for a while. You could use the time to do some thinking."

Mikayla jerked in surprise. Haven Bay was where her twin sister, Megan, lived. Megan adored the place, and the couple of times Mikayla had visited, she'd liked it too. It was quiet. Relaxed. Not her usual scene, but maybe that was the point.

It was a tempting offer. Especially when, for the first time ever, she was uncertain about what step to take next for both her career and her personal life. She couldn't believe Alison was willing to do this for her. But then, if she were Alison, she might also want the woman who was in love with her fiancée to leave town. Her motives might not be completely altruistic. Some part of her wanted Mikayla gone. But that actually comforted her, because it made sense, and it wasn't as though she wanted to see Price on Monday morning.

"What do you think?" Alison prompted.

Mikayla pressed her lips together. In general, she prided herself on not making rash decisions, and this was the epitome of that. But didn't she deserve to give herself a little leeway? The man she loved was engaged to someone else. She might have to leave her job if she couldn't bring herself to face him every day. Perhaps the fact Alison's aunt's beach house was in Haven Bay of all places was a sign she should go.

She considered her options.

One, leave the city to wallow in peace somewhere she'd have access to her sister's wonderfully comforting hugs if needed.

Two, suck up her feelings and continue on as

though nothing had changed while being confronted daily by the sight of her dreams for the future crashing down around her.

There really was no competition.

"I'll do it," she said. "Thank you."

"No problem. Just make sure you pop over next door to say hi to Mr. Gray while you're there. He's a bit of a recluse, and my aunt worries about him."

"No problem." She could check on as many old men as needed if it meant a few days—or weeks—of escape. If she recalled correctly, she had several months of leave saved up. Price would be reluctant to approve it all at once, but after a bit of cajoling, she was certain he'd at least agree to some of it.

"Would you like me to speak to him for you?" Alison asked.

"No." Mikayla straightened. That would be a step too far. She was a capable woman. She could do this. "He owes me a lot of favors. I guess it's time to collect them."

ALSO BY ALEXA RIVERS

Haven Bay

Then There Was You

Two of a Kind

Safe in His Arms

If Only You Knew

Pretend to Be Yours

Begin Again With You

Let Me Love You

Little Sky Romance

Accidentally Yours

From Now Until Forever

It Was Always You

Dreaming of You

Little Sky Romance Novellas

Midnight Kisses

Second Chance Christmas

Destiny Falls

Stay With You

Come Back to You

Always Been Yours

Blue Collar Romance

A Place to Belong

ACKNOWLEDGMENTS

Thank you to my husband, for your never ending support. Thank you to the team who helped me shape this story into its best possible version of itself—particularly Kate and Serena. Thank you to Shannon, for all of my gorgeous covers.

To my friends and family, I love you. You help me to keep going during the good times and bad.

To my readers, you guys are THE BEST! I couldn't spend my days making up love stories if not for you. Thank you for loving my characters and their communities as much as I do.

ABOUT THE AUTHOR

Alexa Rivers writes about genuine characters living messy, imperfect lives and earning hard-won happily ever afters. Most of her books are set in small towns, and she lives in one of these herself. She shares a house with a neurotic dog and a husband who thinks he's hilarious. When she's not writing, Alexa enjoys travelling, baking cakes, eating said cakes, cuddling fluffy animals, drinking copious amounts of tea, and absorbing herself in fictional worlds.

www.ingramcontent.com/pod-product-compliance
Lightning Source LLC
Chambersburg PA
CBHW051133190726
48290CB00006B/1820